Warrior of the Heart

by

MARY ELLEN BOYD

ISBN-13: 978-1-7340881-9-9
ISBN-10: 1-7340881-9-2

Cover model photo© Rehanqureshi | Dreamstime.com
Cover art by Victoria Cooper Art

*To everyone at the
Minneapolis Writer's Workshop,
none of whom were
alarmed by the setting and
all of whom encouraged me
to keep going and not give up
on this book,
all my thanks.*

In those days there was no king in Israel. Each one was doing what was right
in his own eyes.

Judges 21:25

CHAPTER 1

So they commanded the men of Benjamin: "Go and set an ambush in the vineyards. And when you see the young women of Shiloh come out to join in their circle dances, each of you should come out from the vineyards and seize a wife."
Judges 21:20,21

It felt good to sing. The bitter, ugly war was over. It had been a while since she had felt she could laugh, and even now Aksah had to shove the sad thought aside, lest it taint this bright moment. She had spent months grieving, but they were in Shiloh, and the Ark of the Covenant was here. The harvest was over and it had been a good one. It was time to celebrate.

And time to forget.

Laughter rose from the circle of young women as they began to move in the steps of the dance. Aksah hung onto the hands of the maiden in front and the one behind, as she too began to pick up the familiar moves. Left foot over right, a hop and then right foot over left, they all let go for the twirl, hands reached and clasped again in the giant circle, two graceful steps to the right and the movements repeated themselves, faster now, and the songs and laughter soared. Nearby, someone played a harp, and someone else played the flute, nearly drowned out by the happy calls of the circles of dancers.

The women moved in toward each other, the circle tightening, their hands raised as if to grasp a piece of the sky, the sun bright on their faces and then the steps took them back again, the ring widening, their arms stretched as far as they could go and still remain linked. The circle began to move again, their laughter and song a cheerful thing.

No doubt there were others here who hid their own sadness behind the smiles. Aksah did not know most of the girls in her circle, might not see them again for a year, but today they would laugh and dance. It was not so easy to recover, but this was a start, and she would learn again to be happy.

Do not think about your brother, she told herself, *do not think of his wife and little children widowed and orphaned for such a foolish war. Dance now, and be glad you are here in Shiloh, where the Ark is, and where God's favor resides again.*

She made herself listen to the notes, the plinking of the lyre and the trill of the flute, like the birds soaring in the sky overhead. Flute and birds, singing together. The low hills flashed around them as the circle moved, gaining time in the joyous songs, white rocks poking up from the green, the brown tents of the travelers for this once- a- year celebration, tents that dotted the valley and climbed the lower levels. Soon the summer heat would come and the flowers would fade, but today they were all abloom.

Aksah let the colors replenish her as they flashed past, pinks and purples and whites melding into a quilt of springtime.

The circle slowed, and the colors took shape, bushes being bushes again instead of a wash of green, flowers turning into clumps instead of streaks of brilliance. Her eyes were filled with the brightness, the floating music seemed to lift her heart with her feet.

She watched groups of people climb along the tiered hills of grapevines that surrounded Shiloh. Brightly colored robes appeared with each spin of the circle. Men and women, children, wandering through the rows, each turn putting the little families in a different place.

In the distance, the tabernacle curtain came into view, then went out of sight, then back again as she twirled and moved in the dance. Israel's holy house, the very reason they were here, the grey smoke of the sacrifices rising to the blue sky like the music.

The circle wound around again, each scene filling her eyes fresh, untainted by the war's woes. Aksah clapped with the music and whirled again, hardly needing to count in the so-familiar steps.

Near the hill's top, between the rows of staked vines, shadows moved. She lost them as the dance continued, but there they were again, ahead of the small groups climbing up the terraces.

Shadows in the grapevines, vines in places tall enough for a man to lurk, and to spring. Men with the right to capture a virgin, and steal her away.

Men who had shown utter disregard for women.

The back of her neck prickled as the dance slowed to a stop, and the music ended. She smiled at the dancers with her but the smile was strained, and Aksah turned in haste to find those shadows. To be aware was to be ready.

The tiered grapevine rows where the dark outlines had been were hard to identify, now that she was still. No matter which hill she checked, there were no shadows lingering among the thick stalks with their tiny young green clusters, no ominous forms hovering like vengeance.

Despite that, she found no comfort in the lack of movement beneath the tall staked vines on the narrow tiers cut into the hillside, no comfort that there were no rustles through the crowns of fresh leaves other than what the breeze made. The prickles across her skin grew stronger. A warning, a reminder that any virgins at the circle dances were fair game for the men who managed to capture her.

Aksah looked around at all the women from the dance, all the climbers wandering up the paths between the levels of vines, families enjoying the day and the place, all the musicians, then below at the valley encampment filled with people, any of whom could rush to the rescue of a snatched woman at a moment's notice. Only a fool would attempt to seize someone from this busy gathering.

Of course, the men of Benjamin's tribe clearly were fools, to have allowed such a horrible thing to come down upon their heads. What would possess a whole tribe to defend a city of violent men? They brought this war just past on themselves. They had been asked to hand the murderers over for justice, and what was their reply? To fight in defense of those very ones!

What kind of people defended those who would torture and kill? She had asked herself that question over and over for the past few months. The only answer she could find was that Israel's entire tribe of Benjamin had found no crime in the crime, no murder in the murder.

Men might grieve over the nation nearly down to eleven tribes from the original twelve. She would grieve over the poor, dead woman, a woman of Judah's tribe like herself. The concubine of a man who thought so little of her that he pushed her out into a crowd of fiends just to save his own skin, and abandoned her to a terrible death. In Aksah's opinion, six hundred men left of Benjamin were six hundred too many.

Permission had been given for two hundred of Benjamin's survivors, the only men who had not already been found brides, to steal their maiden wives from this celebration. They were nearby, those remaining men, searching for stragglers among the dances. It behooved all of the young women here to be very careful.

She had vowed to be alert, promised herself *she* would not be caught, but her sisters were a worry.

It was a pity, Aksah thought, that even four hundred brides had been found for a portion of Benjamin's entire once-populous tribe. The crime behind the war was beyond horrible. Let Benjamin's name die off now. She would grieve over her brother, her valiant brother who joined the army and died defending justice.

And the woman. Yes, she would grieve over the dead woman, stranger or no.

Blankets lay spread on the level sections of the vineyard just away from the rings of dancers, and baskets had been opened, provisions arranged for any who might be hungry after their efforts. Flat pieces of bread, crocks of soft cheeses and curdled milk, and cakes of dried fruits from last year's harvest. Skins of water and wine joined the feast, ready for the thirsty. Dried strips of meat, too, were placed on fresh cloths.

Men standing guard remained clustered to one side, talking and laughing instead of their usual protective stance, their casual demeanor replacing the expected alert, watchful pacing. Were they *giving* the Benjaminites a chance? Her gaze tracked across, away from the men playing at guarding, past the forming circle, toward the staked vines.

No one looked alert, no one appeared concerned.

Aksah took one last look up at the tall stands of green vines layered across the hillside before turning to the banquet spread out on the wide level place. This opening where the hill flattened before climbing again had been the perfect location to gather for dancing. No doubt during the harvest the farmers did their separating and drying of grapes into raisins here, but today it held women and musicians and dances.

As she sank down on the ground with her piece of bread and the raisin cake, Aksah found she was no longer able to join in the celebration with the abandon of the rest. Somehow, the hill behind her seemed populated with eyes of men waiting the chance to leap out and grab.

Her younger sisters plopped down abruptly on either side of her, pulling her out of her thoughts so quickly she dropped her raisin cake. "Oh!" Aksah clapped her now-empty hand over her pounding heart. "You startled me! Dinah, Deborah, where have you been?"

"Wandering," Dinah said. "With so much to see, we cannot just sit inside the tent, you know. We have not seen some of our friends for a whole year."

"Longer even," Deborah added. So identical, it was hard for anyone who saw them the first time to tell them apart. They all shared the same soft brown color hair, but that was the only identifier of the family link. While Aksah's hair was curly, the twins' was straight. Her eyes were an odd color, hard to determine in the copper mirrors, but it seemed brown sometimes, a paler blend of deep green and grey others, usually when the sun was shining. The twins, though, their eyes were brown, easy to conceal what they were thinking, like now, when they looked at her with innocent faces.

How far from the main congregation had they gone in their wanderings? Groups of silly young women may well have strolled within the grasp of the Benjaminite men. Even now some girls could already be rushed away, and no one would guess. "We were supposed to be careful! Do you not know it is possible men of Benjamin might be around?" Aksah did not mean the words to come out so harshly, but those shadows made her skin prickle, and it was impossible to look at her sisters' carefree faces without feeling the need to push some sense into them.

"So?" Dinah picked up the dropped raisin cake and glared at it before tossing it far away, to land in a prickly bush. Chileab had always said she could throw well—for a girl.

Aksah dared not think about Chileab now. "Do you want to be captured?"

Dinah got to her feet and gave Aksah that superior stare that never failed to rile her temper. "We want to have fun. You worry so. I for one do not intend to spoil our celebration time. We will not be back for another whole year. We are supposed to be joyful, so joyful I will be. Whether you like that or not!" There it was again, that foolishness, the belief that nothing could go wrong because she had decreed it. She put a hand on one thin hip, staring at Aksah as if looking at a much younger sister, instead of at the oldest of the six remaining children. "We are at Shiloh. We come here every year. What could be more safe than to be at the celebration?"

Was she ever that young, Aksah wondered? "Did you pay no attention to what was going on this last year? The woman who was murdered? The revolt? Did you forget about the war? Dinah, do you not realize how desperate the men of Benjamin are? There are two hundred men who would stop at nothing to get themselves a wife before their tribe dies off. Do you remember how close Benjamin came to being wiped away? Those last Benjaminites were given permission to raid the virgins here at Shiloh for wives. Each of us girls here are in imminent danger of capture."

Dinah's eyes lit up as if illuminated by the many- branched candlestick their mother had. Aksah groaned aloud. "But is that not exciting? How romantic to be swept away and wed. Much better than waiting at home for the marriage broker or our parents to decide for us."

"No, it is not!"

The words were in her mind, but they did not come out of her mouth. Aksah turned to gaze at Deborah, the surprise speaker. It was not often that the twins disagreed. Deborah may not like everything Dinah did, but it was rare for her to do so in front of others.

How strange that two so identical people could be so very different.

Aksah looked back at Dinah for her reaction, but for once she was unmoved by her sister.

"Come now, Deborah, surely you have to realize that this is exciting. Every year we come to Shiloh, and every year it is nothing but the same circumstances, the same sacrifices, the same readings from the Law. This is the first time we have ever come when something interesting might happen."

Aksah's mouth fell open. To reduce holy days to something boring? "Dinah! Can you not appreciate what a privilege it is to come here to Shiloh? Do we have a copy of the Law in our village yet? No, we do not. If you are going to learn, you had better pay attention while we are here."

Dinah's shoulders slumped. "Oh, look at you two. Aksah, I know you enjoy the circle dances much more than you do sitting and listening to the priests speak on and on. I saw you dancing just now. Do not become all pious on me."

Aksah felt as if her sister had just punched her in the chest. "How can you say that about me? I do like listening, I try to remember. I am well aware that when I get home, all I will have to draw from is what I retain. I like dancing, of course I do, but I dance because of the joy I get being here. I wish you felt the same."

Deborah cleared her throat quietly, just like she did everything. "Dinah, I like being here and listening, too. I do not come just for the circle dances. We can have circle dances at home, there are certainly enough young women in the village for that. But Aksah is right, our village does not have its own copy of the Law. Maybe soon, but not yet."

This time, Dinah did stamp her foot. "I can quote it better than either of you when we are questioned by our father. Just because you are not as smart as I am and have to listen harder does not mean that I am not listening."

Aksah recalled any number of times when Dinah had given their father the wrong answer when he was questioning them on the Law to see how much they learned.

Unfortunately, she also remembered the more frequent times when the only one who had the right answer, and to the most difficult questions, was Dinah.

It was most annoying.

"This will get us nowhere," she said, forcing herself to be quiet and not raise her voice here at the festival. "I just do not want any of us to be captured by the Benjaminites. They are not men we want to be with. I, for one, do not believe they learned anything from this war. They all ran up into the crag of Rimmon, and hid there like the cowards that they are."

"Now, Aksah, that is a little too harsh," Deborah said in her quiet way. "There were only six hundred of them left, how were they to know that they would not be slaughtered to the last man if they were to show themselves?"

"Not one of them turned over the men of Gibeah after that horrible thing," Aksah said fiercely. She suddenly realized her hands were clenched, and had to make an effort to release them. She did that, it seemed, every time she thought about that poor woman, turned loose to a crowd of violent men. "Chileab died in that war! We never even got his body to bury! This war would have been avoided if the men of Benjamin had had the decency to turn over the guilty ones. But, no, they pretended nothing bad had happened and ignored all the summonses from the rest of the tribes. A whole tribe, all of them, who could not see a murder when it was right in front of them!"

She was doing it again, letting her emotions and her anger run away with her.

"Well, it is all over now," Dinah said with her usual ability to ignore what she did not want to face. "I know Chileab is dead, I miss him too, more than you realize, but really, Aksah, the war is over. We won. I cannot bring Chileab back, but neither will I let myself stop living. And if I want to dance in the circle dances, I will!"

"If you cannot think of me or of Deborah, try to think of Mother and Father and what they would feel if you were suddenly swept away to Benjamin." If they were going to make it through this visit to Shiloh with the family intact, someone had to take it upon themselves to keep an eye on the girls. As the second oldest child—second oldest *surviving* child, she corrected herself—not to mention the oldest daughter, that duty naturally fell on her. She suddenly realized one of them was missing. "Where is our youngest sister? Was she not to be with you?"

Dinah looked over at the nearby blankets with their rich spread. "She was just here. I do not know where she went. She cannot have gone far."

Aksah stood and scanned the ground, up toward the vines growing along the hillside, across the small plain where they sat, where dancers mingled, instrument players talked and laughed, and baskets waited for the hungry, and down the lower slopes filled with more vines. Rachel loved flowers, but she was nowhere to be seen near the blooming bushes or the budding clusters hanging from the propped branches.

Rachel was ten. The Benjaminites would hardly be interested in her. Would they? "Help me find her!"

Deborah rose from the blanket with her normal deliberation and turned to gaze up the hill, while Dinah stared down into the valley. Before Aksah sucked in a breath to scream Rachel's name, Dinah said, as calmly as if they were safely in their house, "There. See? She found Mother."

Indeed, down at the edge of the wide valley holding the temporary village that sprang up each spring, a small familiar form stood by the much-patched tent that belonged to her family. The figure was gesturing at the open door, as if talking to someone just out of view inside.

Aksah refused to let herself feel guilty over her initial panic. Whatever the shadows on the hillside had been, the fact remained that Benjamin had received permission to stalk this celebration, and she had seen *something* up there. It might have been a wild goat, of course, or a deer, or . . . one of so many things.

Olive trees grew in clusters toward the valley where the tent city nestled, the white flowers of the blooms that would become fruit just beginning. Whenever the breeze came up, the leaves showed their silver undersides in a ripple of color across the tree. The last blossoms of spring dotted the brown soil here and there in tufts of yellow, white and pink, bobbing cheerfully among their stalks of green. It was deceptively peaceful.

"Aksah?" Dinah's voice had an edge to it, as if she had spoken more than once.

"What?" Aksah dragged her thoughts from the patched tent.

"You were not listening! I knew it! Well, I will tell you again and this time you had better listen." Dinah's arms were propped again on her slender hips. "During the speeches or not, if I want to walk in the hills, I will. If I want to dance, I will. If I want walk with the young men, and pick flowers, or find a husband, I will do so as well." She pushed her thick soft brown hair away from her face with a rough gesture of irritation, as if it were either push it back or pull it out.

Before Aksah could think of a retort, Dinah continued, "It is not up to you to tell me what to do because you do all the same things. I might think you want us to stay in Father's house, unwed, just because you have not found a husband yourself!"

With that, she turned her back on her older sister, grabbed Deborah's hand, and stomped down the sloping path toward the tents.

CHAPTER 2

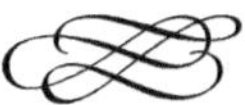

Every one of these men could sling a stone to within a hairbreadth and would not miss.

Judges 20:16

Eliab slipped back over the hilltop, keeping low and moving fast. Off to his left and his right, the other scouts moved as quickly as himself. These last two hundred men were supposed to be safe through today. No one was to challenge them, stop them, or in any way interfere. This was part of the final treaty that brought peace, after all, but every soldier here also knew they were all men of infamy. After they left with their kidnapped wives, what little reputation remained to Benjamin would be gone.

Or would it be restored?

Somehow his tribe's standing in Israel had become confusing.

The only way he would ever be wed was if he stole a bride. The entire nation had taken a vow never to give a daughter to Benjamin. Allowing their daughters to be carried off was not the same as giving, but how much resistance they would face was yet to be seen.

He had noticed the guards, but none of them seemed to be doing much guarding. Eliab still did not believe that once his group came over the hillside, those guards would stand and do nothing.

Today had been the date chosen for the attack.

All it took was for one person to stroll over the hilltop and look. The main group of these last soldiers had tucked themselves in the gullies and were well concealed for now, but once they started across the gap they were vulnerable. And all too visible. He kept his pace down the hillside, glancing over his shoulder every few steps, but no one followed them.

He fully expected the order would come to move when the next dances started. Thank goodness the music carried over the hillsides. Two hundred men, however valiant and skilled they might be, however small the groups they were broken into, would make noise.

He and his fellow scouts ducked behind the peaked hill and into the shade on its opposite side. The group that waited was, Eliab did a quick guess, forty, maybe fifty? That meant there were likely another three groups about this size spreading around the hills, readying themselves to flood over the top of Shiloh's peaks.

Elhanan the chieftain beckoned the three men over. He was crouched on one of the tiers the hill seemed to form on its own, whether by rain or by wind no one could say. Now, however, those tiers made excellent places for a leader to crouch and yet still be above his men so his voice could carry.

"What did you see?"

Abdon spoke first. "There are guards, but they do not appear to be working hard at it."

Elhanan only nodded, and turned to the other two. "Eliab? Heber? Your report?"

Eliab shook his head. "Nothing different, my lord. The guards are strolling about, laughing. Still, we cannot underestimate their reaction. Once we come over the hill, do you imagine they will stand by and let us grab their daughters? I do not."

Heber propped his fists on his hips. "I say let us go over in a wave. I have no one left to care what is thought of me. If I must crack another man's head to get a wife, I will."

Elhanan scowled. "Heber, the war is over. No one is to die today. No one is even to be hurt. If so much as one of us dies, Benjamin will be down to five hundred ninety-nine. We cannot afford the loss of so much as a single man."

His piercing gaze swept over the group. "No weapons. No injuries that require more than your hands." Then a rough single laugh came out of his mouth. "No. Not even that. No injuries at all, to anyone."

That commander's gaze once again washed over the soldiers before him. "It is one thing to wed across tribal lines when the nation is at peace. We must not forget what they think of us."

Heber's hands were still fists. Eliab shook his head. Odd that someone so volatile had come through the war and the humiliation of the last few months with his anger still boiling. They were all supposed to be chastised. Would that not include letting go of at least some of his capricious temper?

As for himself, Eliab thought with lingering pain, he certainly was suffering. No mother, no father, no brothers, not even his sisters were left alive. Out of his family, he alone remained. Whether there was anything left to bring today's wife to, he did not know. The last he had heard, even the nearby city to his father's farm had been burned to the ground.

Would anyone accept that he had nothing to do with the crime? He had been nowhere near Gibeah. All he had done was take his place in defense of his people, try to keep his tribe from being wiped out. To keep Israel from going on a rampage against innocent men.

It had gained him nothing. And cost him everything, a grief that had nearly overwhelmed him these past four months until he wondered why he fought so hard to live. For what, when all he loved was gone?

But Elhanan was still talking, and he had missed the instructions.

No, he realized as his commander continued, he had not. Heber was still taking the brunt of their tongue-lashing.

"Today," Elhanan said, his voice quiet yet still carrying on the motionless air, across the group of watchful, waiting men, "when you capture your women, remember what gifts they are. Your brothers have extended all the forgiveness they can. This is your, my, all of our only chance to keep our tribe alive. We are the descendants of Jacob's most beloved wife, Rachel. We owe it to our forefathers to fulfill this day's purpose. We will go over the hill in a wave, and we will not shout. We will not encourage any hostilities. As Benjaminites, we are here for one purpose and one purpose only. Today we will have wives."

He stood, and Eliab hoped no one was watching from over the hillside that surrounded the tabernacle.

The first notes of the musicians tinkled on the air, and laughter rang along with it.

How long had it been since he had laughed?

Elhanan took off his sword and slammed it point-first into the ground, where it shivered. Nothing could have given the order more emphasis than for their mightiest warrior to leave his sword behind. No man would draw his sword from today on against their Israelite brothers.

Eliab was not going to follow his commander's dramatic gesture, for despite the display Elhanan would be back for it. In a bare few moments, they would all be running for their lives. They dared not do it unprotected. Animals roamed the hills where their path lay.

Eliab watched Elhanan loose the last loop of his rope, and did the same thing. Around him, men got their ropes ready. They all knew what the ropes were for.

Their wives.

The music swelled and Eliab thought he could feel the ground shiver under the dancing feet on the opposite side of the hill. The men all exchanged glances, and then looked toward their chieftain.

"We move, but do not be too hasty. Watch, and plan. Keep to the vineyards, they will provide cover."

Elhanan smiled like a proud father. "You are all wise men. I know you will act with discretion."

He turned and moved around the base of the hill, and Eliab joined his fellows as they started toward the dancing, keeping in the gullies and finding every concealment.

Wives, he thought. And a future.

CHAPTER 3

*The people came to Bethel and sat there before the true God until evening,
crying out and weeping bitterly. And they were saying, ". . . Why should
one tribe be missing today from Israel?"*
Judges 21:2,3

Aksah wondered how long it would take the little rebel to realize she
was heading in the direction she had just been told to go. At least
they were heading out of danger. One worry out of the way, her appetite
returned, and she sank back to the ground. The food beckoned. A quick
glance reassured her the twins had not turned off, they were still on their
way toward the camp and the tents.

The fig cake was delicious, made by someone who knew how to cook
and cook well. Aksah savored the bites, and chewed slowly. The cakes were
small, and before reaching for a second, she gave one more fleeting look back
up to the hill and the vines that covered it.

It was there again, that strange shape she thought she had seen, a shape
that might easily have been the top of a man's head—or a rock badger, or

perhaps even a deer. Except there were no ears sticking off the crown. Another identical shape joined it before they both disappeared back behind the vines running along the hilltop.

Benjaminites!

Aksah leapt upright so fast her head swam. Whirling around and hiking up her robe, she dashed down the hillside after her sisters. Grass poked at her feet through her sandals like flashing needles, and whipped her ankles. The sloped path pushed her onward. Deborah and Dinah had disappeared from view somewhere around the second row of tents, but Aksah stopped at her family's, catching the tent pole to slow her forward flight.

Rachel poked her head out of the flap. "Hello, Aksah. Was that you? It sounded like the tent was coming down. I have helped Mother get the evening meal ready. She said she hoped you were not filling up on the refreshments at the dance because we are having dried goat meat, fig cakes, and cheese on bread." Rachel spoke with complete unconcern. In her ten-year-old world, nothing bad could happen. Even Chileab's death had left her relatively untouched. She had been too young when he lived with the family to remember him as more than a kindly visitor who came from time to time.

Hand pressed to her side, Aksah tried to smile around her gasping breaths.

Ba'ara appeared behind Rachel, a frown on her face. "Daughter, what were you thinking, to run like that, and with your robe up so high?" Shaking her head, she went on, "That is what I expect of Dinah, or even Rachel," her arms wrapped her youngest daughter with obvious affection, "but not you. If there are men here looking for wives, they do not want women who make such scenes of themselves."

At the word 'wives,' Aksah found the air to blurt her news. "Mother, the Benjaminites are here! They are right over the ridge! We have to tell some-one, sound the warning!"

The color leached from her mother's face, and her arms tightened around Rachel. Ba'ara seemed to sink into herself, like a robe tossed onto a bed, but then, as if shoving her grief away for later, she stiffened. "Go inside," she told her youngest daughter, before releasing her with a gentle push into the tent. Then she turned back to Aksah and gripped her arm. "Where are your other sisters?"

Her own hand gripped her mother's. "I followed them down here to the camp, and then they turned away. They must have seen a friend. But the last I saw them, they were safe."

Ba'ara's gaze went past her toward the hillside. Aksah twisted to follow her mother's stare. There was nothing to see, only the dancers still laughing in the joy of the dances' end, and the food baskets collecting a few people to eat just as she had.

No one was alarmed, families continued to stroll along the pathways. Here and there, brighter garments of rare crimson and red flashed among the green grape leaves, proclaiming their wearers' wealth.

Ba'ara twisted her hands together. Almost in a prayer, she spoke, her voice barely heard, "Please let it not be them." If Aksah had not been listening so closely, she might not have caught the words.

They stood in silence for a moment, watching, watching those hills, watching the dancers, watching the families strolling along the trails between the standing vines.

"Perhaps it was not them," her mother said, but she did not sound convinced. Her gaze stayed fixed on the hills, the grapevines, then skimmed the temporary city, what she could see from the cloth walls surrounding their own tent before returning to the hillside again. "They were to take the dancers. They were not to raid from the tents."

Aksah's jaw clenched. "Why could they not wait until the celebration was almost finished? Why come early and spoil it for us?"

Ba'ara nodded once. "What am I saying? We do know the Benjaminites will be close. Everyone knows that, everyone was warned. They *are* our brothers, they are of Israel just as we are. We do not want the tribe to die away." Her voice lacked conviction. "But you are right, I, too, am concerned for our young women."

Then she shook her head. "What am I saying? I am *terrified* for them. Someone will leave this festival grieving for a daughter. Many someones, in fact. The last two hundred men seeking a wife, all of them free to grab whichever virgin they can catch." Ba'ara put her hands over her eyes, and shuddered.

When she lifted her head, grief, the same grief that had followed Aksah into the dance, left its hollow ache in her eyes. "I wish I could follow all my daughters around the festival and hold their hands as I did when they were little. I want each of you married to a man I know, a man the whole village approves. I want you nearby so I can see your children and dandle them on my knee. I want your husbands to understand that we are close and we will hear the news if they so much as raise their voices to you." Her voice caught and she stopped.

The war's cause was never far from any of them, was it? "We must sound an alarm, warn everyone!"

Ba'ara caught her arm before she could leave, and gave her a long, sad look. "There will be *no* alarm. There *can* be no alarm. All know that Benjamin will be here. If you tried to call a warning on your own, no one would support you, or even come to your help." She caught the other arm and held them both. Her strength did not keep Aksah in place, but the grief in her eyes did. Chileab's death could as well be painted there.

Aksah only stared for a moment. Her voice came back, irate. "But, Mother, that makes no sense! We cannot be meant to stand and let them take their pick! We need some defense for ourselves here."

Ba'ara tightened her grip. "Oh, Aksah, do you not see? Benjamin is still our brother. Whatever their wrong, we are all still one nation. We cannot *give* our daughters to them outright, but if these last two hundred are to do their part and join their fellows to save the tribe, we must allow them to take what and who they can."

The calm demeanor of the men standing guard, or at least playing at standing guard, now made sense. "So the men here are willing to turn us over?"

Ba'ara looked away, but not before Aksah saw the water come to her eyes. "I fear so." She cleared her throat. "I believe only the last two hundred men who still have no wives will be here. I do not think we need worry about all six hundred. One would hope the virgins of Jabesh-gilead would satisfy those who received them. I would hope they would not be selfish and take more than one wife per man, but the goal is to let the men of Benjamin capture whatever women they can."

"Not me!" Aksah's hands clenched and unclenched. "I will not be taken! I refuse to become a bride of Benjamin! After they did nothing to avenge *her*? Why would I think they can be trusted with any woman? Whenever I remember what that poor woman endured, I feel ill. And so angry. So terribly angry."

Ba'ara looked back at her, alarmed. "How did you find out what was done? Did you go see the body part that was sent to Judah? It was not something for young eyes."

"I did not *go* to see it. I happened to be standing nearby when the messenger brought it into the village. The wrapping came off as it was handed over, and I . . . I saw." It was something she would never forget, and it had seared itself in her mind and heart.

Her mother pulled her close, wrapping Aksah in protective arms just as she had known when but a little girl. "My poor child. I am so sorry you saw that. Not even I was permitted to look, only your father did, and he told me. It was not a sight for any women, young or old."

Ba'ara let go and brought her hand up to Aksah's face. It was a gesture she had never given up, not on any of her children, no matter their age. "I know you have not been eager to wed. I never pushed you but I have wondered. Why have you not wanted to marry?"

Aksah shook her head, setting her curls free. "It is not that I never want to marry. I would like to, some day." She was not ready yet to reveal the dream she held close, not even to her mother.

The Shiloh, "Him to Whom The Obedience of the Peoples Belong", was to come from Judah. *Her* tribe. While she did not know any more about this person than the deathbed prophecy of their ancestor Jacob, *someone* would have to be his mother. And it would be someone faithful. Two persons equally faithful, both the Shiloh's father and mother. If she wanted even the faintest chance of being considered worthy of such a blessing, she needed a man who shared the same goal.

Until she found that man, she would remain unwed.

That was her dream to keep close. Instead, she gave just part of the reason, the part that would not be mocked. Not that her mother would mock, Ba'ara was too naturally kind, but Aksah's wish, her hope, was just too close to her own heart. "I want to be *sure*. I do not want to resent him later. It would take a man beyond men to encourage the risk. I do not wish to be unfair to some poor man who might guess I regretted the marriage."

Her mother actually laughed. "How like me you are! I, too, was slow to wed. It seemed to me that all the freedoms came to the young. But my parents were kind enough to give me a few years to choose before they said they would pick for me. And then I met your father. I would have given the world for him." Ba'ara sobered, but the smile lingered around her mouth. "Yes, I would have gone to the ends of the earth if he but asked."

Aksah knew it was true. Her father was not tall, not handsome enough to tempt other women. But he was honest, and true, and a hard worker. She had seen him behind the oxen as they plowed the ground, and thought that his will alone kept them on track.

That was what she wanted, a man as good and true as her father. There were good men about the village but none, in her opinion, were his equal. A man one would go to the ends of the earth with if he but asked. It was as good a qualification as she could find.

If she was to produce the Shiloh, it would take a man like that to be equal to the task.

After several deep breaths, she said, "It must have been tempting to keep us at home, instead of bringing us here and living with this threat."

Aksah looked at her mother. Lines she had not noticed before now showed in the shadow of the tent where they stood. Dark circles lay under her eyes, and the outsides drooped as if she had not been sleeping well.

Ba'ara reached out and touched Aksah's cheek again. "I would not stay away from the festival, not even for that. My faith is here. We can get through this celebration if we are cautious."

Cautious? It would take more than caution. It would take constant alertness. "But what about Dinah? She was talking so foolishly. Nothing I said convinced her to be careful. I cannot stand guard every minute. She is like a bird, fluttering all over."

Her mother sighed again. She did that a lot, and for Dinah more than all the others. Her hair had gone completely grey, the last dark hairs surrendering in the last few months after Chileab's death, with no body to bury, no grave to visit. Not even the two grandchildren eased that pain. But Dinah had caused most of those grey hairs, Aksah knew.

Ba'ara had started talking. "—it will be Dinah. I do not wish her to be carted off to that land. If they would not protect one lone woman, how can I be sure they will take care of my child?" Pain laced that sentence. Her clasped hands clutched at her chest.

How can I be sure they will take care of my child? After the crime of Gibeah, how could anyone here, parent and virgin alike, be sure the Benjaminites would be kind to the women they captured? They might all be of the same nation, this might have been a decision made by the wisest men in Israel, but Benjamin had made themselves pariahs. Everyone understood the women unfortunate enough to be caught were unwilling gifts from the nation. All for Benjamin's survival. If the nation had not found this solution, this tribe would have died off. That would have been a tragedy, in the minds of the nation's wise men. Benjamin, the founder of this rebellious tribe, had been the last of Israel's sons, and more important, the one his beloved Rachel had died while giving birth.

Aksah looked up toward the hilltop, just a line against the midday sun. The vines were ancient, from before Israel dispossessed the Canaanites, and tall, their trunks wide and established, the new leaves filling in the crowns and giving more shelter. A Benjaminite could nearly stand up there and not be seen.

But no Benjaminite would be foolish enough to do that. No, stealing wives required strategy and stealth, qualities they clearly had in abundance. When they struck, it would be quickly, with no warning.

Except perhaps a lone, accidental sighting.

The girls came into sight at last, but not among the tents where they would be safe. No, the two matching dark heads were back on the hillside, bobbing in the middle of the brightly colored robes of the gathering dancers. "Mother, I see the twins!" Aksah touched her mother, and pointed. "They are with the dancers." Dinah had likely slipped behind a tent, dragging Deborah with her, and turned around. "That is near where I thought I saw the Benjaminites in the vineyard. I will go bring the twins back."

"Mother!" Rachel called from within the tent, and Ba'ara twisted instantly to the sound of the voice.

"You always were my most sensible child," she said to Aksah, and moved toward the tent opening. "I never had the problems with you that I did with the others. I am only glad that your will leaned toward good. You hated to see anyone hurt. We even had to keep you away when your father slaughtered an animal for food." She slipped inside, the curtain falling behind her.

Aksah smiled at that, and shifted to look back at the girls. Sensible, and good. Although her mother told her that often, she had never given it any mind before. There were better things one could be, she thought, especially if one were to wed. Like beautiful.

What would it feel like, hearing that from a man?

If one were captured by Benjamin, one would be with the very kind of man *not* wanted. Was there anything worse than that? Separation from one's family, and with a dangerous man and no protection of any kind?

She shuddered, and looked up the hill to the broad flat tier that the dancers had claimed, watching the twins in their group. The circle began to form, the music started, the women went into the first steps. Stupid Dinah! Why did she never listen to those with more experience? Aksah walked back toward the hill and started climbing the path toward the dancing.

She had to step lightly to dodge the ever-moving circles of women, laughing and twirling to the music. When she reached the circle that included her sisters, she thought she saw Deborah notice her and quickly look away, but it might have been the dance. She knew better than anyone how hard it was to watch anything when the circle moved so quickly.

There was nothing she could do this moment. She could hardly grab for the girls as the circle went around. Aksah backed out of the way, and sank down on a folded blanket. A few pieces of bread had been left out in an open basket nearby, a feast for the dancers and watchers. Her stomach suddenly reminded her that she had not eaten the first time. She picked a piece and chewed as she watched the circles revolve.

Perhaps it was where she was sitting, perhaps it was that they were suddenly bolder, but an unmistakable head appeared through the vines. Then another, and another, but followed by shoulders and torsos.

She choked on the bread, and spat it out. A scream ripped past the restriction of her throat, all the panic in her soaring over the music, the laughter, and hanging on the air.

The dancers stopped, the music plunked to an end, the notes discordant as the players realized what was happening. More screams filled the air as the women grabbed at each other, abandoning their blankets and food baskets, and started to run.

Dinah shaded her hand and looked upward. Deborah had started to run, but Aksah stared, appalled, across the pressing crowd that tried to carry her along as her sister stopped and looked around to find her twin. Aksah saw Dinah realize the danger just as a seeming army of men came over the top in a wave.

"Run!" Aksah screamed and fought past the bodies dragging her with them as she tried to get to her sisters. "Run!"

She saw Deborah catch Dinah's arm, saw the girls turn, saw them start to run.

And saw the first men single them out. Several swerved in their direction.

"Get out of my way!" Aksah screamed, and pushed back against the crowd. "Move!"

She did not know how she broke free, but suddenly she was in the open. She felt more than heard the people run, the ground shuddered under so many feet.

The men came fast, running along the vine rows toward the downward paths as though their tribe depended on it. The twins were well behind the crowd racing for the safety of the tent village, still so very far away, and the men kept coming.

Aksah grabbed her robe, holding it up and away from her feet as she ran to cut between the men and the girls. She had no breath to scream, she just ran, between them now, they would have to catch her first before they could reach the other two.

The crowd was still ahead of them. A scream rose up, piercing the air.

They had captured one. Aksah ran harder, grasses stabbing through her sandals until it seemed her feet were being lashed. A slope, and a short level space, then another slope, and another flatness, gaining speed as she went. Men were coming from the side, heading toward the thundering group.

Something brushed her back, and her heart lurched. *No*, she thought, but heard nothing.

Her legs churned like a mouse as it raced across the floor. The brush against her back came again, closer this time, the feel of fingers. The hill went level again, her speed slowed.

Run, run, run, her mind chanted. *Run!*

A push, sharp, and suddenly the ground rushed to meet her, her hands flinging out to break her fall.

I am caught, she thought, despair rushing over her. Mother, the twins, Father, the boys, Chileab's wife and children, the house, their fields, the images raced through her mind, and then she hit. Hard.

Her heart must have stopped. If her heart had been beating she would have jumped to her feet and kept running, after the crowd that was nearing the tents. She thought she saw two sets of matching hair running in the group, but that was not possible, was it, at this distance, with her face so close to the ground, with a man pressing one heavy knee on her back, leaning over her, his shuddering breath in her ear as he tied her hands where they lay stretched out on the dirt.

"I have one," she heard a deep voice say, and felt her cheeks grow wet, felt a sob build inside and fight for release, but it could not come out because of that weight on her back. And the band of cloth that went over her mouth, pinning all sound within.

She wept inside instead, screamed and fought inside, kicked her feet against the ground.

"Hold her feet," the man on top of her said sharply to someone else, something tight wrapped around her thrashing feet, and they no longer moved either.

How many men were around her?

Aksah felt her screams continuing, heard their mewling sounds in her ears. Over that her heart thundered its panicked beat, *no, no no!* Her chest hurt, air and screams trapped inside, and that racing heart. Grit built up under her nails as her bound hands dug into the dirt, clutching it, gouging the ground, hoping that tenuous grip would keep her here.

God, help me! Save me!

She was pulled upright, a shoulder went into her stomach and pressed her bound hands into her soft flesh, and the ground flipped upside down. The sky was behind her head, she could not see it, she could only see his tattered robe, see his legs start to move, his sandals flashing their darkened soles against the rocks and grass and soil showing the scuffs and gouges of so many feet. Through the vines, upward toward the hill's flat top, the gnarled trunks and their solid stakes going past so quickly she could not keep up with the changes.

Screaming continued, but outside the din in her head, other women shouting and begging on either side, blending into a thunder of noise from far beneath as the celebration turned into grief.

She, the good daughter, the obedient daughter, the sensible daughter, carried away by the men of Benjamin, away from the makeshift village that only a few short minutes ago was a happy place.

Anger began to sear away her shock. Aksah forced her throat to release, and quieted the cries inside. *Think!* She had to think! If only she had gone to her father, gone to the elders, gone to someone, *anyone* who would have stopped the dances, kept everyone away from the vineyard!

The man who held her changed his angle. No longer running uphill, he skidded and slipped down the hill's far side, but never lost his stride, never released his grip. At last the ground leveled. The sliding became a quick run, other feet pounding the ground as the whole group picked up the pace. All the joy of the day had been sucked away as if some malevolent lung had inhaled it in one quick intake of air.

Her stomach hurt from the hardness of his shoulder and her fisted hands, from the jouncing at every step. She wanted to roll off, but his arm over her hips held her in place, and men running alongside him would catch her before she hit the ground.

There would be time later, she promised herself with gritted teeth. She would get away. She would not, simply not, become a bride of Benjamin!

She shuddered. His arm tightened. It was big, and held her so securely she knew it would take a real struggle to break free. His weapons hung nearby in the wide belt that crossed his body, her cheek rubbed against a knife handle stuck through a loop. More loops in the thick leather held all manner of weapons, some she recognized and some she did not, stained with darker colors that could be anything from old sweat to blood. With her hands bound and trapped between her belly and his shoulder, she had no way to grab any of them.

Her head bobbed with his every step. His worn robe was soft against her cheek each time her head bumped against him, despite her efforts to keep from any contact. The robe was so thin she thought she saw his skin beneath the grey covering. If it had ever been dyed, no trace remained, and the bottom was nothing more than jagged, hanging strings.

Tears leaked from her eyes, dripping up her forehead and into her hair. Her nose began to run, but there was nothing she could do about that. After a few minutes, however, she could not stand it any longer, and rubbed her nose against his robe. Worse had happened to his garment, and why should she care?

Through the film that kept forming in her eyes and clearing, forming and clearing as the tears leaked out, Aksah saw the ground pass by beneath her. Feet pounded on every side, worn sandals flashing up and down, up and down. Or was that down and up? The group kicked up dust from the sun-dried earth, teasing her nose, sifting around the cloth that covered her mouth. Only the tears that kept coming saved her eyes.

The anger still churned, but it could not dry those tears. Aksah's chest squeezed against her skin, her heart burned, her lungs were swollen and tight. She saw her mother's arms stretch for her, play out against closed eyelids, but the vision only brought grief. Inside, she was fighting for her life, her fists beat against this man, her lungs hurled raging words. Inside, her feet ran for freedom until the wind howled in her ears.

The images were false, but the sound was real, her heart's beat growing and building. *Kerthump, Kerthump, KERTHUMP!* The pain went from the bottom of her head—or was that the top now with the world upside down?

Her scalp burned, her face felt swollen, and the pain kept its relentless pounding.

The tears flooded her eyes again, and a sob built. She choked against the gag.

When was he going to put her down? Much more of this, and she would vomit.

In fact, the time was here. Aksah began to struggle in earnest, bobbing her legs against his grip and banging her head against his back.

"What is wrong with you?" He—whoever he was—flipped her up and onto her feet. Aksah wobbled, and her hands grabbed for her mouth. He guessed what was coming. Before she could pull it down, he whipped off the gag without even bothering to untie it, yanking several strands of hair out with the cloth.

"Breathe," he ordered, but the minute he let go of her, her legs gave way. Aksah braced herself on her bound hands and heaved what little she had eaten during that last dance out onto the ground. She scooted away, digging in her heels to push herself away from the tiny puddle, then flopped onto the ground. The world spun around her, and her head still pounded. Her stomach was sore inside and out, and she rubbed it to ease the bruises she could reach.

"I apologize. I was not thinking of your discomfort. I should have been. Forgive me." His deep voice spoke the words close to her face. He must be kneeling. Aksah closed her eyes. She did not want to see the man who spoke so kindly to her. Not yet. Maybe not ever.

A sloshing sound brought them back open. A waterskin appeared in front of her face. "You will want to ease your stomach. Take some. We have little time, so we must make the best of it."

She reached with her bound hands, and he folded them around the skin. It did not have much water, if she drank more than a little, he would do without. He deserved it, was her first thought as she lifted it to her mouth. Her second thought was that this was not a compromise. She had just been ill, this was necessary. Her throat was tight, but the water trickled down.

Every step he took ripped her dream away from her. Shiloh did not come from Benjamin. If she was to keep faith with that promise and hold true to that precious possibility, she had to get away.

"I will not gag you." The waterskin was pried from her hands. She managed not to look up. He went on, "Now it matters not whether you scream, if you even can. If you lose any more food, I do not want you to choke." He—whoever he was, she did not want to know his name—grasped her hand bindings and pulled her to her feet. The ground shifted once, then steadied, but she could not have fallen against the force of his grip.

She opened her mouth to slash him with words, but she made the mistake of opening her eyes as well and finally saw the man who thought she was his. He was huge, this man who had caught her. Much bigger than her father, bigger even than Chileab. She barely came to his armpits, and she had never considered herself a small woman.

If all the men of Benjamin were so large, what had possessed them to be so cowardly in meting out justice against one lone city? And what night-mares had that woman suffered in a Benjaminite city at the hands of men this size before death mercifully claimed her?

Aksah bit her tongue and held the heated words inside, feeling them building in her throat, tightening her chest as the anger boiled and brewed. Dark eyes, clear and intelligent, looked back at her, boasting satisfaction as loudly as if he had a horn to his lips and blared its call. His hair coiled around his head in sweaty curls and hung over his forehead and ears, then merged into the beard. He met her gaze boldly, this man who thought he had caught himself a wife. This was the man she would have to outwit to gain her freedom.

And gain it she would.

No matter the cost, she would not give him anything to use against her. It was not going to be easy. He thought like a warrior, she did not know how to plan like that. Hard as it was, Aksah just met his gaze.

Those dark brows came down, she saw them even beneath the tumbled curls. The smile vanished from his eyes and his lips thinned. "Be angry, I expect that. But remember that this was a decision by the nation, and you will find no sympathy anywhere."

No sympathy anywhere. Her jaw clenched and it took every bit of her will to keep her mouth shut. Her legs were still lashed together, she could not stand without help but needed his large hands on her arms to hold her balance, and that added to her anger.

Her captor leaned down and his eyes filled her gaze. Against her will she noticed their color, a strange dark color, not brown as she expected, not green either, but something in between. A thick rim of black circled the iris. "I am going to untie your feet. If you so much as move while I am down there, if I think you intend to kick, I will toss you back on the ground and hobble you. See how much fun it is to run that way. Because run you will."

He straightened, and Aksah saw a smile curve his mouth under his beard. "Be angry if you must. I do understand, but this is the way it will be. You knew we would be there at the festival. It is just your fate that I was faster."

A haze of red coated her vision. Her jaw clenched, and her hands tried to swing, to wipe that smile off, but only jerked because his hand still held that heavy knotted rope.

He laughed! "Be angry, I expect that. Just remember, I am a warrior. I can outrun and out-plot you. You are well and truly caught."

Aksah felt her eyes narrow. He thought he could out-think her, did he? Now she really did have something to prove.

His eyes narrowed as well. "Believe me when I say I will make you run with your legs hobbled if you kick. Besides, you are tethered to me already, so do not think to run." He patted the thick loops of rope that crossed his body and for the first time she realized the rope around her wrists was of one piece with the rest of it. She could only run as far as the first loop.

A strange noise burst from her mouth. A sob of despair? A scream of anger?

The man bent down and fumbled around her ankles. Aksah felt them come free but remained still. She was not stupid. Another chance, a real one that time, would come.

"We have fallen far behind. We have much time to make up." He released a couple loops from across his chest, a big chest so the rope fell to the ground. "Prepare to run. It will do you good. You want to run, so run."

Turning around, her captor took a couple loping steps and Aksah realized it was run or be dragged. She ran, slowly at first, feeling the rope pull at her hands and shoulders. Her lungs protested, still tight from the sobs that had been trapped inside. Coughing, gasping, she cleared her airway, and picked up speed.

She would not let him know that, despite his long legs, the length of each stride, she was lighter, smaller, and knew how to run very fast. Two brothers had given her plenty of practice. His size against her speed? It might be an equal contest.

Until she tired. Aksah plotted and ran, using the time to imagine vengeance. He had endurance on his side, she had determination and guile.

It took less time than she expected to catch the main group. They were moving with determination, but not running full out as she had been, and Aksah was glad to slow. As she and her captor blended into the group, Aksah saw the other women were all bound much like herself.

Just then, a woman tripped and fell, dragging her captor to a halt. Aksah stopped and watched, ignoring the pull from the other end of the rope. He could just stop. She needed to see this. These men were all Benjaminites, every women here had the right to see how they would be treated.

She would not let herself remember how her own captor had stopped and let her vomit, and then had untied her legs. She would only remember how he laughed at her. Besides, he was only one man among many and they all had to know they were on trial.

As Aksah watched, the Benjaminite who captured her scrutiny hurried back to check on the fallen woman. He crouched in the dirt and lifted her head with both hands, scanning her face. One large hand brushed a spot on the woman's cheek, and Aksah saw him sigh. His beard crinkled, so he must have been relieved at what he found there. Even though she could not see it, she knew he smiled, in part because the woman in the dirt smiled as well.

Then, as Aksah watched in dismay, the man blew more dirt off the woman's hands. *And placed a kiss on the palm of each one!*

The fallen woman's face went soft and tender, her eyes became luminous and every muscle in her body relaxed.

For every softening on the other one, Aksah's own body tightened in rage. Her jaw clenched and the stiffness went both into her head and down her neck. The tightness of her hands ran up her arms and settled in her shoulders.

How could any woman be such a fool? Did she really think the behavior of any man in front of a gathering of watchers was any kind of prediction of his behavior in private?

Something heavy landed on Aksah's tight shoulder and she felt herself be turned. Despite her resistance, she found herself looking at her man. She could smell a deep, musky odor, and knew it was from him. It was not a nasty smell, he had bathed before coming on this trek. To try to win over his captive?

If so, he had grabbed the wrong woman.

He was scowling, his eyes narrow and hard. "Did you expect him to kick her? Drag her back to her feet? Did I hurt you when you needed to be put down?" A sound much like a growl rattled in his throat. "One ugly event, and we are all condemned."

"One ugly event, a rebellion and a war," she snapped back at him before catching herself and pressing her lips together.

"We are not discussing this now," he returned in the same sharp tone she had used on him. "We must keep moving." Turning away, he walked several steps, and then began to run again, and Aksah fell into step as she had before.

The group kept going, and began to spread apart, filling in the gullies between the hills, making the whole plain's base look like it was moving. Was this done on purpose, scattering in case spears or arrows rained down on them?

The sun warmed her face, arms and neck, ankles and legs as the men and their captives hurried across the plain. Benjamin's territory was south of Ephraim's land, where the city of Shiloh was. No one was crying, but perhaps that was because no one had the breath as they were dragged along.

The men found a way to avoid the hilly peaks, Aksah noticed, running around the gullies between each rise instead of trying to drag or carry their prisoners up and over. Without the ups and downs, she knew the captors were conserving strength, and that meant traveling farther and faster.

Plots of escape formed. She could beg the need to relieve herself, and he would have to untie her hands. Although, Aksah thought as she saw him dodge rocks that could trip them, rocks she had not even seen until then, he would no doubt catch her before she had gone ten steps.

And she had imagined she could outrun him? She had not been watching closely enough.

A whistle from ahead sounded, and her captor slowed to a walk. Clearly the group was about to take some rest. She felt the presence of others close beside her even when she could not see them.

Her captor stopped at last, the ever-moving ground stilled. Brown soil, tufts of grass, a cluster of yellow flowers between some pink rocks. From where she stood behind him, she noticed the back of his legs, covered with a layer of dirt. Her legs must look the same, she thought.

Now that she had time, Aksah took stock of their location. If she was to get home, she had to know what to look for.

Trees were scattered here and there, small and scrubby and a few poked above in the hollows of the rolling land, still green from the last of the rainy season's runoff. Flowers bloomed on the slopes, but the blooms were withering now as spring gave way to summer, and bushes held on to the spiny green for a time. She saw the greyish underside of the olive trees' leaves. Tall palms could be seen in the distance. Did that mean there was water, and if so, why were they not heading in that direction?

She thought she smelled the sweetness of the broom tree, but did not see one. She did notice a couple of almond and pistachio trees with their slender trunks and wide crowns. Her stomach growled, and her mouth watered. The nuts would not be ripe for months, but she could remember the taste and longed for a handful of each. Or two, enough to rebuild her strength.

She turned her head, working to memorize the rest of the land. Small green pods hanging in another tree in the distance, the clusters contrasting with the darker leaves, caught her attention. Aksah squinted. Was that a carob tree?

How rich this land was! Were they still in Ephraim's territory? Would Benjamin's land be the same? Between the olives and dates, the nuts, even the sweetness of the carob's odd flavor, no one would go hungry here.

The distant hills caught her attention. Hills, like so many other hills, but Aksah discovered with a jolt of surprise that she knew them. On the family's yearly journey to Shiloh, a journey they never missed unless her mother was near to delivering another babe, she and the other children had climbed around them, ran up them, even gleaned the leftovers of the harvest on them for extra food along the walk. Passing by those familiar rises had been time for celebration, knowing they were nearly to Shiloh and the festival.

If she could find her way this far, or escape before they travelled much further, she could make her way home.

She must not let him know what she recognized. Instead, Aksah turned and looked at her fellow captives. The return journey would be better, safer, if there were several in the group. It should be easy to find others of like mind. There might even be some who had had their eyes on men from their own villages before today, and were waiting for a marriage offer.

Before today.

Would her life break down into before this day, and after? The thought made her ill, all that she would lose. Aksah refused to let herself think of that any longer. She had to get back to Judah, and she would bring whoever she could with her.

To search out women who shared her determination, however, she had to find a way to talk to them.

She tried to count, but the men kept getting in the way as they circled the group. Her balance unsteady with an unwelcome wave of weakness, Aksah absorbed what she could. Some women sat on the ground, others were allowed to pace but only in a circumscribed area. And always, circling the outside, the captors, the men of Benjamin.

A heavy hand came down on her shoulder, making her start and wobble. The man held her steady and pulled her around to face him. She must have given herself away because his dark eyes were clouded with annoyance.

"I will allow for your anger for a short while, but a short while only. Think of us. There are just six hundred Benjaminites remaining in all, as I am certain you are well aware. No one at Shiloh was hurt, you need not fear for your family." He seemed to lean closer, or was it the mention of her family that smothered her? "You kept us from catching the two women. Were they members of your family?"

Aksah jerked. He had to feel it, as close as they were standing, as firm as his grip was.

"Ah. I thought as much." He shook his head, and the drying curls flapped around his ears. "You should be pleased with yourself. You kept us from getting the two in one snatch. They are safe in the bosom of your family. You might think that you have lost any hope of the life they will have, that you are reduced to a future of misery. If so, put that from your mind. And there will be a good life for you. Busy with work and sons and daughters."

Taking a breath, forcing her jaw to unlock, Aksah said in a tone far too polite, "I need a moment alone. If you could untie me." She almost choked getting out the last word. "Please?"

He looked at her, his brows in a slight scowl. "And leave you free? I think not. If you need privacy, I will walk you to a bush and turn my back. I will untie your hands from their double bondage, but I am not going to let you wander about the hills of Ephraim."

He was not done. "I will link us together, wrist to wrist. And know this." His voice grew sharp. "If you think to untie us from each other once your hands are free, I will know if you are ready to run. You see, the instant the rope goes slack, I will be around the bush. You cannot outrun me. You have already learned that."

The man picked her off her feet, one arm around her back, the other under her knees. Aksah stiffened at the closeness. Being held this way, as a man did to a woman when there was some kind of feeling between them, hurt down in her chest. It was a betrayal of her loss of a most beloved brother. A betrayal of her determined stand on the side of the woman his people had murdered, the people who then had gone on to taunt the rest of the nation with her death.

Aksah wanted to squirm, to fight in his arms, but her shoulders hurt from being stretched out in front, her arms were sore from fighting the weight of the rope. Her legs burned from the constant running. Even her feet were sore from the dust that had built between her skin and the leather. She wanted to squirm, but her body was too tired to fight and betrayed her by enjoying the respite.

He set her down on the far side of a bush with great care, and walked around to the opposite side, granting her privacy. She knew, somehow, that he was trying to court her, to treat the captive, this woman he thought he was going to have as a wife, with care and win her over. Or at least start.

He did not know who he had captured. He would never be able to win her. She could not join the army and fight a battle, but she could refuse to submit.

Right now, though, she had to take care of her own needs. Aksah peered through the scrubby bush. She took her time, making sure to tug on the rope every little bit. The crowd was too far away to see the expressions on the faces, but she was not looking for that alone. No, she was looking for actions, mannerisms, anything that might indicate someone who would be willing to turn their back on their captor, to take a chance and run with her.

Assuming their captors let down their guard. She would have to be very alert.

She focused on the assemblage again. There were about fifty women and an equal number of men, a mere one quarter of the number of Benjaminites they had expected. No doubt this group was but one section of the men that had stalked the celebration. They must have come in from all sides, and split up in their flight.

Although it is entirely possible, she thought remembering her mother's words, that no one would pursue them.

Some of the women were tied as she had been, but even as she watched, they were released from their bonds and led away, no doubt to find bushes just as her own captor had done.

One of the women who still sat on the ground, hands tied, was approached by a man. He held out a waterskin, and the woman looked up at him. Everything in her demeanor was soft, the curve of her neck as she looked up, the way she reached for the skin to balance it even as he refused to let it go. As she moved a bit, and lifted her head to swallow the water inside, Aksah recognized her from the fall. She was a plain woman, large ears and a bent nose, but had a face of such sweetness Aksah was not surprised someone had chosen her.

Then the woman smiled up at the man. Aksah could see it even from between the branches. Her mouth fell open as she watched. The man reached out and touched his captive's cheek. His finger slid along it and back behind her ear, brushing away a tendril of hair no doubt.

The woman did not look like she objected, but perhaps she was more clever than Aksah and knew how to hide her feelings. If that was the case, she was very talented in her acting. It was a skill that might need to be learned, although such duplicity sat uneasily in the stomach.

Akash did not realize how still she had become until her wrist jerked. In reflex, she yanked the rope in return. She needed more time to watch so, her captor placated, she went back to studying the group.

A voice interrupted, far too close. "I know you are done. Did you take advantage of the time to plot your escape? Do you believe I am too dull to guess?" With every word he came closer, she heard his steps on the other side of her meager protection.

Aksah straightened. "And where would I go?"

He looked down at her from his lofty height. "I did not stay alive by ignoring signs. Do you think I did not notice what your body told me as we passed through these hills? You know this area. You recognize where we are. So be assured, I will redouble my watch." He reeled in the rope as he talked, wrapping it across his body, each step bringing him ever closer until at last he had come around the bush. "I hope you did what you came here to do, because there will be few stops until we are far enough away that escape is not possible."

CHAPTER 4

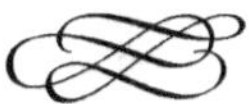

*"As for you, Judah, your brothers will praise you. Your hand will be on
the neck of your enemies. The sons of your father will bow down before
you. The scepter will not depart from Judah, neither the commander's
staff from between his feet, until Shiloh comes, and to him the obedience
of the peoples will belong."*
Genesis 49:8,10

Eliab watched the woman he had captured. She was angry, her eyes
were cold every time she glanced his way, which she contrived to do
as seldom as possible. He had to bite the inside of his cheek to keep the smile
in check. He had not expected to take anyone who was happy to be caught,
but this one was taking her capture particularly hard.

"There will be few stops until we are far enough away." Eliab did not say
those words just to frighten her. He could see the plans running through her
mind. They were easily readable in her expressive eyes. He would have to
watch his back.

She knew the reason behind this war. Her knowledge showed in her face, her sharp tongue, her complete rejection of him. He was unhappy with the way Benjamin had reacted to the crime, but one man against the entire tribe? His voice had never even been heard. He was not among the village elders, though he had been in the army since he was old enough and strong enough to handle a blade and carry a shield.

If anything like that horrible crime were to happen again, he would speak longer and louder. They would have to listen to him. There were only six hundred left, sufficient for each man to have a say. He would never live long enough to see his tribe restored to its former size and glory, but he would know he had done his part to restore Benjamin.

Although he needed this woman to do so.

Eliab hated having to bind her again but he had no choice. None of the men did. Every woman here would run if given the slightest chance, and this one would no doubt lead the escape. She knew the way. They had several days' journey to go before they reached what was left of his family's land. Several days when he would risk alienating her further, several days when she would have to be bound, when she would not be allowed to do the most intimate bodily functions without him being at least within earshot.

He looked again at the woman he captured as he reached the end of the rope. She was on the short side, although most women were compared to him, and lovely, with curly light brown hair that tangled around her fine boned face. She had a smooth nose, and large eyes that were a blend of brown and green, darker around the middle, lighter in the center, and dark again around the rim. Her mouth had full lips that begged to be kissed, although that would have to wait. Eliab chuckled as he thought what might happen if he tried to steal a taste of that mouth. He would have taken whichever woman he caught, but what a delightful bonus that she was so very agreeable to look at.

What children they would make! His daughters would be the prettiest—Eliab caught himself. How easy it was to think in terms of having a whole tribe, a whole city to compare with his offspring. His children would not be the most intelligent, the prettiest, the most handsome. They would be the sole village, the only pretty, intelligent, handsome ones. There would be none to compare with them.

He reached for her other hand. "I dislike having to tie your hands together. I know it must hurt. If I did not bind you, I know you would run the moment I turned my back."

Ah, there it was, that glint in her eye.

"Do not try to lie and say I am wrong." Eliab grabbed for her hand as she pulled it away. He was not going to tell her how easily she revealed her thoughts. Let her think she was inscrutable, let her believe it was a chance guess. "I would think less of you if you gave in too easily." As he said it, he wondered what prompted the words.

And then he knew. He would not want sons who were weak and without spirit. He wanted sons with courage, determination, and intelligence. His newly chosen wife, unless he was totally wrong, had all three.

He did not think he was wrong.

Although, at the moment as they fought for custody of her hand, the woman moving it about like a child's top, him always a blink behind, he was not certain he wanted children with her rebellion.

There were ways to stop her, to block her hand without this nonsense, but it could cause pain and he would not do that to her. She thought little enough of him already. So if they had to play this game of catch-the-hand, he would do it.

There! He snagged her hand in mid-swing, spun her against him, enjoying that brief moment of contact, and wrapped the rope around her two hands together. She tugged against it, hard, and he had to hold tight to keep her from hurting herself. The rope was rough and she had enough already to overcome. Pulling her close, Eliab spoke into her ear. "I told you I did not want to hurt you. See what happens when you fight? Now your wrists will be sore when I release you."

She, Aksah of the tribe of Judah through which Moses' successor, the prophet to take his place, would come, was being dragged away to an unknown future. She forced herself not to think about what would happen if she could not find a path back. So far she thought she caught glimpses of things she remembered, a tall outcropping that reminded her of where the family would take rest from the sun on their long yearly journey to Shiloh, a shimmer that might be the promise of a river they crossed, or a spring where they filled the waterskins and took a few moments to play.

Limestone poked its white head up as it did in her own land, and dotted their route, threatening the unwary with turned ankles.

They were on a path, she could see that. The wear of endless feet and hooves that wore the roots away left trails pointing off into the distance. Here and there she saw shallow grooves in the ground, no doubt the remnants of the last wagon wheels.

She had no blanket, nothing to keep the night's dew off. What would the man do when they had to rest? Would he tie her to himself? Whatever it took, she would be brave. She would find a way to escape, would pit her anger and determination against his skill and win.

Six hundred men for a whole tribe's territory. They would be thinly spread and there would be plenty of room to get away.

If she could remember their path and trace it back. She could hardly turn and run now. The entire group would chase her down, fifty warriors hot on her trail.

No, she would have to be more wily than them, find a perfect time to break free. Maybe at night, but the thought of travelling across this vast terrain, the hills that began to blend one into another, where it would be so easy to fall off a ledge, to wander into a lion's den, to run out of water, frightened her. So many ways to die.

But not at the hands of violent men. Not that, never that.

What was her mother thinking right now? Her father? Her only living brother? The twins? Little Rachel? Aksah's throat closed against the sudden sob that built, and she choked at the strain.

Her captor stopped and looked back, then retraced his steps to her side. She felt her shoulders tighten as he drew near.

"Let me give you ease. Do not fight me." His voice was almost a croon, but she was not that easy to soothe. He would learn that soon enough.

Her captor had told her she prevented them from reaching the twins, but Aksah knew this group surrounding her was not all of Benjamin. These hardly totaled six hundred men. Perhaps others had risen from the vines and grabbed her sisters, men he did not see because he was so busy subduing her.

If only she could be certain the girls were safe, if only she could be certain her intervention had been in time!

She wanted to pray for guidance home, but a little worry started, annoying like an itch she could not reach.

If this plan for brides really was from God, was she breaking faith by fighting it?

That could not be. God would not ask such a thing of her, whose own brother had been killed in the war. Nor would he ask it when she was trying to defend the value of women. From the day she had heard of the crime of Gibeah, she had been appalled by the injustice, the brutality. She had wanted to take a stand, to make the men of Benjamin appreciate a woman's worth. Perhaps there were other women of Israel who were not so affected, who would not feel so broken by being captured.

Granted, the whole rest of the nation had risen in the woman's defense. Yet it had become so much a part of Aksah that *she* needed to do something to defend that nameless victim, even though the dead woman would not be alive to see.

Another part of her harbored a seething anger at the man who had shoved his concubine out of the house and into the mob. He had been of Levi's tribe, not Benjamin's, but that only made men all the more frightening.

Aksah had vowed that she would never allow a marriage that would put her with such a man. All of her, every part of her being, needed to know her husband would treasure her above all else. And lately, she needed to know that nothing would force a husband to send her into a crowd of blood-thirsty men.

Out of someplace in her mind, she heard again her mother's voice, from so recently. *Benjamin is still our brother.*

There had been no sound of pursuit, even as her mother had suggested. It hurt, the tightness in her throat came back. Ba'ara's voice had been so clear on the subject. The whole family had suffered a great loss. How could any of them find it within themselves to forgive a tribe so unrepentant? In none of the reports she heard had any Benjaminites said they were sorry for the crime. Sorry for the battle's loss, yes, but not sorry for what caused it.

Benjamin is still our brother. No one would follow them. Her captor had repeated the same thing.

No, that was not true. A little light started deep inside, pushing aside the hurt and the rising panic. Her father would come. He would. A bargain could be struck for release, and this would be over.

"Are you well?" The man leaned down again to peer into her eyes. "We are near water. Everyone needs a drink, we need to fill our skins for the rest of the day." He smiled. "We have been walking through the heat of the day. That is not good for anyone. My commander has ordered a rest. You stay here, and I will go fill my skins."

Stay here? Aksah felt a flare of excitement through her exhaustion. He was leaving her on her own?

"We are splitting the men into two groups, so each woman will share being watched with another." His eyes twinkled, and he stroked the beard on his jaw as if thinking. "Two women under the eye of one man? I think we can handle you."

Aksah's shoulders slumped. She was quite sure he was right. Bright sun, and still twenty-five men to watch? She would be a fool to attempt it, and had always prided herself on *not* being such.

He leaned close as he slid the heavy loops of rope off his shoulder and let them fall to the ground. "Go ahead and try to take the ropes off your wrists. You would be better served to try to catch a few moments of sleep."

Sleep? While she did not think she would actually be able to drift off, a few moments prone sounded wonderful. The pile of rope on the ground would do nicely as a pillow. Without saying a word, Aksah sank down onto the ground, rested her head on the thick loops, and closed her eyes.

Eliab looked at the woman by his feet. Those expressive eyes that gave away her every thought were now closed against his prying gaze. Unless she was a better actress than he guessed, and he very much doubted that, his woman was already asleep. All it took was the chance to get flat.

He should go over to the well they had found and get in line for filling his waterskin. Twenty-five men with empty skins would take a bit of time,

time he could spend either standing talking to men he had already spent four months trapped in caves with, or he could crouch at this nameless woman's side and watch her.

Strange, despite the hours they had spent tied together, he did not know her name. While he doubted very much that she was at all interested in finding out what his name was, he ached to know hers. They both were now trapped in this solution the nation had thrust upon them, yet there was no reason why they would not find happiness.

He needed sons, but he wanted a family with joy and laughter. Among the nation, the love stores of Abraham and Sarah, and Isaac and Rebekah were legend.

Another, more powerful, reason had been added since the war. His tribe had to rebuild their reputation. It would do no good to have stories spread around the nation about more unhappy women. No, now he and his fellow survivors needed to have the most content wives in all Israel.

Soft breaths whispered through the barest opening between her lips. As he stared at that mouth that tempted him, Eliab realized how dry those lips were.

She needed water, and if he was honest, he was thirsty, too. There was no need to prove how strong he was. The mere fact that he had survived the war proved it. Now he had a new reason to live, and care for himself.

He had a wife depending on him, needing his protection.

Eliab pushed himself to his feet, bent to snatch up the skin, and walked to the well.

Evening closed in, the sun hung low. Shadows stretched long, one hill's shade bleeding into that of the next. Palms could be seen, though little more than dark slashes with soft heads poised tall and proud even in the coming dark.

She did not feel either tall or proud. Even her anger in behalf of the murdered woman was hardly enough to keep her walking. Aksah did not know how much time had passed since he put her on her feet. She was still lashed too close to his belt, and he walked with strong steps ahead. Her own steps dragged, and not just from reluctance. Her endurance had worn thin long before and now only determination kept her moving ahead.

She would not cringe or weep, not in front of him at least. No, she would not be a weakling, even if she had to walk until she dropped. It gave her purpose, a way to stand for the woman, a way to make the men of Benjamin see the value and strength of women.

Even if only the one man watched.

At the evening meal, if it could be called that, just rough bread and sips of water from skins that had become thin and floppy with empty space, the men must have decided their captives were too tired, that no one would dare try to run with exhaustion pulling at them. The sun was slipping below the horizon, the last of its rays would soon be gone.

As discouraging as it was to admit, Aksah knew flight was folly. The group had stopped in the one open space they had seen in some time. The land around was a nearly endless carpet of little mounds, small ups and downs that tired the legs, but this area was flat. Trees were rare in this small plain, and the ones around were stunted, with thin trunks. No one could hide behind them. The nearest hill of any size that might offer a valley deep enough to hide her was temptingly near, but still too far away. Any of the men could catch her long before she reached its shelter. Running toward concealment was out, but she could put one part of her plan into effect and speak to the women.

At last.

The other groups were being fed, women in a large cluster near the small fire, men off to one side in their own separate gathering. They were not far from their captives. Aksah looked at the men and measured the distance between them and the women. She knew the placement was deliberate, far enough away to talk without being overheard, but close enough that the women were well aware they were still under guard.

All of them, men and women alike, appeared worn down from the day, few on either side were looking happy.

Aksah rose from where the man had left her sitting on the ground. Food always broke restraint and there would hardly be a better time to broach her plan. She had little for an offering, but she could bring the nearly-empty waterskin, and a few fig cakes he had secreted away. If he got angry at her sharing their food, he could just find a way to get them more.

He had sacrificed part of his corded belt to bind her hands while he was away. Aksah glared down at his handiwork. It would make things more difficult, but it would not stop her.

Picking up the waterskin and a single fig cake, she crossed the short distance to the rest of the group.

"Greetings," she said as she stopped by the outer rim of the clustered captives. "I have water." She lifted the skin, even though her hands were still bound and she had to use both to hold it. The fig cake was beginning to crumble in her awkward grip.

"We have dried meat." One of the other women held up a bit of linen, and Aksah saw the meat sticking above like a short bouquet.

"I also have a fig cake." Aksah had to set the skin down to open her hand. The cake was in many pieces now, but the other women smiled and took them happily, a little sweetness in a sad time. She took one of the dried meats extended in exchange and bit down. "It is very good," she said after the first swallow.

A few women nudged each other. One of them motioned to Aksah's bindings. "Why are you still bound?"

She looked down at the cord. Her skin was turning red around the edges, she wondered what it would look like when he finally released her. "The man does not trust me. I do not want to be here, and he knows that."

"None of us do," the woman said in return. "But what can we do? It was the decision of the nation, we all understood there was a chance of capture when we went to the celebration."

The worry that had plagued her broke free and spilled out. "I have twin sisters, and I was caught running between the man and them. I believe he wanted to catch both at once, two brides at one try. I would not let that happen, but I thought until the last moment that I, too, would get away." Those annoying tears filled her eyes. "Where are the rest of the men? There were to be two hundred hiding in the vineyard at Shiloh, yet this group is only a portion of the total. I am afraid one of the other bands of soldiers may well have caught them."

The huddle of captives was quiet for a moment, she saw the same worry in the eyes looking back at her. Other sisters, friends, maybe even nieces who might share their same fate.

She glanced over at the men. They looked bigger, more frightening standing so close together. She would not let that stop her. In a low voice, she asked, "How many of you are willing to come with me, if I manage to break away?"

The worry in those eyes turned to alarm. "You cannot do that!" "Run away? How foolish!" "They will kill you if they catch you!" "You are asking for trouble!" "We must be obedient or we will suffer, too."

Aksah held up her bound hands. "You see me? You see *this?*" She glared across the group, looking at one set of eyes after another. "What makes you think any of you will fare any better?"

"He carried you for a while. None of us got the same consideration. Why are you complaining?" A black-haired, brown eyed, sharp-featured woman looked back at her from where she sat on the ground. The woman managed to look down her nose at Aksah even from that position. She was barely of an age to wed.

Aksah met the woman's gaze and decided this one was not coming with her on the escape. "Anywhere along the way he could have turned me loose and I would have found my way back to Shiloh, maybe even back to my home."

The black-haired woman's lip curled in a sneer. "There is no going back. We all knew that. Our future is sealed. We are brides of Benjamin, and that is the end of it."

Aksah stared at her. "Do you know how they treat their women? Have you even heard the tale?"

The woman tossed her head, the dark strands bouncing. "Yes, she was killed. What of it? She was an adulteress, she would have died anyway."

She would have died anyway. Words failed Aksah as she stared back. Those ugly words echoed in her head. Did this woman feel no connection with another of her own sex? What was done to one woman in Benjamin could happen to any! "Her husband had gone back for her. That penalty was eliminated! The entire nation was angry at that woman's death. Even more, the other tribes had to bring justice themselves because the tribe would not. That was the whole point of the war, to teach justice! How can you brush their punishment off so easily?"

"I can because I have to. This is my life now, and I must adapt. As had you. Escape is folly." The bitter black-haired woman rose from where she had been sitting on the ground. "No one will rescue you if you need help along the way. If you think to involve any of us in your folly, you deserve whatever happens. Do not make me bear any sympathy for your bonds. If you wish to be treated as we are, free to walk without ropes or bonds, give up your vengeance."

She stalked away to the far edge of the group.

Another woman, this one seemed about Aksah's own age, firelight picking out a tinge of red in her light brown hair, shook her head as she watched the woman storm off, then turned back. "She is just as angry as you. I pity her husband. She will poison his food someday."

Getting to her feet, she held out a hand, taking both Aksah's in hers. "I, too, heard what was done to the victim. I was not told what part of the body my village received, but my father came home and was sick in the garden. I always hoped to pick my own husband, or at least have some say. Instead of a joyful wedding, I got a capture by a stranger, and hard trip through the wilderness. These are hard men now, seasoned warriors, and they frighten me a little."

"Only a little?" Aksah tried to make it a joke, but the attempt was weak.

"Very well." The woman smiled, and released Aksah's hands. Without that new support the bindings suddenly felt heavy, more than they had even carrying the waterskin. "They frighten me a lot. I wish I had your courage. How can I be sure my . . . husband—" the word seemed to choke her, and she swallowed before beginning again, "—he will not try to punish me for what has happened to his family and city?"

"Who knows why they refused to help punish Gibeah? What is worse—" the words Aksah had wanted a few moments ago were suddenly there, "—Gibeah and Benjamin could not pretend it was anything other than evil, pure evil. The sin of the men far outweighed any sins the woman had committed against her husband. What is worse, all the nation asked was that those who did the crime be handed over for punishment. That was all. And for this, Benjamin came in force of arms to refuse."

She turned to the rest of the group, who were all either listening to her, or watching the soldiers around them with obvious unease. "I lost a brother in the war. Do you want to be wives of men who disregard the Law to that extent? Suppose some day you need your man of Benjamin to stand up for you. What will he do? Will he defend you? Protect you? Or will he leave you on the doorstep to die?"

The plain woman with the big ears, the one who had greeted her captor with such welcome earlier, stood up. In her sweet way, she said, "I never thought to marry. I have a husband now." The words came with a bit of triumph. "Perhaps this is not the way I hoped to get one. But what comes from here depends solely on me, and what I do. If I want to be happily wed, I must see to it that I win him over. No matter who I married, I would have left my family. I would have moved to my husband's land. I expected that all along." She shook her head, almost in pity. "Did you never consider that yourself? Never know the day you married, you would live someplace else?"

"Of course I did!" Aksah fought the frustration that built inside her. Did none of these other women realize what was truly at stake? "It would have been my own choice then, and I would have married a man I respected! How can I respect anyone who fought in defense of the men who committed such an atrocity? Men who defended the city who sheltered them? Do you never think of that poor woman?"

"Yes, of course I do." The plain woman shook her head again. It seemed her way of expressing disapproval. Aksah did not appreciate being at the receiving end of that censure. "Before you blame all of Benjamin, remember her husband, the Levite, who sent her out into the crowd. Should not some of the blame be placed on him?"

Anger overruled all thought. "If not even a Levite would spare his wife, perhaps I will never marry!" Aksah's hands hurt, and she realized they were clenched into fists.

The other woman looked at her with pity. "But you *are* wed. Like it or not, we are all wed."

Aksah's tongue finally listened to her brain and stopped wagging out words. She did not consider herself wed. There had been no ceremony, for how could snatching her from the celebration be considered a ceremony? Her wedding, when she thought of what it might be—might have been—would bring all the villagers together. There would be feasting and dancing, friends would follow her to her husband's house, or to the edge of the village if he lived farther away.

Her stomach knotted as she finished her thought, for much of what she had expected had indeed happened. There had been feasting and dancing, the whole of the celebration had watched her be taken away.

The only thing missing was the joy.

The women had begun to show more unease. Even the one who had shown the most sympathy was looking over Aksah's shoulder.

With a sinking sense of defeat, she turned around. And stared into the face of her captor. His brows were down, his mouth in a thin tight line. "I think you have caused enough disruption, and sowed enough unrest. I should not have left you alone."

He bent and scooped the waterskin off the ground, then took her arm and began marching her to their own campsite. He was silent, and she felt the anger pouring off him.

As they neared the fire, burning low now, Aksah sensed him calm. His steps slowed, and she did not have to run quite so much to keep up.

He pointed at the fire. "I found some wood. Feed the fire. We want a healthy blaze for the night. I need to get water, and there is a stream on the other side of the bank."

The stream must not be a large one, because she had not smelled any moisture, or heard it babble as it tumbled along.

"I will hear you run." He leaned close, and she had to bend back to see his eyes. "Do not even try. I want the fire burning. We are staying here for the night, and I have had enough of you. You think we of Benjamin would stop at nothing to murder a woman? Very well, you should be afraid. Now get the fire blazing, and find something for us to eat in the supplies, since you gave away our food."

Somehow, she did not feel any fear. Perhaps her rage had needed the right target, and he was it. At last she was able to tell one of the Benjaminites to his face what she thought of him, of all of them. Tell him how angry she was that she had been captured, that some of her most treasured dreams had been stolen from her.

He did not wait for her to speak, however. He stomped off, and Aksah thought she could feel the ground tremble under his feet.

He did not untie her hands! If the land had trembled under his angry stomps, it would tremble indeed when she had a chance to vent her rage.

And if the other men of Benjamin heard, all the better.

She picked up the small pieces of wood he had brought, the ones she could handle with bound hands, and fed the flames with greatest care. If not done right, it would burn too low overnight, and animals were always ready to attack anything vulnerable.

A mid-night strike would be an easy way to remove a wife, she thought as she crouched and added another stick to the growing flames. Aksah saw the scene in her mind, the lion or bear creeping toward their sleeping forms, and then a prick of guilt poked her. She knew the thought to be an unworthy one. Unworthy of herself certainly, and possibly of him. He did not go to Shiloh to avoid getting a wife. No, he wanted one. If not *wanted*, at least he *needed* one.

None of which made her want to be a wife of Benjamin.

Aksah stood and gazed into the distance, not seeing anything. Her heart burned, pain crushing her so hard every breath hurt. *Shiloh. Remember Shiloh. To him the obedience of the people belongs.* Israel's dying words to Judah and his descendants. She did not know exactly what that promise meant, what exactly Shiloh was to do, other than that the commander's staff belonged there. That and he came through her tribe.

Of course it was a foolish dream, to think of all the women in Judah she would be chosen, but someone would be the one to become the mother of Shiloh. Why not her?

If she went through with this marriage—the thought made her shudder—

that treasured dream was gone. Once that dream was gone, what would she have to replace it?

Aksah stared at the crackling fire and fought the despair that crept in like the darkness building in the sky behind her. Being of the tribe of Judah, knowing the privilege that was out for some woman, longing to be worthy of it, having that precious hope snatched away by a single tribe's folly threatened to crush her.

Was she really angry at her captor? Or was it not anger at all? Was it instead her heart and her faith fighting for their true purpose?

She heard the sloshing of the waterskin, and pulled her shoulders back. To wilt in front of him, let him see that he could bring her to tears, she could not do that.

The skin was dropped at her feet with a tight *bump* that set the water inside glugging. Aksah did not flinch. Did he think she had not heard him come?

"My name is Eliab." He stopped at her side, and she saw his arm out of the corner of her eye.

He was going to touch her. She moved one step to the side, and bent down to pick up the waterskin. His hand touched it before hers, and the other hand caught her arm. She felt herself being pulled upright, and then she saw his face.

His eyes blazed at her, or perhaps that was just the flickers of the fire. The skin around those eyes was lined, his mouth thin. "I want you to say my name, then tell me yours. It is time we know that much about each other."

Aksah's mouth went dry. All along in her mind he had been 'the man,' 'the captor.' Even 'he' or 'him.' The Benjaminite. The fire crackled and spat, a spark flickered and landed in the dirt, she traced its path from the corner of her eye. Across the short distance between their camp and the main group came the soft murmur of voices, other women talking to their men, or each other.

"My patience is not infinite." The voice was sharp. He took a deep breath, seeming to pull the air from around her. She could sense him wrenching his temper back under control. "I understand that you would rather I had been slaughtered along with the rest of my tribe. Sadly," he held his powerful arms out wide, so very wide, and her eyes followed his gesture in spite of herself. She was playing with danger, there was so much of him, broad shoulders, long arms, long legs, tall body.

He did not stop speaking. "I did not die. I am still alive, and I did only what the rest of Israel decided was my right. I went to the celebration, and there I caught a wife."

His eyes caught the firelight, turning their dark color into a lighter shimmer. His curls were wet again, and she noticed for the first time that his beard had the same water-fresh shine. He must have taken a moment to wash. For this?

He propped his hands on his hips and leaned in close. "Hate me all you wish, but you are my wife and you are not going home. Now. Say. My. Name."

Aksah took a deep breath, past the constriction of her chest, the pinching of her throat. Her eyes burned, but she would not let the tears form. "Eliab."

"I want the rest." His dark eyes pinned her like a knife in a wall. "Give me your name."

Shiloh. Messiah. The Commander's Staff, the blessing on her ancestor, Judah, from his father Israel's inspired mouth.

"Aksah." She did not know she was going to speak until the words were out. *God, please do not take this from me.*

A sound came out of him, like a sigh long held. "Hello, Aksah." He leaned over and reached far down for the waterskin. He untied the string and lifted the sack-like container, holding the narrow neck out to her.

She had drunk before at his hand and it meant nothing. This time, Aksah knew, if she drank from that bottle it would be filled with import as deep as a vow.

She had given all she could. She had given him her name, and repeated his. Looking at the skin, dripping water from the outside, Aksah swallowed past a dry throat. She must be tired, more tired than she realized. It was just a drink of water. Sooner or later she would have to drink.

She had accepted water from others at the celebration.

He set it down. He had not stepped away, was still close. She was tempted to reach out and push him away.

His broad chest inflated and he blew out a breath. "I am sorry it came to this, for my tribe and for yours. For our nation. I understand your feelings, better than you know. You have been stolen from your family and home, from all you know. This is not what either of us would choose from a marriage. But it is done."

"*Done?*" Aksah's voice sounded shrill. Her throat was tight, both from thirst and the calm way he wiped away all that led to this. "Done? You have what you wanted, a woman to produce your children. But I am the same as that woman who was killed, and I bear in myself the wrong done to her. Whatever you permitted to be done to her is a threat to me. If you could not defend her, not even after her death, why should I trust you?"

His hands came down again on her shoulders, his grip so tight she could not wrench herself away. "What do you mean, you are the same as her? Have you already given yourself to another man?"

That was too much. Aksah shoved hard with her bound hands, doubling her strength, and to her surprise she was free. He stepped back. "Of course not! Of course you would think that. Women are either worthy or not to you. We women consider ourselves as sisters, what could be done to one could be done to all. The death of one is a threat to all. And we are all threatened now."

Aksah hoped all the other men could hear. "What woman wants a man who will not defend her? Protect her? Worse, what woman wants a man who defends those who murdered her? When you—" she waved a hand toward the men off in a cluster, but did not turn to see if they were listening, "—your whole tribe, turned to attack the nation that only asked for justice, you attacked every woman in the land. Me! You attacked *me!*"

She stopped for breath. Her heart pounded in her ears, her hands were clenched so tight the cords burned her wrist. Raising her hands so the bindings were visible to all onlookers, she finished, "I never thought to marry a man who would keep me bound to him with ropes."

He leaned down. His breath brushed her face. "I never thought to have a wife who would rather be bound than stay with me." Then he turned and walked off, back toward the river.

At least they both now knew where they stood. And she would not take any of those words back.

Aksah began shaking as the anger and zeal that had propelled her words drained away. Rather than let him see, she lowered herself down to the ground, and picked up the waterskin. Her mouth had been dry when the fight began. Now it was parched, but the water tasted brackish in her mouth and she struggled to swallow it down.

More than her throat felt tight. Her chest was tight as well, and her heartbeats hurt behind her ribs. Her eyes burned but no tears came. She lifted the waterskin for another drink. Her chin trembled, the small shivers that warned of oncoming weeping.

Those shivers spread, tightening her throat further, closing her lungs. She had fought so hard to be brave, to hold herself together, to pray, until every part of her hurt.

Her heart most of all, each beat a searing pain.

She felt the barrier give way, her sorrow and fear and anger and yes, exhaustion, bursting through the tightness of her restraint. With a noisy gasp, the first sob shattered her control.

At last, at long last, she collapsed on the dirt and began to weep, washing her weakness into the dusty ground.

CHAPTER 5

*Then the Benjaminites gathered together out of the cities to Gibeah to go
out to battle against the men of Israel. That day the Benjaminites
mustered from their cities 26,000 men armed with swords, apart from the
700 chosen men of Gibeah . . . The men of Israel apart from Benjamin
mustered 400,000 men armed with swords, and each one was an
experienced warrior.*
Judges 20:15,17

Eliab looked down at the small trickle of water running along the gully
and tried to get his breathing under control. His hands clenched and
released, and for a moment he wished he still had a war to fight, something
against which to vent his rage.

No, not a war. Never again a war.

He had not yet mourned his family. There had been no time, only battles,
forays, retreats, and death. Always death. His whole family was gone, he
knew that. Mother, father, his brothers, even his sisters. Nieces and neph-
ews, cousins, grandparents.

Men who had not even been in the army, who seemingly had no part in the war, came out of cities to attack them on their retreat!

Old men he did not think could handle a spear had found things to throw. Those who had only used the arrow to hunt the hind and the gazelle shot from the city walls, and more of Benjamin had fallen.

How much the nation had come to hate his tribe!

It had seemed so simple at the beginning. Eleven tribes had invaded their land. Eleven tribes! Four hundred thousand men! The ground was thick with swords and shields around one lone city. What else was he to do but join the ranks of Benjamin? Four hundred thousand against twenty six thousand picked warriors plus seven hundred left-handed slingshot men. The best warriors of one side against the best warriors of the other. Who would win? Numbers as in the massive army Israel had mustered, or right, Benjamin defending their land? Or so he had thought at the time.

The numbers, it turned out, were in the right.

His heart burned with the pain of memory.

The first successful battles had been a welcome surprise. It had been the worst kind of conceit, he now knew, to think those first sorties won had been the sign that God was on their side.

Yet what a sight it had been to see the army of Israel running from before Benjamin's swords! His heart had swelled with pride as he joined in the chase, swinging his blade with abandon.

"Run," he had shouted, "run like the cowards you are." He still heard the sound of his voice above the din made by the screams and taunts and dying.

In the end, his taunts had come back to mock him. Four months hiding in the crags of Rimmon, watching the smoke rise from the burning cities. Four months waiting for word from the cities of Benjamin, word that came only in the smell and sight of smoke rising from the burning. The skies had been marked with grey spires reaching toward the clouds, city after city gone, set to the torch.

He had not even been back to his village, but he had been past the remnants of others on this trip to the city of Shiloh and the festival and the tabernacle. Benjamin's cities were no more than burned hulks, crumbled walls, the awful smell of burning that lingered long after the city was passed. Bodies that needed burial.

The men had grown more and more somber after that. Bodies lay across their land, so many warriors who left to fight believing they were doing the right thing and were slaughtered in vengeance. The few left all knew the fate of their tribe rested on them. Six hundred men, all that were left of the once-mighty tribe. It had been a gift for four hundred men to receive wives as spoil from Jabesh-gilead.

That had left two hundred alone to go and raid Shiloh for wives. Two hundred hated men.

At least, *he* was hated. She had been very clear about that, his bright and chosen bride. *What woman wants a man who will defend those who murdered her? Whatever you permitted to be done to her is done to me.*

Until Aksah threw those words at him, Eliab had never considered his actions from the victim's side. He defended those who murdered that woman in battle, with force of arms. He had consorted with murderers, and had not given even a single thought that he had done that very thing.

What would he have done if he had been in Gibeah when the woman had been thrown out into the street? Until tonight he had never asked himself that question. Eliab shifted his shoulders as the thought prodded him. Most likely he would have turned his back and gone into his house rather than confront an entire mob.

He turned around, but could only see the bank that rose above the river. The sky was nearly dark, a faint glow above the bank's top told of the camp. For as many people as were there, the night was surprisingly quiet.

He sighed. At least now he knew what he had ahead of him. She was going to ask for release, but that was not possible. How many other women in that group would gladly slide a blade through their men's ribs?

Unless he had chosen the only one who decided to defend the victim. Before tonight, he never thought women might have had a stake in the war. Wars were between men.

If she had been a man, what a warrior she would have made!

The river burbled at his feet, weeping for him.

It was time to return to the camp. For all he knew, his wife had managed to get her ropes off and was halfway back to Shiloh by now. She probably thought she would run into a rescue party.

There would not be one.

Which meant she would be all alone against the wild beasts.

Eliab vaulted up the bank and ran for his fire, only to stop short. His bride was there, sitting on the ground by the fire, trying to gnaw on a strip of dried meat with her hands still bound.

She had pulled off her headdress and managed to get it around her shoulders, but it was bunched in back. He had not even realized that the night was cooling, and fast, one more thing she could hold against him. The fire flickered on her hair, catching the brown curls in waves of light.

"Why?" He did not elaborate the question, just walked toward her with measured steps, afraid that she still might change her mind and flee. He could catch her but his list of failures would grow, and it was long enough already. *Why had she not run?*

"It is dark," she said, as if she could read the rest of his question.

He sat down next to her, and reached for her hands. She resisted, and he pulled harder. "I am most likely being a fool, but I will take your bindings off."

She had given him this one chance, he knew, staying by the fire instead of fleeing for the hills, she would not give him another.

Aksah held out her hands and let the man—Eliab—start in on the knots. She had an idea what her wrists would look like. They burned. If she was home, she would put some oil on them, but there would be no oil here. Men on the run did not carry fine things like that with them.

How had they survived during those four months hiding on the crags of Rimmon? The pomegranates would have been ripe for the first month or so. After that? Had they killed wild goats, eaten locusts?

The man—Eliab, she had to learn to think of his name, at least until she managed to get away—pulled at the knot. Even though the rope was large to her mind, it looked small in his hands.

She still was not sure which was better, to play at being soft, like the sweet-faced woman who was happy now to have a husband and the chance for children, or to keep faith with herself and defy him openly.

Aksah watched her hands tighten. No, she could not play at what she did not believe.

The rope fell away. Her wrists felt stiff. He inhaled a sharp sound, almost a gasp. "I did not realize it was doing such damage to your skin."

What had been a nagging soreness was actually open wounds. Aksah stared at them in surprise. "I did not know it was that bad." Now that the abrasions were freed to the air, real pain started, and she pulled her arms against her chest, cradling the burning wrists as if that would make them feel better.

"I am sorry." He looked at her, and his eyes seemed sad. But that might have been a trick of the firelight. "Come with me. We must bathe them."

He—Eliab—eased her hands out of their protective hold against her body and pulled her upright. "The river is just over this small bank. We will soak your wrists in the water. The coolness will ease them." Her captor relinquished one hand but kept the other in his grasp. "Come."

He started walking. Why did tall men always forget to measure their steps? She had to half walk, half run to keep up, but a sudden sharp poke on her sole broke her stride. When that foot came down on the ground, the stab shot through her again, a pebble, or maybe even a stone, from the size of it. Aksah gave a skip on the other foot as she tried to shake it loose.

"What is wrong? Am I walking too fast?" He did not wait for her to answer, but he did stop. He had not let go of her.

With the hand she still controlled, Aksah hopped as she slipped off her offending sandal and gave it a sharp shake. Not one but two pebbles fell out, landing on the ground with faint clinking sounds. He had to see them fall, even in the dark. She looked down at the small stones in disgust, their new shadows nearly lost in the rocky ground. "I felt them under my foot."

Eliab's eyes, mere glistening orbs reflecting the firelight, met hers in the growing dark. It was too shadowed to see his expression. "Have you got another sore you need to soak in the river? You are not bleeding there as well, are you?"

He actually sounded concerned. To Aksah's surprise, he released her hand, knelt down on one knee in the dirt and lifted at her foot, throwing her off balance. She grabbed for his shoulder, and clenched a painful fist in his sweaty robe.

Had he done that deliberately, knowing she would have to reach for him? No, she thought, looking down at his curly head, if anything he wanted her to fall. She had certainly caused him enough trouble, he would most likely look forward to seeing her embarrass herself.

Still on one knee, he rubbed the sole of the foot he held off the ground. Aksah tightened her grip on his robe. He continued the stroking. Though he was nowhere near the small spot that had hurt, his fingers still seemed to ease it.

"There is no need for that," she said, because he would expect it, because she needed to push him away. Because that gentle motion felt too good.

"We have much more walking to do in the coming days. It is better for both of us if neither has problems with their feet." He did not look up, just kept soothing the sole with his strong fingers.

It was a battle of wills, one she could not let herself lose.

He set her foot down. "Did you shake all the dust and rocks out of the other sandal?" He did not get up, just remained by her feet, that knee in the dirt.

His curly hair was too close to her hand. Aksah tightened her grip on the sandal. "The other does not have stones in it."

"Do it anyway, to please me." He looked down at her shod foot but made no attempt to take it off. "I do not want you to find yet another reason to hate me. There is no reason for us to suffer pain unnecessarily."

Aksah stared across the barren distance to the large camp of the other men and their women. The two of them were being watched, the fire's reflection showed faces turned their way. She had made herself a focus of all eyes by trying to find others ready to run, was viewed with suspicion, and now both sides of the conflict were interested in what she did.

Being a rebel was not easy, Aksah thought. Her mother's words came again, *my most sensible child*. How disappointed her mother would be! But neither did she want a son-in-law from Benjamin, she had said so.

No one did.

If she was going to escape, it would not be this moment. Aksah lifted her other foot and slid that sandal off. She started to shake it, but Eliab grabbed it out of her hand. With sharp claps, he snapped the two soles against each other. Grass and dirt broke off and rained on the ground. When he was apparently satisfied, he reached for one of her hands and folded her fingers around the straps.

"Now, let us take care of your wrists." He took her other hand, twining it through his large fingers as though there was feeling between them. Aksah had no choice but to follow him toward the edge of the bank. He stepped down with confidence, each foot placed where he would not slide.

She followed him, stepping where he had stepped. He had spent four months living in the wilderness. Somehow he had found food, located water, made shelter in the caves with the others where they survived the cold, rainy season. She would be a fool not to take advantage of the skills he had learned.

The river was lower, the damp pebbles proclaimed its original boundary. The rainy season was over, and soon this stream would be little more than a trickle until the next season's rains began. As they neared where the rocky shore became soft, he stopped. "The river's edge is near." He did not let go of her hand or even bend over to pull off his sandals, just scraped down the back of one with the sole of the other shoe, then toed the second off. He did not bother to set them neatly side by side, but left them sitting in disarray. Aksah bent to place hers with more care. What was the purpose of cleaning part of the dirt off if she just picked up more?

Out of the corner of her eye, she saw him move closer. When she straightened, Eliab took her hand once more and walked forward until she heard the water splash, pulling her behind him.

The water brushed against her feet now too, cold in the night. The sky overhead had lost all the last traces of sunlight, and only the stars gave brightness to the land, that and the moon's sliver.

The rocks were slippery underfoot, and she stepped with care. She did not want to spend the night in a wet robe. No one had packed for this unexpected journey, because of course, none of them were going to be caught. Her changes of raiment were back with her family at Shiloh.

"I think we have gone far enough into the water." Eliab let go of her hand.

Had she known she was destined to run across the hills of Ephraim, Aksah thought as she gave a shiver at the chill wetness on her feet, she would have kept a covering nearby. She rubbed her hands up and down her arms to bring some warmth. One wrist brushed the sleeve of her robe, scraping the sores, and it began throbbing.

"Bend down and splash water over your wrists." His voice was warm, the only heat around. "It will help cool, and cleanse any dirt that might have settled in the rope."

She bent over, but he caught her before she got too far down.

"Tie up your robe before it gets wet." He pulled out a piece of leather from his weapons belt. How many of these strips did he hide in it?

She gave him a narrow look, but his face was innocent, or so it appeared in the shadowy night. The disadvantage of a beard, she had learned long ago, was that it could hide a smile. He held the strap out, and she gathered the skirt of her robe to one side and rolled it against itself, wrapped the thick braided leather around the bunch of fabric, then tied it tight.

It looked foolish, she thought as she squinted down at the fabric all knotted on the side, and it would be wrinkled tomorrow, but it would stay out of the burbling water. She could walk in wet sandals, she could not sleep in a wet robe.

He was standing close. "Bend over. Keep your wrists in the water long enough to cool them."

Aksah did, swishing her hands in the water, letting it soothe and cool the torn flesh. The abraded skin stung, a reminder of her position. A woman of Judah, far from her land. Far from her hope.

Her feet were getting cold, and Aksah's teeth began to chatter. Eliab had been in war, he knew more about injury than she, so she held up her arms. The night air raised little bumps all over her skin. "Is this enough, do you think?"

He must have heard the soft clicking of her teeth, or perhaps he saw her shiver. "I wish you could stand it longer, but you have equal risk now of becoming ill. Let us get out and warm you for the night."

Warm? Other than the fire, she had seen nothing that would serve that purpose, and it would burn down during the hours unless one of them got up several times to feed it. She asked, without much hope, "Do you have any night coverings? I did not see them."

He started toward the bank, his feet splashing through the pulsing waves. She heard rocks on the river's bottom click together as he moved. Without looking back, he said, "I have one outer robe in my pack, but for heat we will have to depend on the fire."

Even a lone outer covering sounded very encouraging when one was this cold, she thought. Aksah made it back to the bank with the same clacking sounds underfoot as Eliab's steps did, rocks sliding and shifting. Her footing was unsteady, something she had not noticed before. Perhaps it was worse now because her feet were numb.

The sandals waited on the river's bank where she had set them. Aksah picked them up, looped them over her wrist, ignoring the sudden sting as the sandals scraped her wounds, and went to work on her hands, rubbing them clean with the sand from the river's very bottom. When she finally felt cleansed herself, Aksah straightened and twisted to get the tension out of her back. Her knuckles dug into her spine, finding the tender knots and working them. Once her body felt like itself, she turned and splashed the last few steps out of the water. The night air hit her wet legs and sent a chill through her.

He was just a tall shadow in the darkness, his head silhouetted over the riverbank while his body stayed mostly in shadow. He had not moved, simply stood there unmoving as a tree.

She released the strap that had held her robe, and the garment settled back down around her ankles, bringing a small measure of warmth.

Eliab waited for her. "I will take that," he said and held out his hand for the binding.

The leather piece seemed rougher than before as Aksah handed it over. She was not a fool to think he would let her sleep without something to keep her in place, but so far he was doing nothing. The suspense made her nervous. Her wrists began stinging again, as if in anticipation. "If you cannot tie my wrists, where do you intend to tie me next?"

Shaking his head, he released a great gust of air from his lungs. "I know you do not believe me, but I do not want to harm you. I would be a foolish man to injure my wife." He tucked that leather piece into his belt, not bothering to look at her as he tied it tight.

"This may come as a surprise to you," she said, and folded her arms over her chest. Heat pulsed through her abraded wrists. "But I do not consider myself your wife."

His head came up at that. Even in the dark, she could see his eyes. Perhaps the moon had moved higher in the sky? "Was there another man waiting for you back in your village?" He looked concerned.

Aksah wished she dared lie, but not even for this would she risk her God's disapproval. She was not certain the judgment would be as severe if one lied to an unbeliever, but—sinful or not—Benjamin had been accepted once more into Israel. If she was to get free and back to Judah, her God would be looking for only the most faithful.

The answer would have to be the truth. She looked away. "No." Until now, it had not been tragic.

"Then I do not see the problem." He was smug now, or should she say *again*. The momentary worry disappeared. "You are clearly of age to be wed, and I have the permission of the entire nation. Now, we need to get some rest." Eliab turned his back on her and started up the sharp edge the river had cut.

Clearly of an age to wed. Her mother had made the same remark, or something much too similar. Look what her reluctance had led her to. Aksah sighed, and followed him up the river's bank, clutching at the spikey weeds for purchase when she slipped.

Their fire had burned down to glowing coals. A lone cloak lay on the ground, something she should have noticed before but had not. If they were to make that work for the both of them, they would have to sleep very close. The nights were still cool. She shivered, but it was not the night that brought it on.

There were too many people nearby for any kind of familiarity. Even so, the thought of this man lying so close to her, this man who still did not see the enormity of the crime but only the aftermath, froze her feet in place.

He came up behind her. Before she could make herself step away from the faint warmth his body gave off, two hands framed her middle. As she jumped with the sudden familiarity, something snagged tight around her waist. Grabbing the hated rope, Aksah tried to pull it away from her body, but it was too tight. She heard the whisper of the rope as it was tied behind her, felt it bind snugly around her waist.

His breath teased her ear as he whispered, "We both need sleep. This is the only way I can think of keeping you here. It is dangerous in the dark. Snakes and scorpions lurk, and lions look for easy prey."

So he had come up with a new way to keep her from escaping. Binding her to him with the knot in the back? Well, she could figure out a way around that!

He turned her around. She did not know what he saw on her face, but his seemed to soften, although it was hard to tell in the dark and under his beard, the firelight at his back. "Do not think you can try to pull this to the front and undo it. I will feel every movement." He stepped away and the binding pulled at her. It had not felt that tight. Was her robe caught in it? He might be right. Getting out of this without waking him might be hard.

"You will be safe tonight. We have been living a spare life these last months, and I do not have a separate blanket for you. Pick up some wood. I want the fire strong, so we both can get warm. I have no desire to get chilled." He bent down and picked a few sticks. Aksah leaned down, and picked up several smaller ones. She had no desire to be cold, either.

If she was to escape, she had to pay attention to how the soldiers survived. As one of them, after all his months in the caves, he had experience that would serve her well. Until escape presented itself, she would have to see which woods he preferred for fire, for cooking. For a walking staff. Aksah looked at the wood bits in her hands.

She knew this particular wood well. These were grapevines. Her father used them to dry and season their meat. Somewhere nearby there must be a vineyard. These could be overlooked prunings of the unproductive vines, dried through the last year, and blown by the winter winds.

Grapevines gave off plenty of smoke.

Only men with great confidence would use this kind of wood for a fire, men who did not care if they were seen. For the Benjaminites to take such a chance, they must feel safe. A chill ran over her skin. She reached for another small piece of wood.

No, she would not let herself give up, not lose trust in her father.

If he was coming—and he *would* come, he loved her, her mother and her sisters, he would not leave any of them among lawless men—what better way to find her than to follow the smoke of a night's fire?

These men of the tribe of Benjamin, who trusted the remaining eleven tribes had forgiven then, had forgotten the values of the rest of this nation. Despite their terrible losses, they had more to learn.

With that conviction, she was able to turn to her captor and hand him the pieces of wood. *Send up the smoke of the grapevines*, she thought, *send it up and let my father follow.*

"Thank you." Eliab surprised her with the small courtesy, and crouched to place the wooden bits on the fire. He stacked his branch and her smaller ones, and Aksah watched the embers on the bottom begin to glow.

As the sweet scent began curling from the flame, the grapevines brought another worry. Did Israel burn down the grapes during the battles? Did they leave the Benjaminites without sustenance? She had hoped to collect the fruit on her trip back, but if the productive trees were destroyed, she might be in danger.

Aksah looked at the wood she still held. These had been picked up uncharred, a hopeful sign that they had not been burned by the leaving army. If there were healthy grapevines, there might be fig trees left that had bloomed as well, and perhaps other plants for eating. She would be hopeful, and attentive. Eliab's hand appeared in front of her face, snapping her plans for escape. Aksah handed the last gnarled stalk over and watched it begin to smoke and smolder.

"Come. We need sleep." Eliab rose, the rope tugging at Aksah's robe, making her move along behind him. Pulling against her reluctant steps, he walked over to the cloak. "I have already told you, nothing will happen tonight. You can sleep in peace, or plan how to drive a knife through my heart, it matters not to me. Do not imagine you will catch me off guard and murder me while I slumber."

"I would not think to." Aksah walked those few steps up to him, and tilted her head back to meet his gaze. The fire's glow tinted his eyes red. "I want no blood on my hands."

Eliab was frowning, she was close enough to him she could see his expression even in the dark. "I am well aware of your opinion of me. I know this makes you uneasy. Right now all you should be concerned about is keeping warm overnight. It would be foolish to risk becoming sick just to avoid being near me." He pointed at one side of the garment. "Spread that open, and lie down on the edge."

Aksah found her hands shaking as she pulled the cape flat and sat down. He had promised nothing would happen. Around them, the rest of the camp was doing likewise, men and women arranging something to sleep on, or under. Other women were already lying next to their captors.

If any were also tied for the night, Aksah could not tell. She had been the only one still bound earlier when she joined the group, but things were likely different when they slept. Bound or not, the women were still there, their very presence was a comfort for each other and a protection. Every woman there knew, herself included, that their bodies would be safe during the night.

Around the perimeter, men stood guard. Against the lions that Eliab had warned her? Or against the possibility that someone would try to run?

Aksah made herself stretch out on the cloak, hugging close to the edge, the ground hard beneath her. She could not relax. No man had ever slept beside her, but in a few moments he would be there on a cloak meant for one, near enough that she would feel his breath.

Eliab knelt at her side, but took his time getting ready for his own rest. The rope between them gave a sudden tug, and she jumped. What was he doing? Removing his weapons? Setting them out where she could not get them?

Movement seemed constant along the link between them. The rope bindings bunched and tugged on her robe, and Aksah stiffened more. Eliab finally finished his task, and stretched out behind her, air still separating them. With a puff of dust and cold, the cloak was flipped over her. It carried his musky scent, blended with the soft fragrances of their walk, fresh air and trees and leather.

His warmth seeped across that space between them, eating away the chill from the rush of the cloak settling. His body was a wall of heat reaching from over her head to well below her feet. Air separated them, warming, but it still gave her privacy. Aksah was about to take a breath of relief in granting her that respite when his big arm came over her waist, pulling her closer. Too close. Her neck prickled with the whisper of his breath drifting through her hair.

Her muscles went tight.

He shifted, and his chest bumped her back, once, twice, and then stayed, solid and unyielding. Gnarled muscles and hot skin overwhelmed her behind and in front, dwarfing her. A chuckle shivered down her spine. His arm across her waist tightened.

"I gave you my word you would be safe." His mouth was so close she felt the puffs of air brush her neck. "I am hardly going to assert my rights in front of the entire camp." Eliab nudged the back of her calf with a knee. "Tell me you are not warmer. If you curl your legs up, you might even keep your toes warm all night. I, on the other hand, will have to sleep with my feet sticking out into the chilly air. Should you want a small bit of revenge, think of that."

Cold feet were hardly an atonement, but at least he had shown a measure, however meager, of understanding that he did deserve some punishment.

Across the camp, Aksah saw other shapes stretched on the ground. They were too far away to see if those men were holding onto their women, to see if she had company in this shocking new situation.

Smoke drifted past her face, carrying with it the woodsy scent and puffs of heat. A spark popped out of the fire, and hit the ground with a sizzle, then went out. From the corner of her eye she saw the stars twinkling against their own blanket of darkness. They were tranquil, steady guides in the sky.

Unlike herself, shivering despite the cloak and the blaze not far away. *God*, she prayed, *what is my future?*

She was cocooned in warmth. Against her will, and despite the weight of his arm and the lump of the rope digging in the small of her back, her muscles loosened. His breath formed a rhythm, in, out, in, out.

Sleep crept in, and Aksah surrendered.

CHAPTER 6

So she said to Abraham, "Drive out this slave girl and her son, for the son of this slave girl is not going to be an heir along with my son, with Isaac!" But what she said about his son was very displeasing to Abraham. Then God said to Abraham, "Do not be displeased with what Sarah is saying to you . . . Listen to her."
Genesis 21:10-12

Aksah walked as if in a dream, or nightmare. Women around her fell into two camps, those who were already beginning to flirt with their new husbands—or captors—and those like herself for whom the situation had become a grueling, frightening ordeal.

Overhead, the sky was bluer than the water of the Dead Sea, and cloudless. The sun shone down with a heat that had not grown dangerous yet, but was still strong enough to dry out her mouth and make her sweat, using precious water that her body needed.

Where was her father? Aksah had put her hopes in him, knew he would come, and the group left a trail so glaring a child could notice.

The hours wore on. No shapes came over the rolling hills. If there were any followers to be seen, even at this range, the warriors would notice them.

Surely he could not be tracking one of the other bands? Two hundred warriors needing wives must have come in smaller groups and left in smaller groups, something she had determined yesterday when she counted the soldiers. If the men had divided into groups of equal size, that meant four bands to trail. Four bands, fifty men in each, fifty captured women to swell the numbers, and leave tracks.

Three other groups, maybe more if this was the largest congregation of Benjamin's wife-hunters. That thought made her shiver. How many groups were there in all? What if this was the most sizeable one, and the others had splintered off like shards of broken pottery? Her father might be chasing any number of paths, trying to find her.

These men were warriors. Benjamin's tribe, nestled almost in the middle of the nation's land, had true soldiers, fighters renowned across the land. She was at a disadvantage from the beginning.

If her father needed to follow each group in turn, by the time he found her it might be too late to return as a virgin. She would claim the month to be untouched allowed for captured brides. That was the last option open to her if she could not flee, her plan to be kept in reserve, but thirty days was not so very long.

Aksah looked behind again and again. The only things to see were the hills marching away to the north, to Ephraim and the holy city, only trees varying from small stands of olives to thick forests in the distance. Flat stretches and gullies alike sported the last of spring's blooming flowers. Beneath her feet was only more brown soil, drying in the sun and the dust shifting in the soft breeze.

The men kept the women walking at nearly their own pace, long steps that ate up the ground. Climbing rolling hills, then down the opposite sides, through the searing rays of the midday sun, ignoring it as it glared in their eyes. She was quite certain she knew one more reason why they pushed the captives at such a relentless pace. It made sure that the women would be tired enough to sleep and the guard could be lightened.

Other than herself, no one seemed to pay the smallest attention to what was behind. No women turned their heads, and Aksah made certain she watched her other captives. Two on the run were safer than one woman alone, and a larger group would be even better.

The soldiers did not look behind, either. It was as if they were confident they had no pursuers. She could not believe, would not believe, that no one dared attempt to challenge these men! No one in Israel was willing to come after their daughters? Such a thing was impossible. Israel's fathers loved their daughters. Cherished them.

Her mother's words returned time and again. *Benjamin is still our brother. Whatever their wrong, we are all still one nation. There will be no alarm.*

Worst of all, those words, *the goal is to let the men of Benjamin capture whatever woman they can.*

Whatever woman they can. Aksah would hear those words echoing and remember her father's face, shining with pride as he looked at his daughters around the table, as he complimented them on their cooking, or praised their weaving.

Mandate or not, she did not believe a man like Saul would let her be carried off without making at least an effort to find her.

Each time the group stopped, everyone sagged onto the ground, glad of an excuse to sit for a few minutes. They all were grateful for a brief pause to eat, to attend to the body's needs, and maybe, if Aksah and the others were quick, to catch a few moments of sleep.

She overheard some of the soldiers grumbling. "What is it with these women? Can they not hold in their water?" "If I were not afraid of being accused of abuse, I would restrict them from drinking so much." "Do you think it a ploy to hold back reaching our homes? I would blame the one with Eliab. She is in no hurry, that is certain."

Aksah gave a start, and then choked down her laugh.

Food came then, carried on the backs of the men as it had the other times as well. Small groups had broken off, and returned with sacks full of fruit and dried meat. Every sack of food brought a whiff of smoke. A haze hung on the air. The odor brought with it the memory of the sacrifices at the holy city of Shiloh, the constant grey cloud that rose above the altar.

Once fed, they would be ordered up and the walking would start again, as they had the day past and this morning, leaving her to forget the smells of burning until the next time it drifted past her nose.

The sharp scent of fire became more consistent with every bite of the small meals provided, dried fig cakes—and smoke, dried melons—and smoke, raisins—and smoke. Aksah recognized the constant smell came from the food itself. With that came another realization, a memory of overheard discussions of the war. Whenever revenge against Benjamin came up in conversations during the first days after the war, someone would mention towns and villages destroyed, every building burned. Now, with the constant smoke teasing her nose and tainting her food, Aksah learned the enormity of those discussions.

Cities burned to the ground. Benjamin, an entire tribe of the mighty nation of Israel, one-twelfth of the population, gone except for six hundred men. That meant there would be no one to help on her way until she got into Ephraim's land, no place to stop for succor, perhaps no house left in which to sleep.

That constant whiff of smoke could mean they were passing those burned cities. Or even burned houses in the middle of farm fields, although she had not thought of destruction that willful.

What a fool she had been, thinking she would find help along the way! Her mind had been lost in its own dream of freedom. As soon as she began her return, she would have to realize she was on her own. With no population, wild animals would begin to take over the land. Did not the prophecy Moses had given of Israelite's punishment for unfaithfulness say so? *Your carcasses will become food for every bird of the sky and animal of the ground, with no one to frighten them away.* Those were God's own words, the judgment waiting for the nation if they refused to remain obedient.

This land boasted many predators, not all of them human. Lions roamed, and bears, even leopards, waiting for the people to be gone in order to take it back. The war had given them their chance. Beyond them, the vultures hovered overhead and clung to perches biding their time to scavenge the remainder.

The city of Gibeah had refused to be obedient, and it was burned to the ground. The tribe of Benjamin had rebelled in the same way, and suffered much the same fate. How long would it take for the rest of the land within its borders to be overrun with wild animals, moving in to places that had held humans?

There were no survivors in this land who might feel pity for a woman's flight. No lone farm family who would give a night's shelter, no small town whose sheds she could hide among and sleep safely during the night. No one to help her on her way.

Not that they would have before. Eliab had tried to warn her. This is what it meant, Aksah thought as she sat on the ground and ate the smoky food. Being a rebel meant being very alone, doing things on one's own, having no backing, no one to provide assistance, not even another voice to keep company.

The return trip took on new weight. Alone against the wild, against the animals who scavenged whatever they thought an easy meal. Alone with only the food and water she could carry.

Should she listen to the other women, give in to the new life in front of her? Or, rather, continue to plan and hope for escape? Aksah chewed the dried fruit and thought. Her head whirled with the anxieties that taunted her as she stared out across the land around them. Hills with valleys where danger hid, trees that hunting animals could hide behind. More hills, more valleys, more trees.

More worries.

There was another reason why it might be taking her father so long to be on her trail. She must never forget the twins. Her last glimpse was them running, with Benjaminites so close behind.

Did her parents mourn their other girls as well? Had Dinah and Deborah been caught? Aksah's lungs clenched as the thought returned, and her throat tightened. Would she ever know?

If her father had to rescue more than one daughter, which one would he go after first? How would he choose? How *could* he choose?

The need to get back to Judah and her family's home grew the further they got from Shiloh. Sometimes during the walk, her heart had felt so heavy she wondered that she did not trod it underfoot.

Her parents had suffered enough loss. One son dead in the war, and herself dragged away by the enemy. She could not give them back Chileab, but she could give them back herself.

Please, she begged her God, please do not let the twins have been caught as well. A foolish prayer if they were already being dragged away as herself, but the prayer, a litany that kept pace with her steps during the endless walking, gave her a measure of comfort.

Another stop, another meal, the sun lower in the sky. Her legs burned from her hips to the soles of her feet. Standing hurt, sitting hurt, walking was agony. The back of her legs had knots pulling tight and sending pain down to her toes, which wanted to curl under the tension. Men strolled through the camp, handing out more dried fruits and meats. Water sacks had been filled somewhere, for they all glistened with moisture on the outside.

Aksah sighed as she took her share from the soldier's sack, sat down and began to eat. They never had much time to eat before the call to walk came from the man who seemed in charge. She would have to make short work of her food.

How much further did they have to go? How much distance had they traveled in this day's journey?

Eliab stopped by her, his large shape blocking the sun. "You look thoughtful. I have learned to worry when I see that face. What torments are you planning for me now?"

More loudly than she intended, Aksah cleared out the last bits of food so she would not embarrass herself by coughing in the middle of her answer. It sounded like jeering, though, and she had a fleeting touch of fear. What would happen when she finally pushed him too far? He was of the tribe that allowed a woman to be brutalized. "Torments! As if I could hurt you! You are a warrior, it is hardly a fair battle."

He crouched down, coming even closer. She forced herself to meet his gaze. His expression held no concern, not even any anger. Instead laughter danced through his dark eyes. "Ah, but you know as well as I that you have already made me a laughingstock among the men. The man who could not control his woman."

Heat rushed up her skin. "I am not your woman! And I am not an animal to be 'controlled!'"

The laughter in his eyes slipped down to his mouth. "That is better. That is what I expected." Then his face grew serious, and his eyes the same. "Throughout the day I see you looking behind. No one is following us. How many times must I tell you, the rest of the nation gave you women to us. No one will come after you."

"My father will." She would say it again and again. "He will."

Eliab stood, and she tilted her head back to hold his gaze. "Somehow, that would not surprise me."

After he left, Aksah returned to planning her escape. It was not going to be easy. Eliab removed the hated rope during the day when escape was impossible with an entire group of both men and women watching. She could see him even now, that rope looped over his shoulder and across his body as he stood deep in conversation, no doubt plotting their route. The other men with him knew what he used it for during the night.

The entire camp knew what he did with it, knew he had tied it around her waist and slept behind her, where he would feel her move. What was worse, what these warriors also must know, was that she was so tired she had not tried to slip away. It would have been a fool's attempt, assuming she even woke to try. The knot was at her back, the rope snug enough that only the most dire struggles would have turned it around. Worse, he fastened it to himself as well, and all had seen him do so. Would she have taken the chance to run if she had awakened and he was gone, off on some manly errand with his fellows?

Yes, she would have run. To safeguard her lineage, to see her family again, she would have grabbed the opportunity for escape. Even in the dark of night, with the unknown threats it hid, if there was so much as a glimmer of a chance of escape, she would have run like the gazelles.

But he had not gone, and she had not wakened.

Women bit into their food, eating with dispatch just as she did herself, knowing this rest was brief. Women about to become brides of Benjamin, to give up hope of returning to their families. About to devote their lives to producing children for this tribe, children who had a purpose themselves before they were even born. Destined to grow and marry and have more children, until this tribe would regain its former glory.

Aksah leaned toward the closest woman. "How are you? Can you walk any farther?"

The woman leaned over and whispered back, "Only if I have to." Staring past Aksah's shoulder, she hissed, "It is so unfair! They are soldiers, used to hard walking. Look at them! Their swords must weigh more than I do. Have you even seen one of them break a sweat? Without us holding them back, they would all be at their homes by now."

Aksah caught herself before she turned around. She knew they were strong, knew most of them were very tall. Her own captor had carried her for that while. Height and strength did not matter to her.

The woman looked down at the food in her hands as if it nauseated her. "My life as I knew it is over."

Something in the sadness there alarmed Aksah. She scooted a handsbreadth nearer. "Did you leave a man behind? Were you to wed someone else?"

A tear ran down the woman's face. "There was a man. Nothing was set yet, but I had hopes . . ." Her voice broke, then trailed away.

"I am so sorry." What else could she say, Aksah thought. For a woman to hold such hopes meant the man had given her reason. There must be two aching hearts in that situation. "I am Aksah, from Judah, in the hills of the Shephelah."

"I am Mara, from the land of Dan. I will be so far from my home. Everything is going to be so different."

Aksah eased over one more handsbreadth. In the quietest voice she could manage and still be heard, she asked, "Would you run back if there was a way?"

Mara's eyes had a spark at last. "May I speak openly?"

Openly? Even though Aksah had a feeling she would not like what was coming, she nodded. "Certainly."

"Everyone here knows you wish to escape. If I were to run, I would have to find someone the soldiers are not watching. But no, I would not run. Exchange something certain for something only possible? No. The man I spoke of might have offered for me, but he might not have. What if I go back, only to find out he chose someone else?"

Aksah stared at her. "Is marriage all anyone thinks of?"

Mara actually smiled. "Not everything, but is it not the desire of every woman?"

"Not at this cost!"

"Hush! Do you want them to hear you?" Mara slid away and went back to staring at her food.

After managing not to look before, Aksah found herself turning around. Eliab was still there with a portion of the men. She looked at them. Their clothes must have been washed before they came to Shiloh, she did not remember any offensive odors, but nothing could hide the wear of four months' hard use. Stains and tears carefully mended marked every man's garment. While the women rubbed feet or legs, the men remained standing, and looked as if they could continue to do so without problem.

The older men must have been cut down during the battles and the subsequent flight, for the army around her seemed in their prime. Not young, but not many grey hairs.

Aksah alternated her gaze from the women, all tired now, and the men, who could only be described as satisfied. Satisfied and something else, something honed fine through this journey. Determination, she realized, that and a cold purpose. They had their captured brides, they would begin rebuilding their tribe. No wonder satisfaction and resolve rolled off them like sandstorms in the dry summer.

"Rise!" The call to move again sounded across the troop.

She got to her feet with the others, taking one more look behind for any signs of pursuers. Nothing, only the scattered trees growing up the hills and perching at the top. Trees that cast patches of shade and held onto the spring flowers at their base longer, shielding them from the sun that could otherwise shrivel them into stubble. Only more hills, more trees, more patches of grass, low-growing bushes that added green to the gold-tinted soil, and the white limestone rocks that dotted the hills, sparkling in the rising sun.

Aksah studied the group as they kept moving forward, men around the outside, women in the center, guarded yet not guarded. Ostensible freedom, but only on the surface.

She hurt. Sand and pebbles had worked their way through the straps of her sandals, like they did every day, and did not dislodge when she shook her feet between steps. She longed to stop and remove her footwear, but the men were impatient with sluggards, so she wiggled her feet back and forth with alternate steps and rejoiced at the few irritants that slid free.

Shadows crept out from the trunks of trees and the hills, and grew longer, the sun began its downward journey. The whistle came, and the camp stopped once again. The women sank down where they stood on the stony ground, grabbing what little rest they could before it would be time to walk again.

A stomach rumbled nearby, and Aksah turned her head. It was the happy woman, the one who was so delighted to have found a husband at last. The woman did not meet her eyes. This was the first time Aksah had seen the happy woman up close since that conversation. Was the woman still glad, or did she now regret her capture?

They all had been stripped down to their very core, attitudes refined by the amount of time they had to think. There was nothing else to do when one walked. Aksah's attitude had been formed by faithful parents, and it pleased her that her faith remained strong even through this hardship.

The men came around with handfuls of food, their weapons belts still strapped about them. A shiver crawled down her spine despite the sun's warmth at her back. She would need a weapon, and Eliab kept them on his person except when he slept.

A shadow cooled her for a moment, and there he was, crouching at her side. He held out the usual fare in smaller measure, dried fig cakes balanced on a handful of raisins, and a small skin swollen from its contents. Water for her dry mouth.

He lowered himself the rest of the way to the ground. When he did that she had learned he was in a talkative mood. Aksah did not know whether to be wary or relieved to have a break in her loneliness, and from the unease that had settled in since the men's odd behavior earlier. She set the skin down where he could reach it if he wished, and took a few raisins, nibbling them one by one to keep from talking.

"We will be going to our homes soon. There has been safety in this group, but we all must go our own way." He looked off across the rolling ground that stretched to the horizon, lingering green still dotting the hills, spring's color where hardy plants grew. They would soon be summer-brown.

He turned back to her. "Some wild animals were seen roaming last night. It is one thing to stand against them in a group this size. It will be quite another to make it home safely when it is just the two of us."

Aksah felt a new shiver. She had thought of those herself. Somehow hearing him, as a warrior weighed down with all manner of weapon, be concerned made the risk of her escape all the more frightening.

He took a gulp of water from his small waterskin, then wiped the last drops from his beard. "The other women are willing to listen to their men. You are the only one who needs to be bound for her own sake." He sighed, a strange lonely sound coming from such a large man. "I will need to sleep at times. We have another two days' walk, I estimate, before we reach my city. I hope to round up as many sheep and goats roaming free as I can, perhaps even cattle, and then it is going to take both of us to get them herded home. They will slow our trip down, but it is vital I have something with which to begin."

Aksah looked at his so-innocent eyes. *It is going to take both of us to get them herded home.* If the land had been prophesied to return to the wild, no doubt the animals would go wild as well, and would be more than one person alone could manage.

The lions and leopards would prowl, looking for easy prey. While she did not want to be his wife, neither did she want him to die fighting off the beasts while trying to keep a flock intact.

He held her gaze. She was almost certain he knew the thoughts running through her mind. The only food she had was what he found for her, the only water what the guides brought back.

"I will not run away. I will help you reach your city." *But after that,* she added to herself, *after that I intend to go.*

He lifted the waterskin again and filled his mouth, watching her over the shiny surface. After he swallowed, he let a long pause hang before he said, "And I am supposed to believe you? Forgive me if I find your words less than convincing."

"I give you my solemn oath." Aksah glared at him. "I have no desire to have your blood on my hands."

"Unlike my hands, laden with blood and death?" Eliab turned his hands over and back as if to display the gore. His eyebrow went up, just one. He could not have said his doubt louder in words than that one raised brow spoke in silence.

She looked down at her wrists, still lingering red and retaining some swelling from the ropes. "You see me as a vessel for your children, a source for more sons of Benjamin. You do not see me yet as a woman of worth, nor do I suspect the other men feel any differently of their women. I want a man who values me above all else, above his sons and daughters, above his land and his flock."

She saw his mouth open, knew he was about to claim those virtues, and raised her hand to silence him. "Do not think you feel those for me, and do not insult me by pretending so. You only know me as a thorn in your side. If another woman fell from the sky, one who was meek and willing, you would gladly turn me back to my parents." The words hurt. Not that she wanted that feeling of being valued from *him*, but if she was to leave, it must be her own idea. Being cast off carried such stigma for a woman.

Why could it not be so for a man? Why did women always have to be the ones with the most to lose? A woman was worthy while she had a womb, but what about when she became too old? Was she then valueless? Her worth depended on creating children for her husband? Could she not have value in herself, *as* herself?

Aksah would find that value, even if she had to make it. She would be known for her courage, and her principles. She wanted to be the kind of woman Abraham's Sarah was, the kind of woman whose husband would be told by her God, "Listen to your wife."

Eliab rose in one smooth move, as if rolling to his feet. "You have given me your word. If you prove yourself, I will let you sleep free this night." His brows came down in a line. "Be aware, though, I sleep lightly."

Sleep free. A lump formed in her throat and she had to blink to keep the tears at bay. It was as if she had been given part of herself back. The privilege to own her nights again.

Prove yourself. "So what exactly must I do to win my freedom?"

"Do not give me any reason to worry that you will flee. Help me collect whatever animals are roaming the land, and herd them with me. Stay with me." He pulled a small linen cloth from a slit in the strap of the weapons belt that went across his chest and handed it to her. "Put whatever you do not eat now in this and carry it with you. I do not want you going hungry."

"Thank you." Aksah rose, as much to be more on a level with him as to reach his gift, and took the small cloth. She dropped in the last few raisins, wrapped the fig cake in it and tied it shut, then rolled the little parcel in her own sash around her waist.

Do not forget, she told herself as she checked the knots, *all he wants are sons.*

"The waterskin is getting low. When we begin moving I will look for a water source." The words came from over her head. Even standing on her feet, he towered above her. "For now, I will leave the water with you and when a new source is found, I will come and refill it. Take care of it."

Eliab gave her a nod and walked away to his guard duty.

He was not doing a very good job of winning her, Eliab thought. He could not remember listening to a woman before, never wondered about their thoughts and dreams. In his mind, women had always been meant to agree with their men, not the other way around.

What did he really know of his sisters, gone now? Did they want more than to marry and have children? He had never asked, they were much older than him, and now it was too late.

Nor did he know if his father had listened to his mother. Did they have long conversations when they were alone? He only remembered them talking about food and rain and the other children. When the woman had been murdered, if his mother had said anything, he had paid no attention. There had been too many discussions going on among the men.

Discussions that had led to war, and brought the entire nation to this sorry state.

This woman, this Aksah, would make certain he listened to her.

His nation's history had recorded that their ancestress Sarah had argued with Abraham, severely enough that God had seen the need to intervene and order Abraham to listen. How strange, Eliab thought now, he had never considered that before. God had *demanded* of Abraham that he pay attention to his wife, and more, God even agreed with Sarah, to the cost of Abraham's first son Ishmael.

What did Abraham think as he sent Hagar and Ishmael away? Many the man who would turn around and blame their other wife, yet no record existed that indicated Abraham was angry with Sarah after that.

Did any of the women in Gibeah order their husbands to go out and help the woman? Or were they all glad *they* were safely inside, away from the turmoil outside?

This woman, his Aksah, would be hard to live up to, he thought, and turned around to search for her in the crowd. She was still standing where he had left her, still alone.

He had the urge to bring her into the group of women, but quickly stifled it. The last time he had given her free rein of the camp, she nearly started a revolt. She certainly tried. What would have happened had he not arrived when he did, Eliab did not know.

He would have to learn to listen to her. The challenge lifted his spirits. Listening to his wife. What a new thought.

It would be a hard life for a woman. She would do well as the village midwife, or even a shopkeeper, but there would be no other women near his home needing delivery, and no others to purchase goods. He had dragged her into this lonely future.

They would all be lonely in the land of Benjamin, men and women alike. Cities had to be rebuilt before they could be populated. Farms would merge with so many whole families gone. In much of the tribe's territory, brothers and sisters would only have each other to play with. Families must of necessity be large.

There was no choice, Eliab reminded himself. Whoever he had chosen, whether Aksah or some other woman from the celebration, there was no choice. He had a responsibility himself, like all the other men here, to save his tribe.

Abdon came up to him. After so many months hiding in the crags, they all knew each other, but this man Eliab knew best, considered to be a friend. Abdon said, "The chief wants the final decision on whether to wait another night before we begin to separate. I have given him my choice. It is your turn. I will take your watch."

Eliab turned to look at his woman. Since the camp had not begun moving yet, Aksah had re-seated herself by their small bundle of possessions. She looked placid enough, but he knew her too well. Other women in the camp might feel the same as his wife, and be only too willing to slip away, should an opportunity present itself. "You know my woman?"

Abdon nodded. A smile hid in his beard, or so he might think. To Eliab, that faint smile was as obvious as a laugh. "I do."

"Watch her closely. I think she still hopes for a chance to escape. She thinks very little of us."

"None of Israel does," the other man muttered as he looked off into the hills. No one had been seen following them, but they chose not to lower their guard. The families had been told they would not get their daughters back, but the rage of their fathers and brothers could well be a fearsome thing. The war was still bitter. On both sides. "We have much reparation to do."

"And rebuilding," Eliab reminded him, although that as well was not far from their minds. Six hundred men to make the foundations of the tribe. They could only pray that God would keep any of the women from being barren. "Just keep my woman from slipping away while I am with our commander. Whatever it takes."

Abdon turned back to Eliab. "Go," he chuckled. "She will be here for the next while, even if I have to lash her to a rock or a tree."

Eliab could only hope so. They were all warriors now, hardened by battle and loss. Surely his woman could not outwit such a man.

Aksah had given her word. How much was it worth? He wanted to believe her, but she had not changed her mind about his tribe, and had not promised to stay once they got to his village.

Ten men were gathered around the chief. He took his place in the group.

"I wished to keep the camp together as long as possible, if only as protection from the animals. We are in Benjamin's tribal land, and men will need to break off soon and head to their family homes." The chief looked around the small group. "Should we separate now, immediately, so everyone will have the whole of tomorrow to begin their own journeys?"

The men began the vote. When asked, Eliab spoke for one more night as a group, but kept his true reason to himself.

He had promised her freedom while sleeping. He had not specified freedom for the daytime, but no doubt she expected it to begin immediately. If he wanted to test her vow, it was best to do it with other people around to watch. Eliab wanted to turn the time back and undo his rash pledge. But he had given his word, he would show her she was not the only one who kept their vow.

CHAPTER 7

Now a garrison of the Philistines had gone out to the ravine pass of
Michmash.
1 Samuel 13:23

I t had been hard to watch her fellow captives walk off with their individual men. Aksah forced herself not to cry as the group had thinned, first in half, then half again. She did not know her fellow captives at all, but they had been a comfort.

Her heart beat faster as the main group thinned, her breath felt stifled in the mid-day warmth, as if there was not enough air to fill her lungs. Soon, too soon, it would be just herself and the man who thought he had himself a wife.

They kept walking throughout the morning, this ever-shrinking group, moving further and further into the land of Benjamin. This part of Israel's territory was more lush than her own tribal land of Judah, where the wilderness went wild and sharp crags filled the landscape as far as one could see.

The sky was still blue, the sun high enough to glare in the eye, when the last two said their farewells and walked off. The men dropped their packs on the ground, pounded each other on the back and hugged, eyes moist. What memories did they share, she wondered.

The couples walked over the nearby hills, tall figures against the sun at the top and then shrinking as they went down the far side until all that could be seen were the tops of their heads, only to climb up the next hill as much smaller dark specks against the dusty brown soil. Scrubby broom trees had started to appear, trees she usually associated with desert.

Were they heading into one?

Trees, greyish olive and tall palm, almond and spreading carob with its fat green leaves, dotted the hills here and there, and the departing men and women would pass beneath them, blending into the shade briefly until they came back into the sun. The carob trees showed the light green pods she thought she had seen before, small and early yet but promising a good harvest for the fall. Patches of green, low-growing bushes and tufts of grass, became only shades against the ground as the people passed them.

And then the figures were gone. All that was left were the clumps of green against the dirt and the dark cast of the shadows on the hills.

It was just the two of them now, herself and Eliab.

The world around them was strangely quiet. It was amazing, she thought, how much noise a group of men and women made, sound she had taken for granted until it was gone. Birds chirped here and there, but trees came only in clumps off in the distance, clinging to the sides of the hills, and she could not see where the birds hid, only heard their calls. Aksah was uneasy at meeting Eliab's gaze.

The land changed from the settled area around Shiloh. The hills grew taller, steeper, more threatening. Aksah stood at the top of one and stared at what was ahead. It looked ominous before when all she saw were the sharp peaks in the distance. Now the view frightened her, and they had not even reached the first climb.

A rocky forbidding landscape split the earth, running from far to the west and going equally far to the east. As if someone had gone across them with a giant knife, the mounts were ridged with sharp slices. Steep, and covered with boulders even from this distance she could see were taller than men. Each rise loomed loftier than the one before. There were no paths, only rocks the size of houses and jagged slabs leading there.

And after that, the deep gash those spiked peaks hid, appearing as only a dark line from where she stood.

The sun was going down, the shadows stretched long. It is a trick of the light, Aksah told herself, as she looked at the black emptiness ahead.

"What is this place?" she whispered to herself.

"This is Michmash." Eliab spoke from behind her, giving her a start.

"What is that?" The name was not familiar, but then she had never thought to be in Benjamin's land. Only the cities that made up its border had once mattered.

Eliab stepped up to her side, standing there without touching. For the first time, his presence was comforting. "It means Concealed Place. It is a rocky mountain, with a wadi in the bottom. The wadi will likely be only slightly wet now, the rainy season is over. The river that runs in the winter is probably no more than a trickle."

That was not a comfort.

"If there is water, we will want to fill our skins." He stared ahead, like she had. Was he afraid of this place, too?

"Do we have to cross it?" She could not seem to get strength back in her voice.

He heard her, he looked down at her, but did not answer right away. "We will not cross it, at least not at this point. There is a pass between Bozez and Seneh. It is not easy, but it is the only way from here," he pointed to the ground, and then raised his finger to point straight ahead, "to there. We can walk all the way around, but that would take far too much time. Finding food will be difficult enough without having to make it last extra days."

Eliab turned and began walking parallel to the gash in the earth. "We need to make camp for the night. Help me find something for a fire." Stopping suddenly, he turned around. His eyes burned with urgency. "Be careful! It is getting dark, there could be scorpions around. I want you to take every care."

Aksah tore her gaze away, and stared at the ground. The shadows made every stone look alive. She knew scorpions. They were all over in the wilderness near her home. A baby on a nearby farm had been stung years ago, and had not survived.

Without moving, her eyes still on the stones around her sandals, she asked, "What will we burn? It is nearly barren of trees here."

"There will be enough. We need to find two sticks long enough and strong enough to knock snakes or scorpions out of our way." He shook his head. "I will not risk either of our lives by a walk in the dark in this part of our land."

She could see that huge gouge in the earth without even turning her head. No, she did not want to risk walking in the dark, either.

At least he was not walking through this desolate place with a woman who had been sheltered in a city where the dangers of the wild were not so common. She knew what to watch for.

Sticks. Long sticks for walking, and short sticks for fire. A search like that would keep her eyes from drifting toward that black cut in the earth, and on the more immediate danger. There were no scorpions at her feet here, Aksah assured herself, and began walking behind Eliab. His weapons poked out from his weapons strap, axe and bow and quiver, knives and sword, and the rope wrapped across him in seemingly endless loops.

All that stood between them and death. Weapons of destruction and salvation.

As they moved along, Aksah was surprised at how much vegetation there was. While the rocky ground appeared barren from the distance, with the rainy season over low-growing bushes and scrubby plants left a lingering green tinge on the ground. She had to smile. These plants were like pieces of green sun hiding among shattered layers of stone, waiting to lift the heart.

Even from where she was well to his rear, easing herself along the broken rocks that filled the area, she saw broken branches littering the bases of those bushes. The brown sticks were small, but with enough gathered up they could have a small fire. Properly tended, something she knew both of them were capable of managing, the rationed fire might last the night.

Large predators were a worry in more lush areas of Israel's territory, but in this barren land she felt a bit safer. Aksah knew she might be wrong, this place might hide more life than she thought, but with just the two of them, the very lack of prey animals was reassuring.

That only left the snakes and scorpions. She shivered. Between those two threats, that still left enough to worry about. The baby was not the only tragic death from these killers. A man near her parents' farm had died from a snakebite, his skin blowing up and turning black before he died in agony.

Remember, her mind chanted, Eliab survived four months in the wild. She watched him stride on ahead over the ragged terrain, steady and confident. His legs were long, befitting his height, and thick with muscle, his burly arms swinging in rhythm. After the past two days in the company of warriors, she knew how fast they could move when they had to. She had watched their captors pace themselves to the shorter legs and less experienced stride of the women with varying degrees of frustration.

The sun toward which they walked gilded him in gold, or perhaps that was just the reflection in her eyes. His head with that curly dark hair turned from side to side, and from where she walked behind him, she knew he was scanning for the same things as herself. Firewood, snakes, and scorpions. While her steps where short and cautious, his were confident. If a scorpion was underfoot, she thought with a flicker of humor, it had best beware. Eliab would grind it under his thick leather sole.

He was not worried for himself, she suddenly realized. If he had been, he would not move with such confidence. No, he was worried for her.

The thought was both comforting and annoying. It had been easy to cast him as the villain when in a group with so many other men, all warriors. Now, with just the two of them, she was afraid she would come to depend on his skill.

Just then, Eliab called, "There!" His long arm pointed at something. Turning to her, his face alight, he asked, "Do you see?" Without waiting for an answer, he loped off across the uneven ground.

Careless man! She held her breath as he sprinted past scrubby bushes and tumbled stones, the lair of snakes.

What if one was hiding, and struck?

He skidded to a stop, and she could only stare helplessly as a rock turned under his foot and Eliab lost his balance. He was going to fall, and just a cubit or two away, something long and low moved through the grey stones.

But he did not fall. One hop, and he was solid on the shifting stones again. There, to one side, she saw what had drawn him away. A thick branch, likely blown some distance in the powerful winter storms, had been stopped by one of the stunted bushes.

What about the long thing that had moved but a breath ago? "Look first!" she gasped, sudden fear trapping the air in her lungs, but he could not hear her at this distance.

Once again, she had underestimated him. Eliab stayed in place, she saw him study the ground, moving his head to cover the area around him. Only when he was certain the location was clear of dangers did he reach down and pick up the branch and hold it aloft like a trophy of war. Twigs poked out on all sides. It had to weigh a lot. Something that size?

Even from this distance, Aksah could see Eliab's wide smile. "A perfect staff!" He started back, but did not allow his prize to distract him, still alert, still watchful. "Have you found any firewood?"

No, she had not. She had allowed herself to be distracted by his confidence and his stride.

Now that she knew where to look for things to burn, it took only a moment to locate the closest cluster. As she went toward the first bush, Aksah studied the ground with the greatest care. He might be able to trod the earth with confidence, but her sandals were not meant for such heavy use, and the openings on the side would let a stinger or fang through. Small insects skittered around her feet, but none of them were any real cause for concern.

Rocks clicked and rang together and shifted as she moved, a harmony of soft sounds. Even though this place lacked trees and grasses, the scents she was used to, the air still mellowed into evening's sweetness. The sun sat on the horizon, the shadows stretched long. Time was running out. Full darkness would come soon.

Look first, then pick it up, look and pick up, stick after stick filled her arms. When she had enough and any more would start falling out, she turned around. It took her a moment to find the landmarks she was looking for, she had covered so much area.

Eliab made it easy to find him. The fire was already burning, however small, a glowing beacon at his feet. How had he done that? And so quickly! She needed to learn, this was a task generally left to her father. She had done it, though not often, and it was very time-consuming. Her job had been to keep the coals glowing in the pit, or the fireholder, not to start the fire from the beginning. Her house had the tinder and the flints at hand, there was no need to scour the ground searching.

Would she recognize flint if she saw some? She hoped so. She thought so. Perhaps his fire-making tools still littered this new camp.

Moving as quickly as possible without raining her treasures of wood onto the ground, Aksah hurried across the stretch of slippery, rocky incline.

Eliab's axe caught the sun's lowering rays as it went up and down, chopping something. As she got closer, she saw what he was doing. The branch he had found was now trimmed, all the twigs gone, and he was smoothing out the sides. As she drew closer, Aksah noticed the pile of sawdust and chips littering the ground near his feet.

So that was what he had used for tinder. Bark and twigs. The sounds from her travels across the noisy rocks must have hidden the noise of his pruning, even the snapping of flint for the so-necessary sparks. Small bits of wood continued to snap off from the main branch against the force of Eliab's axe, soft sounds, and likely the reason she had not recognized his fire-building noises.

Absorbed though he seemed to be, he did not miss her footsteps, and looked up as she drew near. He pointed at a spot to his left. "Well done. Put them there, and they will be close at hand. We will have to keep the fire small, but even a little fire should keep the beasts at bay."

Her very thoughts of earlier.

After the sticks were piled where he requested, she sat on the ground near the fire. He gave her a smile, and she decided to take advantage of the relaxed atmosphere. "How did you make the fire so quickly?"

"I had two older brothers and an equal number of older sisters. I assure you, competition was fierce. My father decided to take advantage of that." A soft sound, like a chuckle, came out of his throat. "When you are one of the younger sons, and your older brother challenges you to see who can do anything faster, it is impossible to refuse."

That soft sound came again. "When it is your sister, the challenge is stronger. Who wants to be beaten by a female, even if she is older? Especially when it is such a manly thing as making fire? My younger brother felt it most. He could make a fire faster even than myself."

Another nubbin of twig snapped off with a sharp strike of the axe. Aksah looked up at Eliab's face again when he paused in his storytelling. The smile that had graced his firm lips now began to tremble. She thought she saw a sheen of tears in his eyes. A tingle of alarm ran across her. Was he trying not to weep?

A sudden compulsion drove her to fill the silence that settled over them. "My mother made sure my sisters and I learned, too, so we could bake bread and do the daily cooking in our home. Making fires without the flint and tinder I am used to is much more difficult."

Eliab did not say anything to counter her sudden babbling as he worked on the stick, but she could tell that he was listening. His lips were once again firm, his eyes, though red, were no longer moist. Aksah decided to continue. "When I can use my own fire supplies, I have been told that I build a nice fire for the oven and have learned to get it just right. I have never burned even one loaf." She spoke with some pride and satisfaction.

He grunted. "Making fire in the open is not a skill that comes easily to everyone. When we were in the caves, we knew our lives depended on what we could catch and cook. When my group saw how quickly I could find good flint and make a fire, I was often chosen to start them."

While they talked he continued to stroke the axe down the side of the stake, and chop lightly each time the blade caught. The little bits of wood left a yellowish pile at his feet.

She had to collect that pile. They would need tinder to make any more fires. Aksah bent forward and began to pick up the curls and chips when he said, "Perhaps when we reach my home, you will bake me a loaf of your bread. I am longing to eat something else other than what I have managed to forage for us the last several days. I think we both would be happy with hot food of some kind." There was a soft hopeful tone in his polite request. Aksah felt him looking at her as she slowly continued to scoop up the wood chips.

It was an offer of peace of a sort, she supposed. She could decline, but then she too was tired of eating only scavenged food, dried months before. Could she deny him the very thing she wanted too? Captive or not, she needed to keep up her strength if she hoped to take advantage of an opportunity to flee one day, and soon.

"I can do that," she said slowly.

A peaceful silence followed her comment, as if neither knew what more to say and both were reluctant to break the new harmony.

Sparks popped out of the fire, and sizzled on the ground. The sun was nearly down and cast its last golden glow on the land. Shadows seemed to be creeping in, even though it was still light enough to see. Her stomach rumbled, but it was foolish to mention it. He had to be hungry as well, and there was nothing to eat. Unless he had managed to hide some dried fruit cakes.

Such fare would hardly be enough, but she would show him she was not a complainer. She could be as strong as he, at least in this. Aksah made herself sit up straighter on the rocks.

Her stomach growled again.

He set the stake aside at last. "I am going to get us food."

Food? Aksah bit her tongue to keep from challenging him. If he could not do what he said, they would both be hungry tonight. So far he had done everything he said he would, but she did not see how he could find food where nothing edible existed.

"Nothing to say?" He raised an eyebrow. "There is food out there, and I will get it."

She remembered that long moving creature, the only living thing she had seen. "The Law forbids us eating snake."

Both eyebrows came down. "I have not broken the Law, and will not start now." He dropped his head back and sighed into the darkening sky, then straightened and looked at her. "Watch, and trust me." Picking up the large bow he had removed at some time while working on the staff, Eliab took his new pole as well, and tied his quiver onto his belt.

Looking down at her from his lofty height, he said in his warrior's voice, "Stay here, and keep on the watch for scorpions."

The reminder of scorpions stopped any retort she might have had. She did not know what she would have said, but the thought lingered that she was not a soldier to be ordered about.

His voice softened. "I will not have you stung. Build up the fire if you feel the need, but keep it modest. We need it to last all night, and I will not have either of us wander through the darkness finding more wood."

How could she lash out at a man whose only concern was for her? Now that he put scorpions in her mind again, she stared at the area where she sat. Her skin prickled as if small creatures were crawling on it already.

Eliab turned and walked into the barrenness beyond their fire. Aksah wondered what he thought he could find. And what she would have to eat this night. Just how hungry was she?

He crouched down, and seemed to disappear into the broken land. As she stared at where he had been, she saw something move in the evening's glow, and recognized his bow as it sliced a black line into the dimness.

The bow stayed frozen in place, and Aksah held her breath as if even an exhalation would break his concentration and lose them a possible meal. Time must have crept past, her arms felt the oncoming night's chill, but she did not move, and the bow became a part of the sky. Their small fire teased her legs with a hint of warmth, but it did not reach the rest of her body.

In a rush of movement in the distance, wings flapped, beating a pattern in the air, and then a bird tumbled out of the sky. Aksah had not even heard the bow release the arrow. Eliab stood, a silhouette against the golden-hued horizon, and walked to where the bird must have landed. Sure enough, he bent over and picked something up. If she was right, he had caught them a quail for their evening meal.

Her mouth watered. Quail. Her father had a pen where he kept and bred some for both eggs and meat. She had plucked quail since she was young, and the feathers would be good for tinder.

His knife captured the sun's last glow as he removed the head. She had to turn away. Although butchering was the only way to get meat, she had never grown accustomed to it, and much preferred to leave the bloody bits for someone else.

Like a warrior.

They needed something to cook on. She should have thought of that earlier! But earlier, she did not think they would really have something to cook. Aksah found several flat stones, and set them close to the fire, adding another couple sticks. In less time than she remembered his path out had taken, he stood before her and handed over the hen. Was it a test?

Aksah looked up at him, and felt a confident smile curve her lips. "Do you think I will not know what to do with this? I lived on a farm with my family. You wanted me to watch you hunt. Now, you can watch me."

So he did. He might have been able to remove the skin and insides faster, but they were not in a race. All he needed to know was that she was capable in her own right. The little bird sat there, bare and empty.

"A knife, please." Aksah held out her hand.

"As you wish." Eliab pulled out a small knife from his weapons belt, and handed it over, hilt first.

She split the bird and placed the parts on the warming stones. With quick, careful pushes, she slid the rocks with their meal against the fire, and sat on the stones she had claimed earlier. She felt his gaze on her, and pretended to be watching their meal cook.

Why not? All they had to do was wait and watch so the precious food did not burn.

Eliab lowered himself down on one of the largest boulders with that grace peculiar to him. "So you lived on a farm."

Would she answer? She had already given him something, that she had lived on a farm. That was a good thing, since he would be a farmer himself, once he reached his father's land.

Eliab tried not to think of that, but how could one wipe out all that one loved from the mind and heart? The loss threatened to crush him. *Do not think of them. Just move on.*

This young woman sitting on the rock below him, watching the quail as if that would make it cook faster, was his future. That very future felt as if it was hanging from a thread. Somehow he had to break through her distrust.

Answer me, he thought. *Say something.*

"Yes." Aksah said. "I lived on a farm."

"A farm? And what tribe did you come from? You know my tribe, it is only fair that I know yours." He tilted his head to see her face better. A difficult challenge, since she continued to stare at the flames.

Was that a glare flashing in her eyes? Or was it just the reflection off the fire, now brighter than the last light of the sun? "I am of Judah." Pride rang through her voice.

Judah was a large tribe, with a lot of land, but not all of it was usable. "Where in Judah did you live? Were you near the Wilderness?"

A faint smile curved the side of her mouth that he could see. "Close enough, but no, before you ask, we did not live in it."

"I did not think anyone did." The Wilderness was legendary for its barrenness. Benjamin's territory had their own barren parts. Eliab turned his head to see how much of the Michmash showed. It was only a black line in the growing dark. He went back to his questions, wondering how long it would be before she stopped answering. Whatever answers she gave, he would take them and be grateful. For now. "How many are there in your family?"

She turned her head, and he was sure now that he saw a glare. "Now? Or how many were there altogether, before the war?"

Ah yes, the conversation between the women that he had overheard in part. Even though he had not caught it all, he seemed to recall that Aksah had lost a brother. While he weighed the options, to ask or not, she took the decision from him.

"We were six before . . ." She took a breath. "Two sons and four daughters." The last words came out clipped.

"I, too, was one of six, as you might have determined, but we were the opposite count. Four sons and two daughters. As I said, I was late in the family. Two older brothers and one younger than myself."

"And where did the girls fit in your family? You said they were older than you. Where does that put them?"

In the last moments, the night had eaten away the lingering light. Despite the only brightness now being the glow of the small fire, he saw her arched brows, could tell she was watching him with skepticism.

"The girls were the eldest, before any of my brothers." He knew where she had been heading. Younger sisters were supposed to bring out protective urges. He had seen it in Aksah, running between the men and her own sisters, only to be caught herself. That argument would not work for him. His sisters had been older than all of them. If anything, they had tormented and teased him, rather than him feeling protective toward them. He had never felt they needed his help.

"Oh." He could see the building fervor, a budding argument, seep out of her. Conversation faded. She looked down at her feet, and then up at him, meeting his gaze for a fleeting instant. "I am sorry."

He did not expect even that much from her. Not this early. "Thank you. I, too, am sorry for your own loss."

Aksah went back to staring at the fire, and shifted to reach another twig. Instead of tossing it onto the fire, she poked at the rocks with the meat sizzling, working them around to ensure they cooked evenly. Once the stones had been adjusted to her satisfaction, she finally did what he expected, and tossed the twig into the fire.

The flames crackled and flared. In the distance some large creature growled, but it seemed to come from across the gash in the land that separated their camp from where they needed to be tomorrow.

He looked over at the fire. "The quail smells done."

"Yes." She reached for another twig.

Eliab caught her hand. "No. It is too hot. Let me." The axe or a knife? He pulled out both. The axe would work best for sliding the rocks away from the fire, the knife for pulling the hot meat away from the bones.

Either they were both very hungry, Aksah thought, or they were both trying very hard to avoid the massive disagreement on the cause of the war that loomed between them. That argument would come, she knew, and part of her longed to get it done. Just not now, when she was so hungry and wanted to eat in peace.

Her mind, however, did not want to stop brooding. His sisters were older. More confident? The kind who could take care of themselves?

Do not think about that now, she ordered her unruly mind. *Eat and sleep.*

Aksah set aside the bones from her piece, and looked over at her companion. "Are we going to save some for tomorrow?"

From the way he stared at the remnants, she could tell he, like herself, was thinking of what they would eat in the morning. The group had lived off the land, scavenging what they could find from houses she had not seen, but the scent of fire gave their presence away. Looking at the area, there were no dwellings, no place to forage for food. If they wanted to eat, at least until they got out of this barren landscape, finding food would be much more difficult.

"I think we had better. We need to keep it safe. The large animals can smell it from great distances, so we will have to sleep lightly."

She knew he meant that he would hardly sleep. Aksah looked over to where the Michmash blended into the darkness. "I will stay awake for part of the night. We both need sleep. If you think you are going to get me across that," her arm gestured toward where her nightmare lay, "I want you awake and alert."

He smiled, his beard's curves obvious even in the flickers from the fire. "I have spent many a night at watch. I assure you, I will be alert tomorrow."

"Maybe alert enough for you," Aksah said with all the firmness she could muster. "But not alert enough for me!"

His smile faded. More seriously than she expected, he asked, "Are you worried about your safety? Or mine?"

Aksah could not hold his gaze, and turned back to the fire. How did she answer that? She could not admit to being worried about him, for it would build hopes she had no intention of fulfilling. Instead, she said, "I am afraid for both of us."

He shook his head, she could see the movement from the corner of her eye. "Very well. Do you want the first watch?"

That suited her well. She had much to think about. "Yes. I am not familiar with your weapons, but if something frightens me, I will wake you."

"Do that." Eliab handed over the staff he had made. "Use this to shove snakes or scorpions aside. If there is anything else dangerous, call for me." The smile came back. "Just do not prod me with the stake to get my attention. I might awaken ready for battle."

Much to Aksah's surprise, she found herself smiling back. "If I awaken you, you had better be ready for battle."

He laughed. "True enough."

CHAPTER 8

*Thorns will grow in her fortified towers, nettles and thorny weeds in her
fortresses. She will become a lair of jackals, an enclosure for ostriches.
Desert creatures will meet up with howling animals, and the wild goat
will call to its companion.*
Isaiah 34:13,14

H ad she really agreed to stay and watch while he slept? She could have
turned around and started retracing their steps. This was her chance
to escape!

It was very dark, and the cavity in the land was too close.

Something moved in the deeper dark of the crevices, and Aksah held her
breath. She knew those movements, knew that shape.

Scorpion.

Another shape came out from the next rock, squeezing out from underneath the small overhang and started to scuttle across the dirt. Eliab slept a
scant cubit away. Aksah lowered the staff and measured her swing. This had

been a game she and her brothers and sisters had played, who could send the scorpions the farthest.

Taking careful aim, Aksah swung, clipping the first scorpion and sending it spinning, but not far enough. The second one scurried for shelter behind a rock. She could have tried again, but an angry scorpion was not good company for the night.

More creatures of the night crept out, and Aksah wished she did not have to ration the sticks so carefully for the fire. How much comfort a strong blaze would be!

The night's watch gave too much time to think. Watch for dangers and brood, add another of the dwindling pile of sticks to the sputtering flames, and brood some more. She began to break up the time between scorpions and thoughts. Swing at the poisonous creatures, and chase equally biting questions.

Leaving Eliab alone and vulnerable was wrong. He would not leave her to risk being stung or bitten by worse than a scorpion, she knew that without a question.

To be sure, their reasons for taking care of the other were very different. She did not want him to suffer, just as she would not allow any person to suffer if she could prevent it.

He wanted children.

It kept coming back to that. Children. But whose?

Her eyes started drooping and her head ached when Eliab stretched and gave a noisy yawn. She had been about to poke him. How did he know when to wake up? Was it a soldier's rhythm, a pattern for all who kept guard? 'A watch in the night,' the familiar phrase, had now come to life.

"We have a rough crossing today," Eliab said as they chewed on the last of the quail. "There is a pass, as I said, but one cannot simply walk over it. The cliff is steep and the rocks slippery. I will help you when we get there. It is not so easy to find, and once found, not easy to climb."

The farther they went, the harder it would be to find her way back.

Aksah fought down the rising panic. If she did not get away soon, there might not be a way back.

For now, it was only forward, deeper into Benjamin's territory. Across more of the slippery shale, the frightening ravine always on their right. The distance was not that much, but the rocks slowed their progress, threatening them with twisted ankles or worse. Despite her experience clambering through the Wilderness of Judea, she took each step with care.

Eliab did the same, she noticed.

He turned around before they had gone far. "We must collect whatever will burn. We will need fuel for later, for the night, and for cooking. What a pity we do not have a fireholder, but we do not." He handed her a familiar thin leather strap to tie the sticks together. "This will help you carry them."

Aksah knew better than to doubt his hunting skills. She picked up sticks, whatever she could find, even fighting some of the prickly bushes to free withered branches that had not yet broken off.

As he had said he would, Eliab caught another quail before midday, and they took time to eat. Part way through the meal, he pointed. "Do you see the crags? Two of them?"

As she looked at the scenery, she realized that there were indeed two distinct points. She had thought them just more of the jagged edges of Michmash, but they were too distinct, almost like gates.

"There is a pass between them. It is still not easy, but we can make it through." He shaded his eyes and looked at the sun. "I think we can cross it before the end of the day." Then he motioned at the remaining quail, sizzling over the fire made from her collected twigs. "Eat what you can, and then we will put out the fire. I want to move quickly. The pass is not where you want to be late at night."

No, she thought as she looked up at the tall stone peaks, and then down at the space between them. This was not the place to cross at night. If she had not been used to the Wilderness of Judea she might not have seen any way to climb up the cliff. Compared to the near-vertical walls of the ravine, the slope was more gentle.

Gentle, she corrected herself as she looked at the pass they would soon be crossing, was not the word to use. Less impossible was a better description.

Eliab took his rope from across his chest where it rested among all his other weapons, and tied one end to his own waist. "I will link us together. I know this area, I can take your weight and help you climb."

His hands were steady as he tied the other end around her waist. He knew this area, Aksah repeated to herself as he finished the knot. He had been here before.

"The rock is slippery, it comes off in scales, so we have to take care. I intend to leave us roped together, but that means if one of us starts to slide, we both will go." As if to emphasize his words, his foot went sideways, and Eliab had to give a couple of shuffling steps to keep his balance. "One does not walk upright here. One goes however one can. Follow my lead." He turned toward the slope that rose, more gently but still inexorably, in front of them. "Hands and feet, now."

Aksah did as he did, clawing with her fingers, digging in with her feet. The two of them looked like children who did not quite trust their legs to hold them upright, she thought, but could not smile, not yet. Rocks stabbed at her palms, her feet slipped on the unstable shale, causing her knees to thump against the harsh layers beneath.

They started up the next rise, grabbing rocks as high as their shoulders for support and pulling themselves past, only to find another in their way. Grab and pull, grab and pull. There were no paths, only sharp slabs leading there and steep sides they could not walk up. They had to use their feet as braces in the few spaces between the man-sized boulders. Hands to pull and feet to brace and push, clambering up the sharp inclines, finding footing, and then the next mount, steeper, taller, more seams to climb over.

Eliab wrapped his section of rope around rocks several times for bracing and pulled her upward, the heavy cord squeezing her middle while she grabbed at any ledge, any jutting rock, and dug in with her feet, fighting the slope that threatened to push her back.

Eliab caught the rope around her waist, dragged her up higher, until she could push herself along with her toes. He fell down next to her and wrapped her in his arms so tightly it was as if his grip alone could keep them safe.

Aksah grabbed onto his robe as close as he held her, and clung. Odd how very secure she felt. Rocks dug into her side, her legs, and stabbed her arm where it rested on the ground, yet she felt no urge to push him away. Her fingers curled into the soft worn linen, holding on as she gasped for breath. Her heart slowed to a more measured pace.

He did not let go, just laid beside her, his arms still tight. "It is easier from here," he said, his voice hoarse.

Oh, she hoped so! Aksah lifted her head away from his shoulders, and saw a slope above her. Just a slope, steep but there were no more cliffs.

Eliab let go bit by bit, sat up, then eased himself to his feet. "One more stretch, and we are done."

One more stretch, she repeated to herself, and reached for his hand as he pulled her upright. Just a few more rocks to pass, just a few more boulders, and then she could see the end. One more grab, a pull from Eliab, scraping, sharp scratches down her side, her legs, and she was up and on the top.

The sky seemed so close Aksah felt she could reach up and touch it. The setting sun gilded the stone and turned the rough land into gold. It was not, she knew that, but after the past days' walk, even the illusion of beauty helped lift her spirits.

Eliab flopped down on the ground and stretched out, staring up at the darkening sky. The moon showed now, a pale crescent against grey. He reached his hand straight up, and his eyes asked her to join him.

It was either brace herself against that hand, use the strength in that strong arm, or have her legs give way. She held tight and he took all her weight and lowered her beside him.

She rolled her head and looked at the dark line of the Michmash. Even knowing the secret to getting through, how would one go across the Pass alone?

· · ·

Morning sun dappled the ground, and found the hilltops, gilding them with gold. The land ahead was devoid of the frightening crags they had left behind. Finally. She had begun to think Michmash covered all of Benjamin.

Aksah wondered how much sleep he had managed last night. They were both so tired and it had grown so late when they reached the top of the pass that he made a rudimentary camp, they had bundled up together and slept.

Or at least she had.

In the distance, green tinted the shadows and valleys. Trees and bushes? Flowers? After yesterday, she would be glad to look at anything that was not rock.

Her stomach growled. Eliab would find something to eat, she knew that. He was a proven provider, a skilled hunter, and there would be food. Animals of all kinds would roam throughout the valleys, and hide in the trees that had to give the tint to the countryside.

Dangling like a final safeguard was the law for captured brides from foreigners. One month without intimacy from the husband. She was not a foreigner, but she was a captured bride and she would demand that month's protection. That law would be her last hope. For one month, he could not touch her.

For that same month her father yet had time to find her.

Eliab leaned down and picked up his bundle from the ground. Aksah jolted back into the present, and took a sharp look at where they were. She had not had the light or the energy to check the toll their climb had taken. Now, as his hand closed on his pack, she saw his skinned knuckles. She looked down at her own hands. A few spots were raw, but he had taken the worst of it.

Eliab straightened and then she saw his legs. How had she missed them? Blood spots streaked his skin, his knees looked like the scrapes would begin bleeding once he moved. Yet he did not even glance at either hands or legs, as if nothing hurt. Her back felt stiff after yesterday's climb. No doubt he was used to sleeping on the hard ground. True, her family had slept on soil with only a blanket to soften it on the way to Shiloh, but the last three nights were so different. Sleep came hard, and each morning she barely felt rested.

Today she felt both tired and sore. It was hardly fair that he could be so alert and move with such ease. If he was hurting, she would feel better if he showed it.

Once the pack was over his shoulder, Eliab ran his hands through his tangled hair, shoving the curls away from his dust-covered face. "We need food and water. The sooner we begin today's journey, the sooner we will find both."

Kicking dirt over the last few coals, he turned and started walking. He stopped after a few steps, and turned back. "Watch for snakes. They might not have found burrows for the day yet."

They made their way down the slope that edged the Michmash. As the hill that lead to the ravine began to level, he made a turn. A clear path pointed the way. The path widened, and tracks showed where wagons had gone. Off to her right, the lighter dirt showed more tracks going in a different direction.

This place was a junction point. Paths branched off from this very spot, a crossroads in the emptiness, and led to other cities, perhaps even to other tribes. The worn tracks of donkeys and carts, visible as hoof circles and straight grooves, left deep lines through the endless dusty brown of the ground. Dirt filtered through the straps of her sandals and rubbed her feet.

How she wanted a bath! Even a stream, which that green in the distance promised, would be more than welcome.

Was all Israel hills and valleys? More ups and downs, not high or low, but her legs throbbed from the previous days' exertions. The wisps of moving air hissed against the sore and scrapes on her legs, and her palms burned from where she had scraped herself against the rocks.

Eliab walked ahead of her, his head constantly turning as he searched for food. Aksah followed, trying to absorb anything that might guide her back. She followed his example of scanning the area as far as she could see, but for a different purpose. Benjamin had been a populous tribe. She could tell from the ongoing trails winding through the gullies and climbing the mounts in faint pale lines that this had been inhabited land.

A hint of smoke hung here, too, as it had on the food the men had brought. Somewhere nearby there had to be the remnants of cities, and there had to be houses for the farmers who dwelt outside them. There were no sounds of people, no shouts from the orchards, no calls to the flocks or herds. No wagons creaking along the trail, either in front or behind.

Or had all the houses been burned just like the cities had, when the armies came through? Would Eliab get to his home and find it a blackened shell?

"If you notice sheep or goats, let me know." He spoke over his shoulder. They had reached the top of a small hill. Grass grew at the bottom, and scrubby plants a goat would love spotted its side with patches of green. More plants had shown up on these last hills, as if they, too, were glad to be away from the ravine of Michmash with its harsh stones.

He kept talking as he walked along the narrow flatness of the hilltop. Little red crowfoot flowers were crushed underfoot, while she had tried to step around them. White daisies still bloomed, sparse here but promising more green in the land ahead. "With no men here, goats and sheep and cattle will begin to stray. They need food and water, and are going to find a way to get them. I do not know if any fences were left standing. The army might well have trampled them in their trek across our land."

Bitterness laced his words, and his chest expanded with the deep breath as he pulled himself away from his dark thoughts. "We must collect all the livestock we can find. They are as much prey for the predators as we are. More, because the wild animals fear man. I cannot afford to let any flocks or herds go to waste if I'm to rebuild the farm."

Aksah had to move quickly to keep up, the hill's downward slope pushing her along as she followed him toward the gully. "You once mentioned having seen lions."

"They are not the only things we need fear." His steps continued to eat up the ground, crossing the small valley that surrounded each incline, then starting up the next hill, shorter than the one they just left, more flowers, more spiny grass, and as always, more limestone poking up through the drying soil. "There are bears and wild bulls that roam the area, especially at night. Even the ibex needs to be treated with care." He looked back from his position above her, and his eyes sent a warning. "Animals will take over the land with surprising speed when there are no people to keep them in check."

Aksah stumbled going up behind him, and tripped over a piece of limestone sticking through the ground that she normally should, *would* have seen. Eliab's tall strong figure, weapons bristling from the belt crossing his back, was her protection. He had survived the war and the months in hiding. He had guided her up the pass, the only way across the sharp walls of Michmash. He would take on whatever threat faced them with courage.

If she were not of the tribe of Judah, if she did not have the possibility of being chosen to receive God's special blessing driving her on, would she consider the risk of leaving alone?

But she did have the chance of the promised blessing to guide her, Aksah reminded herself, and that changed everything.

Eliab stopped at the hill's top, and turned fully around to face her again. "I have weapons."

His thoughts echoed her own. She had just been thinking of them as they hung down his back.

"If you stay close, we should have no trouble. I will give you a staff for protection—and to guide sheep if we find them, as soon as I see a tree that is the right size. You will need instruction." He was looking past her shoulder, his eyes intent on something beyond her. He did not look alarmed, but set down his cloak, the waterskins and the shrinking food supplies they had brought along.

"Well, well," he said. "Just as I expected. Come. There are some sheep out there. I do not think they have had time to go wild, but it has been four months. Who can tell? Come with me and do as I say." Aksah was turned around by the pressure of his hand on her arm. Eliab began moving away back down the hill they had just climbed, confident she would follow as she had been doing all along.

Of course she would stay close. They were chasing loose domestic animals. For all they knew, something else more dangerous was stalking the creatures as well. Lions, bears? Once again, she had proof of how alert he was. She had seen nothing, but then he was taller than herself and might be able to look over the surrounding hills that blocked her view.

He kept talking, but his voice went softer. "We need to come on them slowly so they do not get startled." He shook his head. His curly hair slid across his neck. "I wish I knew the call they would respond to, but we will do our best."

He started along the gully that ringed the small hill they had just climbed before she saw the sheep on the slope two mounds farther away, nibbling at the bushes. A minimal herd, no more than five or six, but it was hard to tell from the tight group.

"I think they are hungry." She kept her voice a whisper, although it was unlikely they could be heard at this distance.

"I doubt it." Eliab kept them moving, his steps slow but deliberate. "We just came out of the rainy season." The strangest sound bubbled from his throat. It took Aksah a moment to realize it was a meant to be a laugh. "I can only hope they are used to people. And lonely. It would be a great help."

They kept moving, the sheep oblivious to their presence. Closer, closer, through the gully between the series of hills while the animals grazed. One of them lifted its head and Eliab stopped as still as a tree. Aksah did the same.

There was no ram, as far as she could tell. If they were all ewes, this might not be too hard. She hoped. It had been four months since they had been with an owner, Eliab had said, and he would know.

Another sheep raised its wooly head as well, only this one saw them. Aksah held her breath and stayed as still as Eliab. This ewe shook her head, ears flapping with the wobbly movement, and gave a soft bleat. To their amazement, she ambled down the rest of the hillside and stopped in front of them, giving another bleat. The sheep behind her finally paid attention to her calls, and one by one started down the hill.

Aksah fought down the urge to laugh. It was highly unlikely all the other animals they sought would be this easy, but they had the beginnings of a flock.

A small ewe bumped her with its head and leaned against her legs, almost toppling her off balance. Eliab slid the rope off his shoulder, and looped it around the neck of the first one to meet them. "I think she might be the leader, at least of this little group." He started back in their direction pulling it along. After the first few tugs it decided to keep up. "Let us see if the others follow."

"If not?"

He shook his head. "Let us not borrow trouble. Come along."

Aksah frowned at the command said in a voice of gentle sweetness, until she realized he was speaking to her in the tone that might lure the flock as well.

In the same crooning voice, Eliab continued, "You seem to have made a friend. If we go slowly, I think they will all come."

So she started walking, and the ewe did indeed follow along, the others joining like links in a chain.

They made an odd procession all the way back to where they had left the rest of their meager possessions on the trail.

There was not enough cord to link all the sheep, but once they had divided their possessions between the both of them, Eliab took the rope and gave her a slight smile. "I think our journey just doubled in time." He gave a slight tug, just as he had on the hill, and the lead ewe began walking along behind them.

Odd, Aksah thought, how even the sound of sheep's hooves helped keep the silence at bay. The sun shone down, tinting the leaves of the plants growing along the trail, sparking along the rocks that marked the path, brightening the trees in the distance. Their shade was always just a little too distant to take advantage of it.

The sheep were remarkably placid, walking in near silence, only soft hoof clumps and scuffs, but here and there a bleat broke the quiet. She could not tell if they were complaints or if the sheep just wanted to make their presence known. Perhaps they were glad to be back among humans again.

Up another incline, and along the trail, Eliab's gaze swept the hills. Aksah suspected he was watching for more than the rest of the flock. Predators might find them an easy meal. He kept that large staff so newly made loose on his grip, ready to flip into position at the first sign of danger.

Throughout the day, they spotted more animals. Some they had to ignore because they were just too far away, some they tried to catch but they were too stubborn, too frightened, or too wild. They did gather up four more sheep, including one very young male not yet ready to leave its mother. Some day he would be a great ram, the foundation of a new herd.

More than ever, she could see how empty Benjamin was. Olive trees grew in neat rows, but no figures came out of the shells of houses in the distance. Houses that had blackened walls and shattered roofs, and always that whisper of smoke. Orchards climbed the hillsides, the fruit beginning on the branches but there would be no one to gather it at summer's end. Fields of wheat and barley, already past the harvest, began to wither in the sun. If not harvested soon, it would be beyond hope.

Would Eliab come back and gather these crops? If she could not flee before then, would he bring her with him to work?

If these last six hundred men all had similar fields to harvest across their territory, they would eat well enough. The first early figs waiting with the aging crops of wheat and barley planted before the war ripped the nation apart, summer fruits yet to come, and after them autumn dates ripening high in their trees as the days cooled, then olives and grapes for oil and wine. So much food and so few to eat them.

Such a thing would be good for those women they had dragged onto their land, women who would no doubt be full with child when the olives came, giving oil to rub on ripening bellies and then babes.

Their small flock reached the top of another hill and they saw—or at least, *she* saw—a bull two rises away. It even now had a harness around its massive neck, proclaiming it had once belonged to someone. Gathering a bull into their wall-less Noah's Ark of animals would be a risk, for bulls were dangerous.

Eliab wanted it, Aksah noticed when she looked over and saw the longing in his eyes. A bull, just think what a prize! But he shook his head and turned away, as he had the other times they had passed animals they could not reach. Aksah noticed a muscle in his neck was getting tight.

Darkness tinged the sky overhead. The sun hovered just above the horizon and cast long, dim shadows. They stopped in the bottom of a gully by a stone trough that spoke of long use. A well with a bucket still hanging from its brace told her they were near a house, although none was seen.

"I wish there was a stream for the flock," he said as he looked over the desolation, the lone well, olive trees, and a straggled field of over-ripe wheat running up the hillside that must have been planted before the tribe knew what lay ahead. No one had remained to harvest the crop. "We will have to set out water, enough for the night."

He dropped the bucket down into the well's darkness. Aksah was relieved to hear it splash on the bottom. Bucket after bucket went into the trough, his strong arms making it look easy. The smell of water and the sound of it washing around the trough's bottom excited the sheep. They pushed past her to get to it, climbing over each other, tangling the ropes that linked them as each tried to be first.

Eliab made a small camp, setting out their few possessions, his cloak, the sagging pouches that held their food, the waterskins. He still wore his weapons belt. Aksah knew he did not dare leave it near her, and she could hardly blame him. She was indeed tempted to take something, though not to harm him as he might think, but to have protection in reserve for when it was time to run.

He would notice a piece missing, possibly within moments of her taking it. Would he keep the weapons close even once they were back to his family home? She would have to find something to carry.

The sheep must have satisfied their thirst, for they moved away from the trough. One by one, they settled on the ground, nestling close.

Aksah looked over the flock. "They hardly know us. Do you think they will stay?"

Hands on hips, Eliab's brows furrowed. "Things have gone well so far, but like you I am unwilling to trust them not to wander off. Silly creatures that they are, they may well believe where there is one human there may be others, and that their shepherds are nearby." He glanced down at her. "Help me find some wood we can use as stakes." Before she turned away, he caught her hand. "Stay as close as you can. If we get out of sight, the sheep are likely to try to follow us and then we have the whole thing to do over again."

Moving about, she found more signs that this once belonged to a family. Wood was easy to find, both from man and from the land's own bounty. Bits of fencing, broken branches from trees she could not identify yet, even a stack of logs waiting for a winter's heat that was never needed, all good for keeping sheep in place for a night. She added her finds to Eliab's pile and sat down next to him as he sorted through them. Pieces that broke easily when he flexed them were set to one side for the night's fire, the others made a much smaller pile. He did a second check and picked out the longest ones.

"These should hold up. I think if we stake the animals that seem to be the leaders, the rest will stay put." He picked up a rather good size rock she had not seen at his side and rose.

Not knowing what he expected of her, Aksah remained sitting while he worked his way through the flock, checking for the sheep that already had ropes around their necks. He started pounding the pieces of wood into the ground. The sheep shifted at first, but settled easily.

Eliab did not meet her eyes as he staked the last sheep, pounding in the post to which he secured it with a rock. "You gave your word you would not flee before we reach my land."

"You could claim this land if you wished. You have no one to challenge you." She waved at the empty hills blending into the growing dark.

He dropped the rock on the ground. Even in the twilight she saw anger glitter in his eyes. "I have my own land ahead. Without any brothers to share, it will be larger than it had been, but acquit me of greed."

She got slowly to her feet, to meet him on equal ground. "I intended no insult. I merely meant that someone will have to care for the harvests around us. I have been noticing the fruits and grains, as I know you have. It is a shame to leave it to waste."

He stalked toward her, every step deliberate. "And will you be here to help? Will you load baskets on wagons at my side? Will you thresh grain with me?"

Aksah did not answer, but neither did she look away.

He stopped within reach and glared at her. "I claimed you according to the rules. I know you wish to run for your old home, but I cannot let you go. If you choose to make your life miserable, that is up to you, but do not think you can destroy *my* future. We will have children and we *will* rebuild my tribe."

Aksah held up her hand to keep him from getting any closer and glared back. "You wonder why I am so reluctant to become your wife? You want to rebuild Benjamin. Well, I am frightened by the kind of sons you will raise. I want one thing more than anything else: to know I am safe. But not just myself. I want all the six hundred women you of Benjamin have taken to be safe also. Not just this week, or this month, but for the rest of their lives. I want to know that your tribe of men has learned from this awful war. You all heard what had happened in the town of Gibeah, everyone heard. You all knew—or were supposed to know—the laws on murder."

Propping her fists on her hips, Aksah kept going, she could not stop her mouth, or the thoughts that had been locked in her brain these past days. "What do you think your entire tribe did? The other eleven tribes, from Reuben all the way to Ephraim, came and asked for the murderers to be handed over, and what did you do? You denied them their call for justice and met them with force!"

Eliab's eyes narrowed. "Do you know how many men were in that army that stormed onto our land? Has anyone told you the count?" He paced a few steps away before turning back. His fists at his sides were knotted so taut the knuckles were white. "Four hundred thousand men! Four hundred thousand men came to our boundary! What were we to believe?"

"You had time to think before that!" she scoffed. "They sent a delegation to request the murderers. You had time even before they arrived. Did you need to have someone come to tell you something evil had happened?" With courage she hardly expected, Aksah moved closer, shouting his words into his face. "What did you think when news of the murdered woman came? That was long before the big army. What did you think when you received a part of her body? That, too, was before Israel sent the army of the eleven other tribes. How did you think that poor woman got those marks, so that not one piece was unscarred? And you did nothing!"

"What were we to do? The husband was of Levi, he was not even a Benjaminite." Eliab winced when the words came out, she saw him, but she would not let that appalling statement escape.

"So the only ones worth saving, the only ones you would bestir yourself to avenge, are your own people? The men with blood on their hands in Gibeah, they are of Benjamin's people, so you avenged *them*? You charged into battle because Israel asked for someone of your tribe to face judgment?

If the poor dead woman had been of Benjamin instead of Judah—*my tribe*—and the crime had been done against one of your own, then would you have done anything differently? Would you have judged and punished Gibeah? I hardly think so. I think you could not be bothered to defend a woman, only a man."

"That is not what I meant." He caught her arms. "Remember, her husband handed her over to the mob. For that we must turn the men of Gibeah over to the other eleven tribes for judgment? What did that Levite imagine would happen when he pushed her out the door? He did nothing Abraham's nephew Lot did not do. Or have you forgotten that part of our history? Lot offered his daughters to another mob. You would paint us black and let him go unaccused?"

"There were angels in Lot's house!" She screamed the words, her throat burning with the effort. "Do you think for a *single moment* those angels would have allowed anything to happen to Lot's daughters? What is more, I think the Levite sent her out because he was still angry with her for her adultery. I cannot belong to a man who thinks anger is a good reason to risk his wife. A man who would sleep all night instead of going out to find her."

He let go of her with a little push, and stepped back. His voice was quieter, but then he had not screamed yet as she just did. The sheep shuffled around them, the argument making them nervous. "You are missing my point. Why does all the blame fall upon us of Benjamin? Why not blame the Levite?"

Aksah folded her arms and glared at Eliab. "Oh, believe me when I say that I do, indeed, denounce him as well. None of the men involved remains blameless. Guilt is guilt, and Benjamin is thick with it." She propped her hands on her hips. "Why is it so hard for you to accept blame for the crime? Why can you not say what Gibeah did was wrong, and that Benjamin should have turned the men over for justice? You have never admitted guilt. You have never even said the woman's death was a crime. How hard would it have been to leave your tribe and join the rest of Israel in standing for right?"

His hands fisted again, but they remained at his sides. "I am not a traitor! I chose to stand with my tribe!"

"You see? You did it again!" Aksah wanted to scream in frustration. "You still cannot say a crime was committed! You ignored it. You have ignored it all along! All you will say is how *loyal* you were. Yet, when I choose to be loyal to my tribe and my fellow women, you become angry." She stepped closer. "Say it. The woman's death was a crime."

White spots showed on his cheeks above the beard. "You wish to narrow it down to just one wrong? It is not possible. Her death was only one of many crimes in this whole event."

Her throat burned as if screams still fought to be freed. "*Still?* You spread the guilt and think to distract me from blaming Benjamin? It will not work."

His eyes were dark holes in his face, and his hands were still clenched. "Were you on the battlefield with me? Did you come home to find your house and land had been ransacked? Did you hide in caves to keep the remnant of your people alive?"

"My brother was killed in that war! I lost my oldest brother, only he fought for the right side." The mention of Chileab choked her throat, forcing her to stop just for a moment.

He leaned toward her. They were not that far apart now, not in distance. "Yet in that you can find no sympathy for my loss? You would condemn me forever? You would condemn all my fellows forever? How many times must I say this? *I was not there!* I was not in Gibeah! I was not one of those men!"

Aksah's throat released. "What can I say to make you see? You refused to defend her. You stood up for the wrong. That I cannot forgive."

He flung his arms wide, his own frustration in the movement. But his hands did not move toward her. "So tell me, since you know so much about the crime, how were we to find which men in the city were the guilty ones? She was alive when she arrived back at the house where they were staying. So these men were to be charged with murder when the woman was still living when she left them? At what point did it become murder?"

The woman was not left dead? She made it back to the house alive? Aksah had not heard that. Was it even true?

One sheep gave a bleat, another echoed it, much like children pleading with their parents to stop fighting. They had had enough.

"Tell me your father would have done differently."

"My father has four daughters," she said with more restraint because of the sheep, "If he had been of Benjamin, he would have fought for that woman, no matter that he had to leave his tribe and join the army of the other eleven." She wished she knew her sisters' fates. Wished she could see her mother again, could sleep in security in her own house, knowing that her father would stand guard for them.

"I am sorry for your brother. I did not know him, nor did you know my family. My mother, my father, my brothers and sisters. I even had a living grandmother and grandfather. Are we to compete with the magnitude of our losses? The whole nation is grieving. Do you think any came out of this without pain?" Eliab ran a hand over his hair. When it dropped back to his side, she noticed it was loose, no longer a fist.

Was she trying to claim the greater loss? She did not think so. It was not the loss, great though it was, that fed her anger, but the injustice.

"You are not happy I am your husband. I am sorry for that. The nation gave you to me. You have two choices. Hate me forever and have us both be miserable, or finish with your anger. We cannot go back and change what happened. We can only go forward. I acknowledge your grief. I understand better why you felt such anger. Let us both call a truce. I ask that you try to see *me*, Eliab, when you look at me, and not a Benjaminite."

Leaning down, he picked up the bucket where he had set it. A dark curl fell over his eye when he straightened, and he ignored it. The air was quiet as he wound the bucket's cord around the brace.

Eliab walked over to their little camp, and retrieved his cloak from the ground. He came back with calm steps, as if he, too, had listened to the sheep's pleas, and handed it out to her. "Here. You can sleep with it. I will take guard for a while."

She wondered if anything had been settled at all. The air did feel purged, everything finally aired. "The sheep will keep me warm. They will be all around me. You, on the other hand, will be in the open. You need the cloak."

"The night is warm enough for me. You need it." He still held it out.

Aksah did not want to admit that the night air had begun to cool her arms. He did not look cold, and his arm holding the cloak did not waver. She accepted it, even made herself say, "Thank you." Her foolish tongue kept going, but perhaps she meant it to. "I will stand the second watch."

To her surprise, he nodded. "I shall let you." He bent again and collected the long staff, then turned away and walked to the far side of the flock, and along the crest, stopping just before the hill began its downward slope. Aksah knew he chose that position to watch for anything that would come creeping through the hollows, but it felt a bit like he might be testing her as well.

Will she keep her word and stay?

Aksah wrapped herself in the warm fabric and lay down on the ground, picking out rocks from underneath her until she could be comfortable. The sheep shifted much as she had, squirming and wiggling until they, too, had found their own snug beds again. Fluffy coats brushed against her back, she felt the wool even through the cloak.

The moon was bright, the stars joined it. Eliab would be able to see danger approach in the faint light they gave, she was certain. As would she when it was her turn for the watch.

Something nudged her, a firm, purposeful nudge. "Aksah," the nudge said, and it came again, only this time the touch stopped on her shoulder. The night air did its bit to wake her. The dark felt oppressive. Only a small fire that had not been there when she fell asleep and the sliver of moon gave any light.

Eliab removed his hand. "Promise me that you will not run tonight, and I will try to sleep, at least a little."

He needed his sleep, especially since they were going alone through such barren territory and their lives depended on his being alert. Aksah sat up and rubbed her eyes. She struggled to her feet, bringing the cloak with her. If she stayed on the ground, she would fall asleep again. Her body had not caught up, and she staggered. Eliab caught her with his big hands gentle on her, holding her upright until she was able to stand up and walk.

Aksah reached down to pet one of the flock that had wandered to the edge of its rope. "I will be warm enough. The sheep will be close by." She pulled the cloak off and held it out to Eliab.

His eyes glittered in the dark. Perhaps that was all he could see of her as well. He held out the staff. "This will keep an animal at a distance, but long before you need to use it, call me. I will come." He did not let go as she tried to pull it away. "Tell me you will not run."

She stared back at those shining orbs. Either she was learning his face well, or her eyes were growing used to the dark, because she thought she could see his expression, the weary lines around his mouth. "I have given you my word once. I will keep it."

"I keep my word as well," he said, ignored the cloak in her hand, and walked toward the sheep.

The night was quiet. Aksah leaned against the staff and looked off into the shadows deep in the hills. She did not want to admit that she was relieved to know he was nearby in this deep part of the night.

She stared into the darkness and listened. The sheep shifted behind her, making contented sounds much like snoring. They must have been afraid, used to pens and people bringing food, perhaps even the sound of children in the background. Eliab was tucked between some of the sheep. She saw his feet sticking out between two of the wooly creatures.

He had left her the cloak. It was warm enough when one was standing guard, she realized. The cloak would be better served as a blanket for whoever was sleeping, but he had refused it twice already.

The night was quiet. That left plenty of time for thinking. Too much time, in fact.

It hurt to admit that she needed to think about what Eliab had said. Her anger had become something familiar, almost necessary, if uncomfortable. Anger was a heavy burden, however justified it was.

What did she do now? If she let go of the grief and became a compliant wife, what about all that had driven her? Her dream of being faithful enough to even have a chance to produce the Shiloh? Could she give that up?

A new pain stabbed her like a knife through the heart. How could she sacrifice that? What would keep her faithful then?

The darkness pressed in, and Aksah shivered even under the cloak. Only the moon's pale light let her see. Might there be lions, or bears crouching in the gullies? She held her breath and listened over the heartbeat in her ears. The sheep were quiet, their soft breaths sighing in the air.

Other than that, the night was undisturbed. How silently could a lion move? She had never seen one.

She did not know how long she waited, still, listening to the night, before she was able to relax again.

The staff felt sturdy in her hands, but it was so heavy! At best she would only be able to take a small walking staff, not this one that was meant to be a weapon. If a lion came out now, her voice was her best defense. Eliab was only cubits away. He would awaken and fight off whatever came because right now she was all he had to continue his family name.

No, that was not fair. He would come because it was in his nature to defend. Defend her, defend the sheep. Defend his tribe.

She was not the woman he would have chosen, she knew that. He would have preferred another woman, a meek, mild type. Aksah stopped the thought. There it was again, the blame that always came up when she considered their situation.

I was not there! I was not one of those men!

Stay or leave, could she learn to view him as himself? Nothing would wipe out what happened and bring the woman back to life. How much of this lingering anger was grief over her brother? And how much was righteous fury at the woman's fate?

A sheep shifted, and settled again. A sudden breeze caught the edge of the cloak, stirring Eliab's scent into the air and loosing the soil from the tops of the nearby hills. She blinked at the sting of dirt against her face, and her eyes watered for a moment, until the dust washed away and her view was clear again.

The sky was even still the same, black spotted with white specks, and the lopsided slice of the moon, a circle with a section taken out. Moonlight gilded the grasses growing over the hilltops that surrounded her, and tinted the rocks of their path.

In both directions, going forward and going back. Like herself. Walking forward while her heart and her faith pulled her back.

The wind's interruption had given her thoughts a chance to sort themselves out.

It was not all grief for Chileab, she decided. Grief was there, would be for a long time, even if she arrived back at her parents' house. The loss might be all the more severe there, where his absence had been most keenly felt.

Eliab shifted on the ground, his breath breaking for a moment before it settled again into rhythm.

Eliab. This man who had stolen her and claimed her for himself. Who had upended her life.

The wood in her hands gave her a welcome distraction from her thoughts. She needed to practice. She would not have someone to defend her when she was alone.

When she scanned the area, nothing moved, not even rabbits. Other valleys might not be the same, might be populated with large beasts looking for food. She needed to be aware of that. Aksah hefted the staff. Could she swing it hard enough to ward off an animal intent on attack? If she could manage this pole, she could handle anything smaller with more skill.

Eliab was still asleep, she saw when she glanced over across the span from her place on the hilltop to where he slept, by the fire and the sheep. Was a staff harder to manage than a scythe? She had seen her father and brothers swing that in the field. Closing her eyes, Aksah tried to remember how they had stood, how they had swung. Legs wide enough to brace themselves, hands apart on the handle. A different handle, she remembered now, with one upright grip.

The stance was hard to duplicate with just a long staff, but Aksah knew she had to get it perfected before she was ready to escape. The men had been down to their loincloths as they stood legs apart. She took off the cloak. Her robe impeded her posture, but she did what she could, standing braced, hands apart wide on the rod. One more glance to make sure both man and sheep were far enough away not to be annoyed.

The first swing was awkward, nearly knocking her off balance. She staggered for footing and tried again, and again.

A hand grabbed the staff as she prepared for another attempt.

"What are you doing?" Eliab's hair was mussed from sleep, standing up on one side, packed down on the other. His eyes were bleary, she could tell that even in the dark.

"Practicing," she said, glad she could be honest.

"If you see anything coming, scream for me, I told you that. I sleep light." He pulled the solid stick in her hand, but she did not let go.

"Give that back to me!" Aksah clung to her end. "I need the practice. What if it comes too quickly? What if you are on the far side of the sheep? Do you not want me to be able to do what I can?"

"Defense is my responsibility."

"Then why even give me a staff? Am I just to lean on it?"

"I told you to call me, that I would come." He did not let go, but neither did she. They glared at each other. Finally, he released it. "Fine! Take the thing. Try not to hurt any of the sheep."

"I was nowhere near the sheep!" She almost lost her grip on it. The end thumped against the ground. "If you give me only a stick for defense, you had best let me learn to use it." She leaned down and picked up the cloak. "You need this more than I do. The night is warm enough when I stand." *And practice*, but she did not add that.

He held her gaze in the moonlight for a moment, then took his cloak, stomped back to the sheep and wrapped himself in it before settling down again.

Eliab listened to the staff go through the air. She did not have enough strength to fight off any animal. A rabbit, maybe, or a badger. But a lion? A bear? Even a wild goat? No.

If she wanted to think she was strong enough to defend them, let her think it. And if she also wanted to think she had him fooled as to her true intentions, let her think that also.

She still wanted to run away, and he knew it.

The cities were burned. Scouts had found charred remnants of houses on the trip so far, but that did not mean the armies had destroyed everything. He could only hope there was something left for him to bring her to. If she had a place to live, perhaps she would be less inclined to make her way back to her family and her tribe. A house still standing would be a great help.

She was indeed a woman of rare spirit. What had he done to her, stealing her from Shiloh? He did not want to break her, nor did he want to admit she was making him think about the war in a different way. Since capturing Aksah he now thought of the woman who had died so brutally as a real woman, not as the annoying beginning of the end of his tribe. Had that poor concubine possessed his wife's spirit? According to the story circulated after the murder, she had run away from her husband, apparently alone. And stayed with her father for four months. That, too, spoke of a woman with courage and determination.

Or fear? Perhaps she was afraid of what her husband would do when he caught up with her. Eliab squirmed. He did not like the thought that yet another woman feared her man. How many women lived lives in fear? What were Aksah's words again? *I want all the six hundred women you of Benjamin have taken to be safe. Not just this week, or this month, but for the rest of their lives.*

Aksah hardly seemed afraid of him, but then perhaps he was seeing false courage, like a little spitting cat trying to hide fear behind her arched back.

The staff swung again, and he heard Aksah lose her balance. He smiled into the darkness. *Think of our sons*, he told himself, *think of the spirit they would show.*

He closed his eyes and made himself relax. Perhaps he would get a little more sleep before it was time to get up and take the staff away from her.

CHAPTER 9

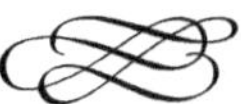

*"and you see among the captives a beautiful woman and you are attracted
to her and you want to take her as your wife, you may bring her into
your house . . . She will weep for her father and her mother a whole
month, and afterward you may have relations with her; you will become
her husband and she will become your wife."*
Deuteronomy 21:11-13

Trees began to fill the landscape now that Michmash was behind them. Clusters of the greyish wild olive and spreading sycamores grew among the valleys and up hillsides. They must be heavy with the coming crop although any there blended in with the leaves, but it would not be ripe. With no one here to prick the sycamore fruit to speed the ripening, those trees might not give a crop worth eating.

Figs, on the other hand, grew close to the path, the fruit brushing their heads on the lower branches. The early crop was nearly ripe, tempting them to pluck a few, but they both knew better.

"Two weeks will make all the difference," Eliab said with regret as he turned away from yet another dangling fruit.

Tall palm trees surprised her, yet another fruit to wait for. And always, growing in large swaths in every open space, the ripe brownish wheat and the lighter-colored barley with its heavy drooping head.

He had stopped several times to catch more birds. Between the need to hunt and the growing flock of sheep that slowed their pace to a crawl, plus their own needs and the privacy required, their journey seemed as if it would never end.

A shape off in the distance caught her attention, and Aksah turned her head to get a better look.

A house, coming in and out between the rolling land and the trees. Several small hills over, it appeared to be in perfect condition. Not everything had been burned, then.

There would be places for security and shelter. All she had to do was find them. She would pray, Aksah decided, and hope that God would bring her home safely.

A fig dangled close to her head, and she dodged it. As she did so, her gaze landed on the field of wheat running along the right side of the path, waiting for harvest. Figs and wheat and barley and dates. Eliab could not possibly manage that work alone.

Guilt stabbed at her. She had not wanted him to suffer, but what else would happen if he was left to all this work?

Bleating and commotion came over the hill's edge. Eliab crested the rise, using his staff as a barrier to keep the sheep moving. They needed a pen, she thought, and soon.

Eliab gave her a twisted smile. "So you saw my home."

That house was his? They were there? Her first thought was, *at last.* Her second was, *what if his was indeed the only shelter?* Then, on a rush of panic that made her heart skip, came the realization that now the countdown began. Thirty days to find a way to flee, or be lost to Judah forever. "I saw a house, yes. It is yours?"

"Yes. Mine." He rested the staff on one end, and stared ahead. She thought his shoulders slumped. He seemed so unbreakable that it was always a surprise when he showed signs of weakness. He must be tired, just as she. "Your husband is now a wealthy man in animals, even land. I will have to claim whatever is around, fields and orchards and olive trees, just as you said before. There are no neighbors. I had them, whole families of friends, boys my age that grew into men with more families, girls that were friends to my sisters that did the same, before . . ."

He sighed and shook his curly head. "Well, that only brings up what we will not discuss." An odd sound, a laugh perhaps, whuffed out of his mouth. "I had told you to put it aside, yet now I find myself thinking back. The memories are . . ." He trailed off. Another great breath, and Eliab pulled himself back up to his great height. "Someone has to bring in the food, someone should eat it, or sell it. We are the only ones around, so the duty falls to us. We will have a busy life."

Eliab swung the staff over his shoulder and began walking toward her, easing around the sheep that milled across the hilltop. Aksah stepped behind the ewe. "I am a captive," she said. "I claim my month."

"What are you talking about?" He did not stop but his steps slowed, as if his confidence had taken a blow.

"I claim the month wait for captive brides. It was given by Moses, and I demand it." She had to shift position again to keep the ewe between them.

"That was for Canaanites. You cannot apply it to yourself." He did not turn around, just stayed in place with his back to her, as if waiting on what she would say.

"It was for captives. You might not consider me one, but I do."

Eliab felt himself turning as if going through honey, so slow, until he faced this woman he had chosen. She was claiming the month for claimed Canaanite brides? *If you go to war against your enemies and you see among the captives . . .* His hands clenched on the staff. It did not say Canaanites, much as he wished it did. It was meant for them, of course it was, but he could hardly limit the meaning just to outlying nations.

His bride's eyes were alarmed as she stood behind the ewe. She was weighing him, daring him to argue on this.

One month. He watched those wary eyes turn toward brown while his mind raced ahead, looking for ways out. Did he count from now, today? Or push the days back to the date of the actual capture, the time of the festival? He thought of the delay, more time in the confines of a house after time already spent on the trail.

Adding on thirty days? No. But a portion of a month? As he looked at her rigid body, he saw fear beneath her courageous front. Eliab did not like to admit it, but she was just part of the rest of the nation who felt the same way. Had he not already known that, Aksah's fierce words brought it home clearly.

He wished he could bring his own curses down on the men of Gibeah who had brought this whole tragedy down upon their heads. "Very well, we will compromise. We have been together for five days now. That leaves you another twenty-five days."

He could almost see the anger pulse through her body. Her fine brows came down in a scowl, her cheeks were flushed. "We cannot count from then. We count from now, today! The Law says you are to bring her into your house and *then* the count begins. Wandering through the wilderness dragged behind you on a rope hardly counts as being *taken* to your house." She kept the ewe between them, but the animal was getting restless.

Poor creatures. Always getting caught in their raised voices.

He ran the rest of that law through his memory. *You want to take her as your wife. You may bring her into your house.* Of course she would be right. She had spent time thinking on this. He held her gaze and hoped she did not see him weaken. There had to be another way out.

Aha! He bit his lip to keep from smiling. She had forgotten one part. "Are you willing to have your head shaved?"

That surprised her. Her whole body snapped back as if he had struck her. Those changeable eyes went near brown with disbelief. "Of course not!" She reached up and held those rich waves in clenched hands.

"That is the next part of that law, you must remember." He added with relish, "Since you know the law so well."

Aksah bit her lip. Her hands came down from their protective hold slowly, ever so slowly. Eliab watched her think. He did not intend to enforce that part of the Law, but neither did he want to give her the full thirty days.

Resignation settled on her face, in her eyes. "I would not like it, but if I am to be obedient, I . . . suppose . . . I must." Her voice lacked the conviction of but moments ago.

He looked at her long tresses of curly hair. Did she seriously think he was going to permit her to shave it off? "I release you of that command." He watched her confusion, knew what she was thinking. If he gave her this release, would she have to release him as well? "We are not the kind of enemies the law was written for. I think I can overlook that part, and then you—"

The relief that washed through her when he released her for the need to shave her head evaporated faster than dew in the sun. "How can you say we are not enemies? Of course we are, so I will follow the law in its entirety. When we get in tonight . . . I will shave my head myself."

Her throat was tight on those last words. How could she have forgotten that part? He must have thought it a joke to throw it in her face.

He shook his head and pushed his way through the sheep. On the other side of the obedient ewe, still standing as her barricade, he stopped. Pushing his hair out of his eyes as he looked down, he said, "Aksah, there is no need for all this. I will not require you to shave your head if you agree to reduce the thirty days by five. You see how reasonable I can be?"

She looked at his eyes. The truth, she had often been told, was in them. The mouth could smile a lying smile while the eyes spoke honestly.

His eyes, deep and dark and knowing, held a challenge. A faint smile quirked his lips. Twenty-five days. Aksah had to look away. She had no intention of being there for twenty-five days. She hoped to be gone in less than a week, now that she knew they stood on the edge of his family land and the wandering was over.

Which direction led to Judah?

She looked back at him, trying to meet his gaze equally. "I agree. I will give you twenty-five days."

He shoved the ewe away and stopped so close she could feel the heat from his body. "You do not lie well." He lifted her chin with his finger, and his gaze seemed to bore into her like a hot knife. "I have more at stake than you, and I do not plan to let you steal it from me."

Aksah's stomach knotted. She had been taught to be honest and the falseness was distasteful.

Eliab caught her hand. He smiled down at her as he gave it a light squeeze, but then did not let it go. "Come, stay close. We may be able to sleep under a roof tonight."

Unlike when she carried it, the staff did not bounce on his shoulder as they walked down the low slope and then up the next one. With each step they drew closer to the house he said was his.

Then they were there. Aksah felt a strange curiosity as she looked at the house where he was raised. Despite being only one story, the house looked surprisingly large. Two windows spread wide apart and covered with lattices fit on the house front, with what must be the main door of the home separating them. How many rooms did the house have, that there would be so much space on a single wall?

Mud bricks made the walls, and bits of limestone whitewash still covered the red. They would need to recoat those walls before the wet season came, or the bricks would begin to wear.

Something aggravated the animals, perhaps the lingering scent of another flock, or perhaps some of them had come from this land. Whatever it was, the sheep began to shove and bleat, pulling Eliab from one side to another as those on the leads tried to break loose.

Aksah took advantage of Eliab's momentary distraction with the flock and walked across the span of drying plants and grasses to the door. Dangling through a small hole, the leather strap that lifted a hidden locking bar up over interior braces—a familiar sight, her home had a lock just like this. No one was within to answer a knock or the leather would not be still hanging in welcome through that hole.

That drooping strip spoke, as clearly as words, of the emptiness inside.

The door nearly fell upon her when she tugged the leather. Eliab must have caught up with her, because his big hand caught the heavy wooden door before it hit her.

"Take care," he said as he propped it open and stepped around her, leading the way inside. "We do not know what waits us. Beware of snakes as you step."

While the warning was thoughtful, after the broken state of the door Aksah would have entered with caution anyway. Like Eliab, she was not sure what awaited them, but her first impression was a good one. Light streamed in, making the rooms bright as day.

What a lovely house, she thought before the reason for the dazzling glow became clear.

The back wall was gone! The house was completely open to the outside. Eliab—or Eliab and herself together—would have to rebuild that side of the house. How long would that take?

Until this moment, Aksah did not realize just how much she wanted to sleep under a roof. Even if only for a few days, she craved the protection and security.

But for now, she needed to see what the house held. The first room to greet her was the main living area. Right now it looked as though all the furniture in the house had been thrown into it. Even so she could see it was broad enough for a family to be together, each member taking care of their own household chores while sharing time and conversation. A man could weave leather into ropes while his wife ground grain into flour and the daughters worked on the loom. The sons could carve wooden utensils or polish the harness bits for the oxen and donkeys.

On her right, coming off this family area, two doors obviously led into individual rooms. To match the space across the front of the house, those rooms must be deep enough for several people to share. The girls could have one room while their brothers took the other.

The doors were shut, blocking any view of what was inside. Aksah did not feel it was her place to snoop, not without permission.

She turned to her left. A third of the length of the house looked straight into a broad food and dining area. The remaining two-thirds was another room, with another closed door. She focused on the open food area. This was a place she felt she could enter freely, as no wall separated it from the open area. Cabinets lined the front wall, with open shelves above. Straight ahead, a tall, narrow table lined the wall, no doubt where bread was kneaded and food was cut and prepared.

Right now, though, that fallen wall, opening the house to the outside, drew her. She stepped across the room, walking around furniture, based on legs and what might be benches or tables, tipped over and piled upon each other, then stopped near the edge of the hole and looked at the brick that had once been the back of the house.

Relief rushed over her. Her knowledge of house-building was not vast, but she knew enough to see that the wall had not been destroyed, the bricks had not shattered. Instead, this part of the house had just fallen down in one piece, or most of a piece, although no doubt with help.

Raising it up might be difficult. No doubt the bricks would separate, although it appeared from her initial examination there were no cracks. They would need to make mortar to seal it into place, but once they got it upright and anchored, it would be as good as new.

Or so she hoped. She would not leave with the house open to the outside, a perfect trap for any predator on the hunt.

Twenty-five days before their bargain ended, before he could claim his rights, and every minute of the time counted. She would have to work hard this next week. Seven days to help, seven days to get the farm in a shape that would not torment her conscience. That would leave eighteen days to make good her escape, to cross the land toward Judah.

"I am sorry the house is in such bad condition." Eliab's hand came down on her shoulder, making her jump even though she had heard his voice first. "I do not know if any other houses in Benjamin were left intact. All the cities were burned, that much is certain. I cannot guess what the rest of the men have found. Do any of them have houses, even with one wall missing? Let us go outside."

Eliab took her hand again and led her back toward the door they had entered. "I dropped the staff and ran for you when the door started to fall." Eliab paused and looked around the room, still holding her hand. "There is still furniture left. We will need to see if anything is broken. If we have to sleep on the floor for a few days until we find what all can be salvaged, well, I —*we* have slept in worse places."

They were both quiet for a moment. Yes, they had indeed slept in worse places. Then he looked down at her and smiled. "The floors feel solid, it is not likely anything would come up from beneath, but anything could have slipped inside through that open wall, from snakes to much bigger beasts." He gave her hand a playful shake. "Although if anything large was here, they would have shown themselves by now. They might have left signs behind."

Aksah rubbed her sandal across the stone floor. Sand and dust scraped underfoot, blown in by wind or carried in by soldiers. Or, as Eliab suggested, tracked in by creatures looking for shelter against the winter rains. "I smell nothing yet," she said with a cautious sniff, knowing what signs he referred to.

"It might have dried by now. With the wall open, it would be hard to pick up traces."

"I see no scratches," Aksah said. The whitewash inside was in quite good shape, unlike what had been exposed to the weather. She looked around the main room of the house. It was long and narrow. Doors opened off it, one on either side. No doubt sleeping quarters. "If something like a lion or bear had come in, surely they would have rubbed or scratched?" Why wander back outside in the cold and wet when there were all manner of places here to hide their dung? Yet the air was fresh. Perhaps the threat of man remained strong enough to keep any beasts away.

Eliab scanned the part of the building they could see. "Perhaps." He seemed to stand taller. "Perhaps it has not been long enough, perhaps the scent of man still frightened them away, and nothing did come inside."

Aksah blinked, startled that his mind was so in line with her own thoughts. His hand still held hers.

Eliab started walking again, drawing her past the propped door and out into the full sun. He turned around. "It would be ideal if nothing lingers in the house. Before we settle for the night, I will make certain nothing is inside. We need sleep, and food."

· · ·

The sheep still waited, nibbling on the grasses and plants around the house. Aksah suspected they were glad to have a respite from the endless walking. Eliab released her hand once they were through the door, and picked up the staff from where it had fallen, using it to guide the animals into a line. With gentle nudges and the restraint of that long staff to keep them close, they began to head around the house.

The fence of the sheepfold, they found when they walked the flock down this unexplored side of the house toward the back, was still intact. Why the fence had not been broken she did not know, but it still stood. The second, larger pen on the far side, reinforced with stone, still stood as well.

"The well is still there," Eliab said, passing the stone circle that proclaimed its presence as he ushered the sheep along. "I must check the water. And find a bucket."

Aksah looked again at the wooden bracket, and sure enough, though some rope remained wrapped around the crosspiece, the bucket was not there. She did not have time to fret, though, as the flock continued on their way, and carried her with them.

The sheep seemed happy to walk through the fence gate, as if they sensed that once inside they were safe. Aksah smiled as she saw them find a place on the ground and prepare themselves for a rest. They knew, they must know, that they were not going to walk any farther.

"We need to get the water troughs filled." Eliab looked over the pen at the stone water trough that sat undamaged, and smiled. No, glowed.

Yes, from the first time since they . . . met, a kind of contentment radiated from him. Not what it would have been before the war, she was certain, but she thought she saw a bit of his future in the way he stood, the line of his shoulders, the softening around his mouth. He seemed to be assessing his empire, counting all the sheep and planning for whatever cattle he caught, weighing the repairs to the house. "If the buckets have been left, they should still be by the well." Instead of catching her hand as he had suddenly developed the habit of doing, he held his own out to her and waited. His eyebrows went up in a question.

Aksah looked at his outstretched hand, and at his eyes, measuring, hopeful. It would be foolish to refuse. She reached out and took it. He tightened his grip, holding her firmly. A sigh went through his body, soundless, a soft-ening of shoulders, a relaxation of the muscles.

Her conscience stabbed her. It was wrong to raise his hopes. It was also wrong to twist her hand away now, so she left it where it was.

"Stay close to me," he said. "I know the wall is down, but I need to examine the full extent of the damage." Eliab started off to the right, behind the house. Like herself, he did not look left, toward the sheepfold, but right, toward the rear of the house. And like herself, he stopped when he saw the rest of the destruction. Unlike herself, however, he had weapons to draw. He dropped her hand and pulled out his bow in one movement, then had it re-strung, nocked and drawn before she could blink.

The entirety of the house was open, not just that main room. The whole back wall lay on the ground, exposing the rooms behind two of the doors she had seen from inside, closed tight. Now she saw what those closed doors had hidden. Nothing ominous, just rooms. Neither of the ones on the left or right of the main one was large. Had there been an animal inside either of these two, there would have been little space to swing a sword or staff.

Nothing moved within. Eliab stood alert as he scanned the nearest room, the arrow point moving only enough to cover between the walls. Without turning his head, he said in a low voice, "Stay here. I need to check the rest."

This was not a man to disobey, not when he spoke with such authority and stood with weapons drawn. He moved forward. In the stillness of the hot day, Aksah heard what had made him so wary. Within the house some-thing scrabbled. A thump, more scrabbling sounds, and out of the far room, the room Eliab was approaching with silent steps, burst a flash of brown.

Eliab's bow swung upward, the arrow still nocked. He shook his head in disgust. "Hare!"

He had not shot the animal. It was unclean by the Law, it could not be eaten by faithful Israelites, but he had not aimed at it even for sport. Aksah stared at him, and had to force herself to look away before he saw what must be in her eyes.

It would have been easy to let the arrow fly. Yet he had not, but had let little creature escape. They would have to do a thorough cleaning of that room but the hare was free and unharmed.

It said much about him. Soldier he might be, but not for love of killing. Now that the house had been checked, he released the bowstring, and began putting his weapons back in place, the arrow back in the quiver, the bow sliding into a broad loop in the weapons belt.

Her gaze sharpened as she realized she was looking right into their room, or what she assumed would be their room once the wall was back upright. She made out the shape of some windows in the tumbled bricks, the latticed covers hidden beneath the grass and flowers that had sprouted during the wet season.

"See if you can find a pail," Eliab ordered as he wandered off back toward the well, retracing his steps to the side they had already walked the sheep along as they went toward the sheepfold.

She wanted nothing better than the freedom to look around. Aksah kept her eyes on the ground, moving aside the drooping grasses and anything else that could hide a pail. And there it was.

The rope that should have fastened the bucket to the well was still tied to the handle. How the pail got so far from the well she did not know, but the vessel had no cracks, and did not look damaged. "I found it," she called into the air.

"Bring it to me." Eliab's voice came from that other side of the house.

She found herself swinging the bucket as she walked back. "It does not appear cracked or worn," she called. It seemed important that he know.

He did not wait for her to appear, but called his answer. "Excellent. We have always had more than one."

Aksah rounded the corner of the house, and blinked at the pail hanging from the crosspiece. She did not have a chance to ask where it came from before he spoke.

"I have good news also," Eliab smiled at her. "The well appears to be in good shape."

Aksah handed the bucket over. "It will certainly need washing. We will know if it is still usable then." While Eliab swished it in the water, she pointed at the hanging bucket.

"Mine was inside the well. It is a good thing the rainy season did not end very long ago, it was floating high enough to grab the handle with an axe."

He unhooked the first bucket, dripping with water. "Help me fill up the trough." He reached out for hers.

"The sheep come first," he said as they walked to the trough just on the other side of the fence. The whole flock smelled the water, and abandoned their settled rest to crowd around. The first bucket in the trough was drunk before Eliab even finished pouring.

The second pail went into the trough. "In the wet season there is a small stream on the far side of the pen," he said as he turned around, "but it is dry already now the rains are done." They began walking together back to the well.

He paused to look at the fallen wall when they passed it. "I want to get the house sealed up tonight, if possible." He turned to her. "What do you know of housebuilding?"

"Nothing." A burst of enthusiasm kept her mouth going. "My father is very good . . ." Her voice trailed off as she realized what she was saying.

"As was my father." Eliab leaned close. "That leaves me with only what you can do to help." He turned away and heaved a sigh, his great chest expanding and then contracting on a gust of air. "I could use them here now." He ran his hands over his head, as if soothing an ache there.

Trip after trip went from the well to the trough, to the well again until the limestone trench was full. The sheep decided they were content, and once again rested on the ground. "We have to make sure they do not get thirsty during the night," Eliab told her during one trip, as if she did not understand.

But he could not know how very familiar she was on a farm, she realized, since she was a stranger still to him.

"There should be ground wheat in the house. Once we get them watered, if you make some bread dough, I will uncover the oven."

Uncover the oven. The family must have known the armies were coming, and taken what measures they could to protect their farm, including hiding the clay oven. They would not have left something so vital in the house. Not when the armies were expected to burn the houses as they had the cities. How fortunate they were that the soldiers had been content to pull the wall down and assume the rest of the house would fall with it.

Only this house had not come down.

Finally Eliab removed the pail from her grip. "Go inside, see what you can find for food. Dried fig cakes would be fine, just something to pad our stomachs."

Aksah looked to her right at the flattened wall and the open room beyond. Food. He was no doubt correct that there might be food in the house. Any wheat would have been harvested a full year ago, since this year's crops were still in the fields around their path. Properly sealed, it could last a long time, and they would be glad to have it. Fig cakes would be kept in clay crocks, and perhaps there would be dried fruit left over from last autumn. The war had begun after the late harvest of the fruits and grapes and olives, and they might remain as well.

Once she made her way around the house and back in through the propped door, Aksah turned toward the room where the family would have eaten. A line of crocks was still on the open cabinet, where the wide top made a fine surface for preparation. While three containers were open and empty, four sat still sealed. Aksah carefully wedged out the wooden seals, each pressed in so tight it took slow but determined wiggling to ease free.

Raisins in one, and wheat grains in the next, then a whole crock of dates, even dried meat. What a treasure! Her stomach, which had been politely quiet, now rumbled at the smell of food.

Preparing the wheat came first. Eliab was right, they needed bread. If they were very fortunate, there might be a hand mill still in the house. Aksah looked at the pile of chairs and other objects and sure enough, down on the floor she saw the unmistakable hollowed shape of the mill. Dragging it out of the jumble upside down, she heard the grindstone rolling beneath it.

Their bread would be a small loaf, with the grinding having to be done first and then time to bake. She rubbed the mill, then gave a sigh. It really needed a wash. She could hardly grind grain in it while dirty.

That done, she uncovered an unbroken bowl. Aksah rubbed the bowl clean, and scooped some wheat. The loaf would have to be made without leaven, she found no yeast, but they were Israelites, they were used to unleavened bread. A drinking cup sat at the back of one of the open shelves. She stood on tiptoe and grabbed for it.

Eliab came through the fallen wall, a dripping bucket in his hand. "I thought you could use some." He set it on the floor at her feet, reached up and pulled out the cup that had been just too far back to catch.

"Thank you." Aksah took it from him and waved toward the crocks. "There is plenty of food, even dried meat. We will not be hungry."

"Not for a while, at least," he said, and turned and left her. His hair was wet, she noticed as he went across the room. He must have taken time to rinse off. How she wanted a bath herself! She would make time after the cooking was done. She would need it more then.

Scooping out a cup of water, Aksah rinsed all three utensils out, the mill, the bowl and the cup, rubbing them until her fingers squeaked as they slid along, then tossed the dirty water through the broken doorway. Her feet scraped on the sand that left a film on the floor. She could not prepare food in a house that was not clean!

She examined the serving room with more care. Tucked along one wall, so wedged into the corner that it had been invisible, was a broom of straw. Draped over the point of the wooden handle was exactly what she needed most, a small square cloth of linen that looked as if it could be used to clean surfaces.

Such as the tall, narrow table that had seemed so much a part of the wall that she had overlooked it at first. The perfect place to chop vegetables, or set a bowl to mix dough.

A broom, a table, and a cloth.

Aksah set to work, and soon that room, and most of the main living area, were as clean as she could make them with one wall open to the air.

Now for the grinding. Eliab had said nothing about finding the oven. If she had to, she would put the dough in a covered pan and cook it slowly.

One comforting thing about grinding grain, Aksah thought as the pile of flour spilling over the edge of the mill accumulated on her scarf, was how well it released frustrations. With a chuckle, she went back to her chore, back and forth, back and forth, adding more wheat berries as she went along.

Some time later, she had the simple dough ready. Where was Eliab? She looked across the field visible from where she stood. Had he found the ovens? Walking over to the open wall, she tried a shout. "Eliab?" No reply.

Even though he was nowhere to be seen, she smiled at yet another thought. One whole open side of the house certainly helped to see what was happening outside. If he showed up anywhere, she would see him coming.

"I found the oven."

Whirling around, hand over her heart with the surprise, she saw him standing in the opening of the door. Air whooshed from her lungs. That was the one place she had not thought to look. Using the door when one had an entire wall to enter?

"The fire for baking is started. It should be hot soon."

Aksah met him in the middle of the room, still jittery from the start he had given her. "That is what I needed to know." They were both so stilted and polite. "I already mixed the dough. It will be unleavened, there has not been time to make a sourdough mixture."

"If it is fresh rather than stale, I will be delighted." He stepped aside as she walked past him, toward where the bowl with the moist dough sat.

He slipped back outside. Aksah collected the bowl, followed Eliab, and found the oven already heating, smoke rising from its top. How his family had managed to hide it, she did not know, but she was certain she had not seen it when they first walked up. Their forethought would keep Eliab and herself fed for a few weeks, long enough for her to store up food.

For herself and for him.

The meal was awkward. Somehow it had been easier to eat when they were clear enemies. Now they had a truce of sorts. Here, in his dwelling, he wanted the barriers between them gone.

"I had almost forgotten the taste of fresh bread," he said with a sigh as he broke off another piece. "You did not overstate your skill."

She felt heat creep up her cheeks. "That is kind of you to say, but unleavened bread is not difficult."

Eliab swallowed his mouthful. "You forget, I have not had fresh bread of any kind in months. Not even manna could have tasted as well to me." He broke off another piece and put it in his mouth, nearly groaning in delight.

Warmth crept, not up her cheeks this time, but around her chest. She did not know what to say, so took another handful of raisins, something to chew instead of having to speak.

"We will not be able to seal up the back of the house tonight," he said once he was done eating. Dried meat and raisins and unleavened, crispy bread, with fig cakes waiting for the morning.

Aksah looked up at him from her own meal. "No?" While she was not looking forward to raising the wall after all the work she had already done, she had hoped to sleep safely for the first time in days.

Eliab pushed his plate away. "I found several cracks in the wall. They did not show at first glance, but it will help us because once we try to lift it, the bricks will separate into sections. I think the two of us can put the wall up that way. For tonight, if we can just lodge it against the house, we will be safe enough. I will stay awake and bake limestone."

"Can we not do this tomorrow?"

"Someone has to keep the limestone burning all night, the fire cannot be allowed to go out. We need to use the ash. I need you to chip away the old mortar at the breaks. We will add that to the limestone. If all goes well, tomorrow we will mix the ash and the limestone, and begin sealing the wall where it separated. The ash will make it set more quickly, so we have to be prepared to work fast and steady. We do not want the mortar to harden before the next piece is in place."

He set his empty plate aside. "Let us get to work while there is light. Whatever we can do tonight is that much less for tomorrow." He reached over for her plate and set it on top of his. "Let us get the mortar off the lower pieces first, before we stand them upright."

With his usual calm stride, Eliab walked over to the pegs on the wall by the outer door. While she had been baking the bread in the oven, he must have decided wearing all those weapons was unnecessary, because when she came back with the warm bread, his leather belt had been hung on the peg.

Now he pulled the axe out of his loop and brought it back. "Use the back of this, not the blade, and begin chipping. My father had several larger, heavy stones he used for chipping limestone, and I found them while looking for the oven. I will use the stones. If we can get the mortar off the bottom and the top of the lower sections, we can stand them upright for tonight. We should take turns again keeping watch, and stoking the fire. I have a collection of limestone, my father kept it on hand for repairs. Once we break off the old mortar from the sections, we can add it to the kiln and get it melting as well."

"Kiln?" This was the first he had mentioned that.

One of his dark brows went up. "Did I forget to tell you I found my father's kiln as well?"

A puff of laughter startled Aksah. "Yes, you forgot that. I only knew of the oven."

Eliab smiled. "This farm was always well-supplied. We managed to handle most of the repairs without going to the city."

She pointed at the pile of furniture. "I have not had a chance to look through that. I do not even know if any of it will be usable. What if it is all broken?"

He leaned over her where she sat on the floor. "I will fix what I can. What cannot be fixed, you will help me determine what it can become. If it is only good now for firewood, we will burn it. But if it is a simple broken leg on any of the tables or chairs, we can cut the other legs down to match, and it can be a bed or a chair for an infant or child."

Eliab caught her hand, and gave Aksah a gentle pull. "Up now, and we must get to work. We will look at the furniture tomorrow, when we have a wall."

She let herself be tugged up to her feet.

Those who work in combed flax and those making white fabric on the loom
Isaiah 19:9

They had started early, shortly after sunrise, but now, after the whole day's hard work, the wall was up. Their hands were raw and skinned from chipping the old mortar from each wall break last night until neither could see in the dimness, then from lifting each section today before the skin could heal. More cuts came from pushing the wall's cracks tight to seal them, letting the heavy sections slide along the mortar until the fractures were gone. Both of their backs hurt, even their legs were shaking.

The gaping hole was closed, the lattices over the windows back in place. The house was secure. Secure except for the door that still needed the pivots and leather replaced. "Tomorrow," Eliab promised as they sat on the floor and sagged against the wall. The house was much darker, and Aksah found she missed the brightness.

Ah well. All she had to do was walk outside to find sun. Or open the shutters. She looked at the door, propped in place, and the shutters, shut now while the mortar around them cured, and leaned back against the stone wall.

The pile of furniture still sat in a jumble. They both stared at it, but neither felt like getting back up for another chore.

"Give me your hands." Eliab reached for her closest hand from where he sat at her side. "I have some skill in healing." He met her gaze. His eyes were serious. "I do not want you to be hurt."

I do not want you hurt. What a kind thing to say. It had not been possible to get through the day's work unscathed, but how nice that he had tried to keep her from injury. She had seen it throughout the day, he always took the heaviest work, the sharpest edges. It had seemed practical. Very well, it *was* practical.

Still, those words ran through her head again. *I do not want you hurt.*

Aksah held out her hands, palm up, for his inspection.

Eliab took one and turned it over, sighing as he saw the sores the day had left. "You have some bits of rock imbedded in your palms. They must come out." He lifted her battered hand and placed a kiss on the sore palm. His beard tickled her hand, and heat ran up her arm, fanned by the whisper of his breath. She wished she could see his eyes, but she could only see the curls of his dark hair, and he was busy looking at the damage. "I am sorry this is what you came to. My wife was to have a solid house, her own furniture, plenty of new blankets, and a fresh mattress that she did not have to make on her own. I wish I did not need to work you this hard. We had to be safe tonight, and I did not see any other way."

The hurt in his voice sounded, felt *real*. That spot on her hand where his lips had been was still warm. "Nor did I."

Aksah watched as Eliab rose, muffling a groan, and walked over to the weapons belt, all the arms of war still hanging from their holders. She had seen him care for them, each washed and polished after every quail, every catch for every meal. He pulled out a knife and came back over, lowering himself with another muffled sound.

Eliab flipped the knife. With care, as if he feared his touch would hurt, he picked up her hand again, and held the knife over the scraped palm.

Aksah turned her head rather than watch. Watching only made it hurt worse, she knew from previous experience of injuries. She rushed into speech. "I was afraid of what might climb through that open wall."

The sharp point probed at one particularly painful split. She flinched. Eliab immediately stopped, or at least the pain ended. Instead, he took over the speaking, talking in a quiet voice. "This was a safe, secure place to live. We have—had—orchards. I do not know if they are still intact, but we saw plenty of others on the journey. I have not gone to look yet, but there should be wheat growing on the field behind the grove that borders the sheepfold. If it is there, we will have to find a way to harvest it. The winter's wheat might be shriveling on the stalks. It has to come in, whatever we can salvage."

His knife stuck one hard jab. Aksah jerked at the pain, looking down in spite of herself. Blood welled around the sharp point. A bit of rock slipped out of the hole it had made going in. And that was just the first one. She saw other breaks and tensed at the pain waiting inside.

His hands were in just as bad shape, but his were mostly burns from heating the limestone, and splits from where the brick had broken the seared skin open.

Sweat beaded on his forehead just as it had during the day's work, and dampened his hair, encouraging the curls. "I am sorry if that hurt you." The words came out as if through gritted teeth.

Aksah looked up at him. His jaw was clenched so tight she could see the muscles bulging along his neck. And he was only removing pebbles from her palms.

He took a deep breath and rubbed his dusty, battered hand over his forehead, catching drops of sweat before they could fall. "Give me your other hand."

The palm he had just finished bled in small spots. Either she had been harder on this second hand, or he was being less gentle. Sharp jabs sent quick flashes of fire through her palm and up her arm.

"This one is deep," Eliab said and his fingers tightened on hers, stilling any movement.

No matter how hard she tried to be strong, Aksah let out a cry when the rock finally came out. She felt it let go, felt it scrape the walls of its tunnel in her skin as it was dragged out.

"Stay here. I want to pour some water over your hands before you go to bed." He rubbed the knife on his robe, stood, and staggered before he caught himself. He swiped his forehead again. "That is over."

"What about your hands?" She rose at the same time, and found herself reaching for his hand, the one without the knife, before she realized what she was doing. "You are wounded more than I. You need care as well."

He did not move, just stayed there with his big hand in hers. He glanced down as she looked up. The air was very still, her heart thumped in her chest. He did not seem to be breathing.

"I have recovered from worse injuries than these small scratches." He pulled that hand away and stepped back. "I thank you for your concern. I must check on the sheep."

"Eliab." Aksah could not let him go out without at least checking his injuries. She caught at his robe, and he stopped. Her grip was not that strong, but he stayed in place, his back to her. "Let me check your hands. Come back and sit down. The sheep will not die of thirst in the next few moments. Let me look at them."

For some reason, a shudder went through him. She felt it run through her knuckles where they rested against his back.

"I tell you, I am fine." His voice was rough.

"And I tell *you* I do not believe you. At least let me see." Some strange urge made her say, "Unless you are afraid to show me?"

"No. I am not afraid." He turned around, the skin tight on his face. "Very well. Look if you must."

He walked back to the wall and sank down, rather like a sulky child, she thought, amused. How unlike him. He was the ultimate tough soldier, yet he did not want to receive the same care he had given her.

The burns she had glimpsed were starting to blister. Aksah did not think anything she did would make them heal faster, so she turned her attention to the splits and breaks. Aha! she thought. He had chips in his hands as well. He probably could not feel the grit under the skin because of the pain from the rest of the sores. "Your knife, please."

Curly hair tumbled around his ears as he whipped his head around. "Do you want to get even with me, or do you really need it?"

"Look at your hands! Of course I need it." She held out her own hand in anticipation, and met his dark gaze. Those frowning brows did not intimidate her, not after he had worked so hard on her own injuries.

With a sigh that sounded almost like a growl, Eliab handed over the knife, hilt first. "Here. Be careful. It is very sharp."

That deserved a laugh. "I have used a knife before," she said, and turned it around. Between the burns and the cuts, it was hard to find a place to insert the point, but she took her time.

"Just do it," he growled again, and Aksah laughed again.

"I promise you, I will get started in due time." She looked at the split that had caught her attention, and bent his hand to open it a bit more. Yes, there was indeed a bit of something in there. Angling the point, she began to probe. His hand never moved, never flinched. The knifepoint caught the white bit, scraped with a grating sound, and then she worked it out.

He still did not move. Aksah went on to the next puncture, and the next and the next. When she felt no more hard lumps as she ran her thumb over his palm, she put his hand down, and reached for his other one. A drop of sweat landed on his palm. Like he had moments before, Aksah swiped over her forehead, then dabbed her sleeve on his palm to dry that lone drop.

Somehow the second hand seemed to take longer than the first, just as hers had. At last she was done. "Now, I think we should do what you said, and wash our hands. I would hate either of us to have dirt work its way back in."

But her legs did not want to stand. Her knees felt weak, and her hands were shaking.

"I will bring in a bucket. I need to water the sheep. I might as well do both at one time." Eliab braced one newly scoured hand on the floor and pushed himself up, pulling his feet under and getting his balance before he rose.

Aksah watched him walk toward the door, surprised at the strange humming in her ears. Leaning against the wall, she closed her eyes and waited for the sound to subside.

. . .

Eliab eased the door into place after he stepped outside. Tomorrow he would have to find a way to fix it. For tonight, he would wedge it shut as best he could before they settled and hope that God would keep them safe, because both he and his wife needed to sleep.

As embarrassing as it was to admit, and he would not dare to say such a thing to Aksah, he was truly tired. Tiredness had become a way of life in the last several months, but he did not remember being so drained. Was it being back in the empty house, wanting to hear his father's voice, his mother's laughter, and knowing that would never be?

Or was it just today's work? If so, and he was this exhausted, how must Aksah feel?

First, the sheep. After he went inside, Eliab had no intention of coming out again until morning. When the trough was filled, he had to grab the fence pole for a moment before he could make that last trip to the well.

Next, he rinsed out the bucket. After both of their efforts on the other's behalf, it would hardly do to bring in a pail with dust or seeds floating on the surface.

At last, he was back inside. Eliab wedged the door into place. He turned around and nearly dropped the pail. Aksah was slumped on the floor, her head resting on her arm.

At the soft sound, a very sweet snore, Eliab managed to breathe again. She was only sleeping. He must be tired, to have his first thought be that she had died.

Asleep or not, her hands had to be washed. Her headscarf sat on the top of the cabinet, so he pulled it off and got a section wet. She might not sleep through this, but she might, so he knelt down on one knee and picked up a hand.

Aksah jerked upright so fast they nearly banged heads. "What?" Her eyes did not open, he was not certain she was awake.

"I am merely washing your hands. I did not mean to startle you. I thought you would want them cleaned."

"Oh." Her balance was precarious at best, and her eyes still had not opened. "Yes."

Eliab kept washing, finishing one hand and picking up the other. She tilted forward, and her head thumped against his shoulder. It was so tempting to set down the scarf and hold her, if only to keep her from falling over, but that might alarm her. Instead, he just relished the feel of her head against him. He did not know how long it would be before this happened again.

At last there was no more excuse to linger, and his legs threatened to cramp. Eliab forced himself to ease her away, and down onto the floor. She curled back into the position she had been when he first entered, head cushioned on her arms, legs tucked up under her robe.

If only she had fallen asleep on his cape! He did not think he had the strength to lift her and get her settled properly. Ah well, he told himself. She had slept on the hard ground before and survived.

He made short work of rinsing off his own hands, then shoved the pail aside. Tomorrow morning he would pour it out and rinse the pail clean again. Right now, they both needed sleep.

Stretching out on the floor next to Aksah, Eliab pulled his cape over the two of them, and closed his eyes.

Aksah yawned a loud yawn, smiling at the sound. She stretched, then groaned at the sudden pain from her abused muscles. Her eyes popped open.

Eliab's face was less than a handswidth away. Memories rushed in, the last few days coming back in a rush, that first blissful ignorance gone as the weight around her heart settled in again. "Oh!" She did not know what else to say. Jumping up did not feel possible yet.

He smiled, but did not move either, just looked at her as time seemed to stretch.

His hair was rumpled and came to a point, as if the curls on one side had slid to the center while he slept and become stuck. She wondered what her own hair looked like.

His skin had lost the pale, stretched look of the last two days. Traces of the dark circles that had been a part of his exhaustion still remained under his eyes, but Aksah knew they, too, would fade with more sleep.

Even his lips were flushed with health now.

The room was quiet. No sounds came in from outside, or at least, she did not hear them. Eliab's eyes seemed to darken. She saw his hand twitch as if to move, then still. In a gruff, morning voice, he said, "How are you?"

Heat rushed up her face from her neck, she could feel it prickle the skin. "Sore."

"I feel it, too." He sat up with a groan, but Aksah was sure that sound was more for show than for real. After rubbing his eyes, Eliab stretched wide, his arms so long the closest one covered the space between them and crossed her where she still lay at his side. She watched that arm as it stayed overhead while he enjoyed the stretch, but he never lowered it and it did not touch her. Crackling sounds came from his spine. "Ahhh. That feels good."

He smiled down at her. "Now I am ready to take on the day. I intend to find the field and see how my wheat is doing, or if it is even there, and check the orchards. Then the door needs to be fixed." The smoothness she was used to seeing was back as he rose to his feet and crossed to the cabinet where the crocks were. "Do we still have fig cakes?"

Without waiting for an answer, he started pulling out the wooden tops of the crocks and peering inside. "There they are!" He plucked out several, leaned back against the cabinet as he took a healthy bite, and swallowed with barely a chew. "I think I might have to slaughter one of the sheep. We need meat. Perhaps not today, but it needs doing soon."

Aksah's mouth woke up and started watering at the memory of mutton. "If we can find a drying rack, we can dry most of it. Do we have enough salt?"

He swallowed another bite. "If not, I can check the houses around and see what I can scavenge. We should smoke part of it, so I will look for good trees, too, those with fragrant wood." A pitcher sat near his hand, and Eliab picked it up, smiling as he heard the water inside swirl. He lifted it to his mouth and drank.

Aksah bit her tongue. How like her father. He never thought to ask for a cup first, but always drank straight from whatever held it, pitchers, pails, bowls, anything that held the liquid.

Eliab must have broken his fast well enough, because he turned to leave. At the doorway, he stopped and looked back. "We need to fix the inside of the house, now that the outside is back in place. While I am gone, look over the chairs and tables, and see if any of them need repairing, and if they can be."

Go through the furniture. She had something to do that would keep her mind busy. Keep her from thinking about the strange moment when they looked at each other and everything became confusing.

Several fig cakes were still left. Aksah took one of them, and picked up the pitcher. Eliab had left very little water. Pail and pitcher alike went out to the well. She tried not to watch for him moving through the distance, going to find the wheat, as he had said he would be.

Morning ablutions and a quick meal over, she turned to the jumble of wood. Woven rush seats became a chair, another odd piece on second look became a bed frame. Short round legs attached to a long top. Cracked pottery, some small pieces with handles that might have been cups. After a slow walk around the pile, she figured out which piece would come off first. The rush-seated chair, its legs somehow woven into the bed frame. A careful pull, with a twist, and the chair came free.

The pile groaned, then shifted, as if that chair was the knot that held it all together. With a scraping thud, the jumble of wood and other bits fell in on itself, thumps and scrapes and shudders. Nothing cracked, no wood gave the sound of breaking. Perhaps everything that would break already had. Taking it apart would be easy now. She grabbed another set of legs that appeared connected to each other, and lifted them free.

Another chair. They had two chairs now, made by a rough carpenter, capable but not skilled. After the chair came the short legs of what was not a small table after all, but a bench. More turned legs attached to a long top—a table for dining, big enough for a house of children, too big for her to lift. Just the right length for that bench to fit under, where many children could sit. Then another chair. The count was up to three. Three chairs and a bench. The house and furniture had survived, but the family was gone. All but Eliab.

She felt a pang of sympathy for the people who had lived here, had worked to make their own possessions. Losing Chileab had been horrific, the grief sometimes doubled her over, and she would have to stay bent, hands on her knees, until her heart could lift enough for her to stand.

That was one loss. How many did Eliab mourn? Not just brothers and sisters, but mother, father, cousins, friends? From outside, the sound of Eliab's whistling drifted inside.

It would hurt him to see these chairs, to eat at the table that lay upside down on the floor. Would he hear echoes of his brothers and sisters? The voices of his mother and father talking—or arguing, as the case might be? While her own parents seldom argued, she had heard others do so.

He had told her they were all gone, but seeing the house abandoned, only their belongings remaining, drove it home.

No wonder the men of Benjamin's tribe had been so desperate to find brides.

Aksah began turning things over. Chairs to match the ones she had already found, another bench, even batten sticks proclaiming that somewhere there had been a loom for weaving. A big family just like her own. She was so far from her brothers and sisters, but she would see them again.

Guilt prodded at her. Where would Eliab find another bride? Would he raid the annual festival again next year? Or had they only been allowed this one chance?

If she left, what then for him?

Was her own dream worth it? She flinched at the thought, a gasp breaking free and echoing in the empty house. Give up her lifelong dream, driven by her faith, of the chance to be in the line of the Shiloh—for him? Be tied to Benjamin, no longer be of Judah? All hope of being the mother of the Messiah would be wrenched away from her. She would be the mother of Benjaminites.

Could she do that?

A bleat from outside broke through Aksah's thoughts. How long had she stood here, staring at the thick wooden legs poking into the air? She glanced back at the benches. Without children, they could be used for guests to sit on, cushions layered that visitors could adjust for comfort against the brick wall at their back.

Cushions. She looked again at the remaining stack of wood but saw no pillows there, nothing soft. No bedding. If Eliab's family had wanted to hide those, where would they be?

As she looked around, Aksah took stock of what was still there. The crocks remained, filled with the rest of the food they had just eaten, as did the plates and cups. Breakable things would not interest soldiers who had to carry them. Who wanted to arrive home with broken pottery?

Despite all that remained, perhaps the house had been plundered after all and the furniture was left because it was too heavy to carry. Blankets and cushions would be taken. Everyone needed more blankets, everyone wanted more cushions. Soldiers would find them easy to haul away.

Annoyance at the thieving soldiers jabbed her, soldiers who had taken the supplies she now had to remake. She left the table where it lay. Eliab would help her. If he wanted to eat on it, he would have to.

Now for the frame of the bed, missing the rope that would be wrapped between the sides to hold a mattress.

A mattress Eliab would need her to make.

Aksah gave a tug, the frame slid free of the table. It teetered, suspended on its side. Without the rope that made it firm, the frame was loosely connected bars that vibrated and wobbled. She grabbed the long side bar, and tugged. Her eyes went wide as the long sides and end pieces swayed, shuddered, she squeezed her eyes shut and leapt backward, and then the momentum flipped it over, landing with a jarring thud. After the noise subsided, she opened her eyes. Flat on the floor like it should be, it was a big enough bed to hold two adult people, or several children.

Struggling with the heavy wood of the bed, Aksah worked it across the floor and into the room that would be theirs—or his. She had to tilt it back sideways to get through the doorway. It scraped a shrill bark on the stone. The long beam would be marked from now on, a scuff from where she had dragged it. Aksah stepped over the legs and scooted to the front. It had to be easier to pull rather than push. Aksah grabbed what would be the top—or bottom—and tugged.

The bed suddenly lifted completely off the floor. She stumbled, her hands tightening on the wood to keep her balance, and looked up, knowing who she would see.

Eliab hooked the bed's side rail over his broad shoulder, and his arm flexed and bulged as he held it in place with one hand. "You did well, wife, but this is too much. Allow me to help you." He walked it through the door, Aksah backing up with it. His eyes twinkled at her. "I have it. You can let go now."

"Oh!" She looked at her hands, still holding the bed's board. "Oh," she said again, released her grip and took a step back. "Yes."

The wooden frame moved past her, floating above the grey stone. He made it appear so easy, this man. He stopped at the very spot she wanted the bed to be and set it down. They both looked at it sitting there, on the floor, like a topless, bottomless box.

Aksah felt her lips twitch. She could not look over at Eliab. Had he thought bringing a bed into the room would make it seem more permanent, more intimate? Nobody would be sleeping inside that bare frame any time soon, not until they made a new mattress. The sun's angle threw shadows part way across the floor through the lattice of the window, but those lines were all that filled the open interior.

Eliab's unhappy sigh drew her attention. She turned, and laughter finally broke free. He was shaking his head, one corner of his mouth pulled his beard into a wry smile. He looked just like Rachel did when her favorite toy was taken away.

That did it. Laughter burst out, peal after peal. Aksah finally had to brace herself with her hands on her knees while whoops shook her body.

Deeper rumbles poured out from beside her. Eliab had one hand braced on the large bed leg next to him. His other wrapped around his middle, trying to hold in the barks of laughter that Aksah knew were making his sides ache.

"There is no way . . ." his voice melded into another whoop, "that we can sleep—" Aksah saw him stare down at the empty frame, and he was off again, roaring his mirth into the air.

After a few more peals and whoops, the laughter faded into groans. Aksah managed to straighten and held her aching sides. She had not laughed like that in—how long?

She looked over at Eliab. He still leaned on the round leg, and sucked in deep gulps of air. When he saw her looking at him, he smiled, and it was warm and full of mirth. Lines crinkled around his eyes, easy lines that showed he had once smiled often. She felt her own mouth curl in a smile she was certain matched his.

The mood was so pleasant she did not want to break it. "There is no mattress," she said.

His eyes still twinkled with lingering laughter. "I noticed that."

"Mattresses take time to make." She would not think how many steps were involved before the bed was ready.

His smile faded, but his eyes were still happy. "I have a lot of sheep to shear. We have to get the ropes across the bed, too."

Her smile dwindled too, taking the laughter with it. "I have to see if your moth—" she caught herself. "If there is a spindle in the house." A drop spindle was so small, so easily hidden, it could be behind the crocks, or tucked around the cups. "I will go look."

Eliab moved toward the door of this first sleeping room. One of his hands clenched on the frame. "I found the sickle, and the sledge, and the winnowing shovel. We need to go out and harvest my crop, and soon. Tomorrow at the latest. After that we must go to the farms around us. Whatever we can harvest, we had better get it done. One of my neighbors had a storehouse. If it is still there, I think we should fill it as soon as possible."

"Why do you not have one of your own?" Aksah saw Eliab's face and knew instantly it was the wrong question to ask.

"We did have one. It has fallen over, and shattered. I can only hope my neighbor's is still standing." He turned and walked across the main room toward the outside door. Aksah listened to his sandals scuff along the stone.

Eliab knew how to laugh. Really laugh. Those moments had been sweet.

A smile tugged at her mouth in the remembering. Honesty forced her to admit—if only to herself—that she would like more of them. More laughter, more teasing, more smiles.

Once home, how long would it be before another husband was found for her? Would she share the same connection with the new one? Would they be able to stand and laugh until their sides hurt like she and Eliab just had? Sometimes the matchmaker did well, sometimes not so well. Even those who found their own mates did not always succeed like they had hoped.

Aksah moaned, and rubbed her hands over her face. For the first time, forgiveness and forgetting seemed almost possible. She had to admit, no matter how hard it was, that he was a decent man.

If she clung to her lifelong dream and left Eliab here alone, what kind of betrayal would it be? If she let that dream go—at the thought her throat went tight. Her mind wanted to reject the idea outright.

The possibility of Shiloh coming through her had become entrenched inside, but could it be a habit now? Habits could be broken.

CHAPTER 11

*Your God is bringing you into a good land, a land of streams of water,
springs and fountains flowing in the valley plain and in the mountainous
region, a land of wheat and barley, of grapevines, fig trees, and
pomegranates, a land of olive oil and honey, a land where food will not be
scarce and you will lack nothing.*
Deuteronomy 8:7-9

Eliab slung the large, dusty sack over his shoulder, gripped the sickle, watching for the sharp blade, and pulled the shed door closed behind him. Tomorrow Aksah would be beside him, raking the sheaves and tying them to make them easier to carry, but today he should get the first part of the field harvested.

The wheat was past ripe, it might be drying. The weather had been warm, so he had hopes that the grains would not have begun sprouting within the head. The anxiety kept him company all along the empty pasture toward the small forest. He wondered if the fence was still on the far side of the trees. They wanted the cattle, should he be fortunate enough to catch some, to be able to keep cool, but not to get into the field beyond.

Particularly now, when they were starting over, and with old grain plants besides. Whatever wheat was still standing, they would have to find a way to use it.

He heard Aksah's laughter echoing in his mind as he walked through the thin stand of trees that separated the meadow where the sheep were grazing and the field where their next year's seed would be found. And planted, when the rains were due.

His feet followed the familiar path into the shallow woods. The air was still, the leaves dangled, barely moving. A couple of carob trees grew just back from the path, giving themselves away with their shiny roundish leaves. Deep inside the branches, he could see long green pods dangle in clusters. He did not remember these trees growing here, but they must have been. Perhaps they had not been mature enough to catch his attention, despite their glistening leaves. Now he would have special food for cattle, if he could round the animals up and get them penned in the empty fence next to the sheep.

As he walked further into the trees, Eliab was glad to see that not enough time had gone by to hide the route to the field. He and his brothers, and his father and grandfather, had walked this day after day, first for the planting, then watching for weeds, and even later checking to see when the head showed them it was ripe. They would come out more often as the wheat grew near harvest, to pinch the grains and see how firm they were, to watch the golden feathers grow long and wave in the wind.

His thoughts drifted back to the house, and Aksah. He and his wife had laughed together. His heart lifted with a hope he would not have dreamed just days ago. He knew she had been plotting ways to leave, trying to decide how to get back to her family's home.

The sack caught on a branch, and Eliab stopped to pull it free. Why did she have to be of the tribe of Judah? More than any other tribe, Judah seemed to be the one especially blessed by Israel's God. Why would she want to give that up to wed someone of his tribe, now especially cursed?

If he had asked God for a wife that would make his heart—and his body—

sing, that woman would have looked exactly like Aksah. She did not seem to know just how appealing she was.

He ducked under a branch that hung too low, and felt the sharp blade of the sickle brush ever so slightly against his leg. If he did not want to come back bleeding, he would have to be more careful.

Fool that he was, he had agreed to give her twenty-five days. When he agreed, he had known it was not going to be easy, but he had not expected *this*, this daily struggle against his growing desire. Not just for the ultimate act. Yes, that, too, but now, after they had begun to work as a team, he found he craved this marriage more than ever.

A real marriage, a blending of their lives, the kind of unity his parents had, and his grandparents. He wanted her to be with him *willingly*, to *want* to share his life just as he wanted to share hers, not just to feel like she was there on sufferance, waiting for her chance to escape.

He had watched her hair slide over her shoulders, soft and curling, and he wished he had the right to touch it, to push it out of the way when it became annoying. Her eyes changed with her mood, darkening almost to brown with anger or surprise, lightening to green when she was happy or laughing, which he would love to see again.

The trees came to an end at a tall fence of wood and stone. The field of gold spread out in front of him. The beards of the wheat stood upright and still in the air that right now did not move. He would long for a breeze by day's end. He saw both wheat and barley, and remembered helping his father plant them.

At the edge of the field, Eliab adjusted the sack, and grabbed the first stalks. With a quick slash of the sickle, he chopped off the wheat heads, and dropped them, beards and all, into the drooping bag. Then he moved to the next stalks, and did the same thing.

It was a good way to keep his mind off his wife, he told himself.

It just did not seem to be working. No matter how hard he swung the sickle at the stalks, no matter how full the sack got, he could not get Aksah's merry laugh out of his thoughts.

. . .

There had to be something in the house to prepare. The crock with the fig cakes was nearly empty, the wheat had not enough grains to make a single loaf, and the dried meat was long gone. Their fruit, as Eliab said they had an orchard, would not be ripe yet, but he was going to harvest wheat. If they had barley as well, she could make bread from either. He wanted to slaughter a sheep. Perhaps he would find time today.

He needed to know how little food was left. The meat was more important now than the wheat. They could nibble on the raw grains, or she could add barley to stewed mutton.

Aksah found a basket, and headed outside. She knew about where the fields were. If Eliab was harvesting wheat, he might be happy to let her cut some barley. Even without meat, there might be other plants she could use to make a tasty stew for tonight. Some early food might be edible. The figs they passed were so close to ripe that maybe a tree or two might be producing an early crop, and have some ready to eat.

While she was out, she should look for plants that could go into Eliab's mattress. Somewhere along here, based on what he had said, she expected a path to the field.

And there it was, plain as could be, a worn track through the ground, along the edge of the empty pasture that someday should hold cattle. She followed the trail, making the long, long walk through the grass and into the trees, the path pointing the way by the noticeable gap between the trunks. Birds fluttered and chirped, but while she heard them, none of them dipped into view. Leaves swayed, but that might be the faint breeze that came out of nowhere. The breeze would be helpful for winnowing away the chaff, assuming there was barley for a stew.

A sound caught her ear as she walked along the space between the trees, a soft swish repeated again and again. Even before she broke through the trees, Aksah knew what that sound meant. It was a sickle cutting through stalks.

Was it only wheat? If he had begun on the barley, how much simpler the evening meal would be!

Her first sight was Eliab as he wiped the sweat from his forehead with his arm. Before he could reach for the next cluster of stems, Aksah called out, "Eliab?"

He whirled around, the sickle coming up as if it was a sword. The tension drained away, and the arm with the sickle lowered. "Aksah! Why are you here?"

She started toward him along the front of the field. "We are nearly out of food. I thought to make a barley stew. Did you grow barley, as well as wheat? I thought I would look for greens to add. There is no meat, but that can wait until tomorrow."

He pointed to the far end of the field. "The barley is down there. I see you brought a basket. Did you bring something to cut the stalks?"

She shook her head. "I do not need much. I am just happy you have some. I thought I would snap off the heads, and get them soaking."

Eliab pointed again toward the far end of the field. "If you know what to look for, I can only apologize for the walk."

She raised her hand in dismissal. "That is not so far." Shifting the basket where it sat on her hip, she started through the wheat, being careful not to brush against too many of the drooping heads. Even so, she heard the tinkle and rustle of the ripe seeds as they popped loose and rained down on the ground. Ah well, the birds would be happy.

While she started snapping off the barley heads and dropping them into the basket, Aksah let her attention wander to the plants around the field, anything that would work for food—or for a mattress or baskets or—so many things they needed. Off to her right, out of the way of the field, she spotted fruit trees. The first to catch her attention were the olive trees, on the part of this land closest to the house. Beyond them the orchard proper, where clusters and rows of fruit-bearing trees marched into the distance. Pomegranate, fig, black mulberry, and juniper, the unripe berries still white. Towering date palms flourished at the far edge of the orchard, hinting at water nearby. A pool, perhaps, or a small stream, perhaps the same one that fed their well.

No wonder this farm had the feel of prosperity. Large, heavy furniture, crocks filled with food, even the substantial basket she carried. She wondered what the plunder the armies had taken looked like. How fancy were the pillows? The coverings? The bed she needed to replace so soon?

Grasses had taken advantage of the land's abandonment to grow freely between the wheat and barley. She should pull them soon, before the ground hardened and only a spade would free the roots. As she looked at the ground by her feet, Aksah saw the exact greens for her stew. Purslane, a soft leaf that would add both color and taste to the stew. Now she wished for a knife, but since she did not have one, she would just take the plant and trim it at the house.

Aksah set down the basket and knelt near the base of a clump. It took a steady pull, but the plant let go. She moved ahead, pulling stem after stem, laying them across the basket so the dirt fell off before she got back to the house.

She reached for another stem, only to stop short and stare at the plant right at her feet. Who thought it would be this easy, even though it grew freely across the land? The jagged green leaves, the tall branching stem, the long flower with yellow petals. Wild lettuce, exactly what she had thought to use when the time came for her to run. The plant she could put in his food and make Eliab sleep heavily enough to let her slip away undetected.

Before the last day or two, there would have been no debate. Before they ate together, before they climbed the pass of Michmash together, even before she watched him hunt that quail, she would have snatched those leaves up. But the first doubts about her once-chosen path threw her into confusion and opened the possibility of staying.

She settled back against her heels and looked at it. All she had to do was reach out and pull. It would hide so easily among the plants she already had in the bowl.

Another patch of wild lettuce caught her gaze, and another. It was a veritable garden, all she needed and more.

CHAPTER 12

"Everyone in the open field who touches someone killed with the sword or a corpse or the bone of a man or a burial place will be unclean for seven days."
Numbers 19:16

Several days later, Eliab walked in after feeding the sheep their morning grain. "I have been thinking," he said as he poured water from the pitcher on the shelf over his hand, splashing into the vessel beneath. He always tried to keep himself clean. Whether it was yet another attempt to woo her, or just his natural manner, she appreciated it. "We need to start gathering the stray animals. It would hardly surprise me if some have found their way back to their homes and are hungry and thirsty. They need care, shearing and milking and feeding, and to do that we must bring them here." He rinsed both hands off in the bowl, and rubbed the moisture over his face.

Aksah looked up from her place on the floor, grinding flour at the hand mill. Eliab brought the stalks from those fields back in great bundles, and threshed it here. He seemed always to be covered in a light coating of white, with bits of husk and stems decorating his hair and arms.

The kernels were drying out from not being harvested in time. Once each load of threshing was done, the kernels came in to her basket after basket, pot after pot. The crocks were filling back up. One had been set aside for flour, and with all her baking, she struggled to keep it full. Soon they would need more of them to hold the harvest, or else Eliab had to get the storehouse back upright.

But that was for another day. Every time she thought about him having to replace the storehouse alone, working hard and fast to protect the seeds, a strange tightness wrapped around her inside. He was so tired already that he fell asleep every time he sat down.

They both worked hard, while that empty bed frame sat waiting for the mattress. To do that, though, she still needed a loom and a spindle. The fleece was building up, pending those two pieces.

It seemed the Israelite armies had indeed taken them as plunder.

"We need to locate more crocks for storing food." Aksah looked at the flour accumulating on her scarf of linen, washed and spread wide. It was the only fabric they had to spare to keep the wheat off the floor. It was time and past to weave a true cloth. "And a loom. And a spindle if we can," she said, "so I can begin spinning."

"The first thing we have to find is a wagon to carry everything home." He walked over to stand next to her. "Do you suppose you have enough flour today for a loaf of bread? Can you stop now? I crave your bread all the time. We might be able to find homes untouched like our own, and if all goes well, we might even find food in them. And crocks." He gave her a crooked smile, and the skin around his eyes crinkled in easy lines. "And a loom and all the other things we need."

Heat warmed her cheeks. *He craved her bread.* It was a sweet compliment, and made all the grinding and mixing and baking worthwhile. Aksah checked the pile of flour once more. The flour crock was nearly full already, this bit would bring it to the top, enough for several loaves, and then she would have to move onto the next pile of grain that he had threshed.

Eliab worked harder than she did. And that was hard indeed.

She was tired of spending so much time on her knees. She smiled up at him, or at least at the prospect of going for a walk. "Yes, I can stop."

"Good." He slapped his hands on his thighs. "What can I do to help?"

"If you can bring the crock?" She picked up the scarf by its edges and watched the fluffy powder roll to the center.

Eliab checked several crocks before making a satisfied sound in his throat. "Here it is." He left the wooden cover on the cabinet top and carried the pottery jar over. Aksah rose and poured the flour in.

"Shake out the cloth and hang it up," Eliab said as he walked back to the cabinet and re-covered the flour.

Her back felt tight as she straightened fully upright, and Aksah twisted left and right to loosen the muscles. One spot in the middle wanted extra attention, and she pressed her knuckles against that tight spot. Ah, that was better.

She walked to the door and stepped outside, taking a breath of the hot air. If growing things and green had a scent, she thought, this was what it would smell like. She hardly expected a refreshing day, it was growing too warm for that, but just to be free again! Her scarf showered powder into the air as she snapped it several times. She would have to remember to wash it, she thought as she hung it on one of the pegs by Eliab's weapons belt.

Dust had formed a light film on the belt.

She turned her back on it, and walked outside. The door opened and closed easily. Eliab had worked hard to make it fit, and it was now secure.

A shadow fell over her, long in the early morning sun. A hand appeared in her view, palm up, waiting.

Eliab did things like this from time to time, and she found it harder and harder to resist his attraction. Aksah took his hand, and tried not to consider just how easy it was.

His fingers curled around hers, and he smiled, not just his mouth but all the way to his eyes. "Are you ready?"

"Yes," she said, and hoped he did not read more into it. The days of that month were slipping past, faster and faster.

They walked with the sun at their side. Stretching out, their shadows blended in the ground, two people merging into one, then separating, only to overlap again with their strides.

He glanced over to the glowing orb. "We will be walking with the sun at our side both ways. We do not have to worry about it in our eyes on the way back," he explained. He gave her hand one gentle squeeze before letting it go. Aksah knew somehow that he timed all of his touches with the greatest care, never pushing them long enough to make her uncomfortable. No, it was not his touches that made her uncomfortable. It was her reaction to them.

They walked in silence for a while. The sun had not become too hot this time of day, and birds did their own calls. The forest stretched along the left, the feathery tamarisk, the spreading sycamore, the little thorny locust, and pines. To her delight, she believed she saw a pistachio tree. Aksah grabbed Eliab's arm and pointed. "Eliab! Is that what I think it is?"

"You have to be more specific." He looked down at her.

"A pistachio tree! How lovely if it is. We can have nuts from it! I can bake them in all manner of things." And then she stopped herself. *We* can have nuts from it?

He did not give her time to brood, though. "My mother used to bake cakes with them, and dry them for something to carry into the field for a quick meal." He frowned as he stared at the forest. "My brother often got sick from them, so she used other nuts for him, or baked breads with figs and dates." His head tilted to catch her gaze. "You are not bothered by them, then?"

"Oh, never!" A laugh bubbled up. "They are my favorite! I could eat them all day."

He managed a laugh himself. "They are my favorite, too." He looked back at the forest. "They are not ripe yet, or I would walk over and pluck us some." He did an exaggerated sigh. "But alas, they are just beginning to develop. We might both get sick from them, and that would never do."

Conversation lagged again, but it was not the tense, heavy silence of their early days. Aksah tried to think of a word for it. *Comfortable.* Yes, they had found a measure of comfort in the time they spent together.

The ground was beginning to show the first signs of summer. Grasses showed brown at the tips, and the soil was dry. Their feet kicked up the dirt that had dried in the sun, and would get even more dry as the fierce heat settled in. The flowers that marked their trail away from Shiloh would now be only curling leaves like the ones they passed, wilted to preserve themselves for the rainy season. The birds flapped from one tree to another in the distance, making a pattern of movement in the trees.

Their shadows kept pace with them, stretching out to the side.

"Look." This time it was his turn to point. "Our closest neighbor." His voice caught at that last word. "The house was not burned, just as mine was not. That bodes well for our search."

As they drew closer, they noticed the white shapes of sheep simultaneously. "More sheep." Eliab said.

Aksah glanced up at him. His mouth turned up in a smile, she could see it even around his beard. The work was much for one man, but it also gave him wealth. How many men could boast a flock the size theirs was becoming? Benjamin's men needed whatever respect they could get, even if it came in the guise of sheep, she knew.

"I will see what the animals need. We cannot walk them back without watering them at least. Perhaps there might even be a wagon, and donkeys to pull it. You go into the house and see if there is anything to salvage." He patted her shoulder, and gave her a gentle push toward the stone house with the window lattices pulled tight.

Who had closed those window coverings? The family, against the approaching army of Israel? Or the army itself, after plundering what remained?

Stepping up to the door, she gave it a push. It creaked open on its pivots, and stale air leaked out. A nasty stench overlaid the staleness. Aksah covered her nose, pushed the door fully wide with her foot, and backed away to let the rooms freshen, but that awful stink remained. She held her sleeve over her nose and thought the food must have gone bad. After several moments the house smelled better, and Aksah stepped into the darkness.

Oddly, unlike the jumble they had found in Eliab's house, this one appeared untouched. The chairs and cushions were shoved out of the way as if the family fled in a hurry, but they seemed to be all there.

And a loom!

Aksah turned to the shelves at her left. This house was built exactly as her own, at least in this part of the building. Food preparation area to the left of the door, living space directly ahead. Curtains hung from several doors to the right that must hold the rooms for sleep. Aksah knew if she went in she would find beds.

She did not want mattresses that had belonged to others, even if she could forego the task of making one.

Another whole family gone.

She did not want to go into those curtained areas, or through that door to her right. Somehow it seemed too private, this empty house.

That heavy odor in the air still lingered, a low bitterness that made the head ache and the stomach turn.

Crocks just like the ones in their house sat on shelves, as neat as the wife must have left them after their last meal. Aksah walked over, took a bracing breath in case the foul smell came from any of them, and started removing lids. Flour, raisins, and dates, dried figs, nuts, no doubt from the last harvest before the war began. One even held dried meat. All were fresh and clean, she realized after she took a deep breath from inside the crocks to block out that underlying stench that hung on the air.

Recovering them with the tight wooden lids, she hoped Eliab found a wagon, because there were so many jars here that the two of them could never carry all in one trip.

The lattice in the middle of the wall needed to be opened. She should have thought to do that first, before she checked the clay containers. The little latch gave way easily, and Aksah shoved them wide. Daylight poured in through the window, bringing brightness to the room.

Eliab's face appeared in the opening, startling her. "Stay inside." The words were short, his voice harsh. He had a shovel over his shoulder.

"What is it? What is wrong?" It had been a pleasant day, and she had almost forgotten the evil that had sent them here. His rigid tone, his stern face, cast a pall over the day's cheer.

Shovel. Her gaze was caught by that shovel. The smell. That nagging smell was the faded odor of death and decay that had seeped through the lattices but had not been able to go away because no one had been here to open the windows.

Aksah whirled around to stare at the curtains that she had not wanted to breach. Had the army killed the family where they hid?

Shivers ran over her skin, bringing the little hairs upright. She would not go in those rooms, not even if ordered. The food had been covered, it was still deemed clean, but she did not want to see what her hus—Eliab had seen.

Scraping sounds came from outside. A grave, or maybe two.

To keep her mind occupied, Aksah began carrying the crocks to the doorway, but not outside. She did not want to see what Eliab had seen, nor watch him bury what he had found.

Once the crocks had been neatly lined up, she checked around the room again. A wooden bin sat in the corner, waist-high and as long as a man but narrow, the lid closed tight. She stared at it. Her parents had one just like it in the corner of their house, where they stored the large earthenware jars of wine.

It was also large enough to hide a body.

Common sense took over. Anyone who had hidden in such a place would be able to climb out once the danger was past. No, if anything hid in that bin, it would be wine.

Wine would be nice. It was such a common part of a meal. She knew of drunkards, but somehow did not think Eliab would ever have that kind of weakness. In the short while she had known him, she had come to see him as a man of great determination and willpower. He would never tolerate such a flaw.

Aksah marched over to the bin and grabbed the handle, jerking it open.

The sweet aroma of wine drifted upward, making her mouth water. A ladle hung on a hook inside. The wine had aged, and was rich and deep. How Eliab would love this! She could not lift jars this big—and they were indeed large. As tall as a child, her arms could not even go around them.

A sudden clatter came through the window. She whirled around and stared at the blue sky visible through the opening, but the sound did not recur. Perhaps Eliab had dropped the shovel. Perhaps it was not as violent a sound as she imagined. Heavy iron and copper tools could make a lot of noise just by being dropped.

A shovel would make that noise if it was flung in grief or rage.

Feet scraped at the doorway, and she turned around, her hand still motionless, holding the ladle. Eliab stood there, his robe soaked, water dripping onto the ground. Wet curls stuck to his head, as though he had taken a bucket and dumped it over himself.

"Wine?" Eliab stayed in the doorway, but his gaze went to the bin. With the air in the house now clean, of course he could smell it even from there. Aksah could almost feel his thirst from where she stood.

"Yes, and good wine, at that." Aksah held out the ladle. "Would you like a taste?"

She did not mention the reason he ordered her to come inside. Nor did they talk yet about why he stayed in the doorway, although Aksah had no doubt he would say something soon. She ladled another scoop, walked over, and gave it to him. He took it, being careful not to touch her.

He drained the last swallows and set the ladle outside on the ground before straightening and facing her. His face was hard, the skin grey underneath the dust overlaying it. Anger and grief, their nearly constant companions of the early days, were back. "I did not touch the bones, but I should still follow the law. I will remain outside."

Bones. She did not want to ask more. In this land, bodies began their journey to dust very quickly. After the months of the rainy season, while the men hid in the caves and Israel mourned and worked out a plan to recover his tribe, no doubt the whole land of Benjamin had begun reclaiming the dead.

"We will have to come another day for whatever you cannot carry. I feel fouled." A shudder seemed to ripple along his skin. Eliab's gaze went from the neat line of containers by the door to that bin in the corner of the room. "If you can find jars small enough for you to carry easily, fill them with wine. I do not want to touch anything. We will bring what we can today. After my week of purification, I shall get the rest."

He sighed and turned away, looking at something out of view. "I had found a wagon and got it ready before I found the first . . ."

Bodies, she thought, filling in what he did not say. Thank goodness he had done much of the hard work before he saw what was left of his neighbors. "There is a loom." The initial excitement had faded, but they could not let this chance go. "It will require another trip. I will carry what we are bringing today out to the wagon." Those containers waiting on the floor caught her eye. "I can carry them, I have already proved that."

He nodded, and turned back to her. "The sheep are ready to come. They had wandered back into the pen. Silly creatures, they stayed there, even though the fences are nearly gone. I am hoping they will follow us when we pull away. They seemed very glad to see me."

"Did you find cattle? Goats?"

A suggestion of a smile pulled up his mouth. "Yes, and yes. We will hope for the same with them."

She looked back into the house, and glanced at those curtains. "Let us go, then. I find I do not wish to stay any longer."

The cattle pulled the wagon in a steady rhythm, as if they had missed feeling the traces and were glad to show what they remembered. The crocks clinked against each other along the uneven ground, but she knew how to pack a wagon. Everything would arrive intact. One could hardly grow up on a farm without the skill of wagon-loading.

Aksah watched the animals as they worked. They had grown round and lazy in the last months, with the rain feeding the grasses and the wadis running with water. It was good they were found before the heat settled in and the grasses dried. Eliab said they would soon have carob pods to feed the animals, and they could keep the troughs full so the cattle and flocks would not go thirsty.

The wind had picked up, and dust whirled around them, catching in their mouths whenever they opened them. But that was not the reason they did not talk.

No, the bodies Eliab had found outside his friends' house was. He had busied himself herding the sheep and goats together while she loaded the crocks into the wagon. One nod from him, and she had urged the cattle into movement, leading their new stock.

Words kept surfacing, but the wind and a hard-won restraint locked them inside. He had buried his neighbors, but her family did not know where Chileab even lay. Somewhere in the large graves that now dotted the land of Benjamin, certainly, but where?

Grief was walking with them, was it not? She caught him wiping his face several times, and even now he walked well behind the wagon. The sheep made a wonderful excuse to stay at the rear, and Aksah pretended she did not see his red eyes.

The war was fresh again. In both their minds. Dead friends, bodies found.

The pistachio trees did not catch her attention going back. Eliab said he would harvest the nuts once they were ripe. Aksah wondered what she would remember when she ate them, the lightheartedness of the journey out, or the heaviness of this return trip.

Their own home appeared on the horizon, growing closer with every step. She would be cooking food taken from his neighbors' house, if not today, then soon. She could disguise it, blend some of the dried fruit with their own food, but he would know. How many meals would it take before he no longer thought of his friends' house, their bodies, when he ate?

"Can you carry those crocks inside?"

Eliab's voice made her start. The cattle ignored her sudden movement and kept their steady plodding, the hooves making a muffled drumbeat on the ground.

Aksah stopped and turned around at his voice, ignoring the sense of relief that he was still speaking to her. He did not meet her gaze, he was too distracted by the goats, butting each other or stopping to nibble at the plants beside the path. "Yes. Of course." She did not know if he was listening, but kept speaking just in case. He had extended the olive branch, she would grasp it. "I got them into the wagon, I can certainly take them back out."

"Good. I will take the animals into the pasture behind the house, then I will put the wagon away." He turned his back full to her.

Odd that the sun still shone. She caught up with the cattle pulling the wagon, and pulled a hair out of her mouth that the wind had caught.

That one small bit of talk must have been all Eliab was prepared to say. The walk continued, silence once again her companion, silence and the cows yoked to the wagon. Some sheep had scurried ahead, and played around her legs, happy at having people in their lives again.

At least, living people.

It was a relief to reach their house. Aksah tugged the cattle pulling the wagon to a halt in front of their door, and turned around. Perhaps now that they were home, he would look at her.

Instead, Eliab was busy herding the flock around the side wall. Water must have lured them with its scent. Both sheep and goats began shoving and leaping, harrying him with their antics.

It made a perfect excuse not to look at her.

She had pushed him away so much that to have him now pull back from her felt odd. Hurtful. Even though she understood the reason for his surge of grief and resentment, just as he must have understood hers, it still was like a thorn under her skin, scraping and gouging.

This was not the time to brood on it. She wanted a respite from her thoughts. Right now, there were chores to do, crocks to carry, the cattle to release. Thank goodness for busy work, distraction from an uncomfortable emotion.

She picked up the first crock and nudged their door open with her shoulder. From the back, the noise increased as the sheep clustered there.

He had said nothing about her joining him to usher the animals into the separate fences. The crock thunked at she set it on the shelf. The bleating continued, and the cows lowed in harmony. Eliab surely must need help. One man with all those animals?

The rest of the crocks could stay on the wagon for a moment. Aksah walked around the house. The sheep were almost all inside the fence, the trough a powerful lure. The goats found their way in as well, shoving between, and even over, the slower sheep.

The loose cattle began to plod around the house, their big heads wagging as they walked. Their pen was next to the other, smaller sheepfold, the two animal enclosures side by side for a distance. But the cattle's gate was wider, and their pasture went far back, following the wooden bars down to the forest. The trees would fill in the path to the neighbor's house, she knew, grow thicker until Eliab had a family, sons to wield an axe and keep it open.

Would he tear down his friends' house and leave the stones to dry in the sun? Or would he bring them, one by one, here to enlarge his own house?

He seemed to be managing the herds alone. Aksah went back to her assignment. The cattle at the door still stood placid in their yokes.

The food came first. As she brought in the crocks, she could see the cows continue along the house wall, a slow-moving stream making their way toward the pen. Sheep bleated, a familiar sound, and goats added their own complaint. Water splashed into the trough, a sloppy sound mixed in with all the animal noises.

With this many animals, they would need the troughs at the other house. How long would it take before Eliab was ready to go back? That house was not his only neighbor, not his only friend. How many other houses and farms nearby held the same nightmare, the same bodies with no one to bury them? Aksah shuddered, closed her eyes and gripped the crock tighter. She was glad he had kept her from seeing what he had faced.

How long would it take before today's tension eased?

Work. That is what she needed. Aksah looked down at the crock in her arms. Food was food, she decided. They had to eat, and this trek had been necessary.

Dried meat would soften nicely when boiled in a little bit of water. She would make soup, and put the dried fruit in cake and bread. They had flour and in plenty now, at least for several days. While the meat was softening and cooking, there would be time to get the baking started.

If he wanted to talk about what he had found, she would be ready to listen.

Eliab stopped in the doorway, looked at the bowl left on the shelf for him and shuddered. He could smell the dried meat. They had not butchered an animal for several days, one of the reasons for today's journey.

Today's jaunt was supposed to be easy, a simple trip. Why had he thought the land was already cleansed of the dead? The bodies had rotted in the rainy season just past, but parts remained, enough so he could identify who they were.

His stomach turned. Aksah was looking at him when he raised his eyes.

"I made bread." Was that sympathy he saw? "And your favorite fruit cakes."

"I must not come in for a week to fulfill the purification. You know that?" Eliab tried not to look at the soup. He wanted to back away from the door, away from the knowledge of what he had seen today.

"I expected that." Aksah reached for a round flat loaf of bread, and tore off a few pieces. The fresh scent eased his stomach. She pulled a plate off its shelf, and set several pieces of the freshly baked loaf on it. "You need to eat. Here."

The plate was warm on his hands when he took it from her. "Thank you." He looked down at the plate, everything so fresh and fragrant, and then back up at her. "The week will go quickly. I will make sure you are safe but I will remain outside." He raised one eyebrow. "After all, you still feel my tribe and I have much to prove, do you not?"

Her mouth lifted in a smile, but her eyes were still serious. "I have no objections to your living by the Law. I will help you make a bed out by the sheep. The nights are warm. The sheep kept us warm along our walk, they will do the same now."

Eliab turned and walked away with the plate filled with her baking. She had smiled just now. *I have no objections to your living by the Law.* Even those words had no sharp edge, only acknowledgement that in this his actions were right and proper.

His tribe had fallen into disrepute by their failure. Setting up a farm did not give much chance to show he could do anything but plow and thresh and shear. Hardly a way to redeem himself in the eyes of a woman who held the law in such regard.

But seven days living separate, a week of admitting to uncleanness?

Perhaps this day of ugliness would be a good thing after all.

.   .   .

Aksah watched Eliab walk away. For the briefest of moments, she had thought he would be sick looking at the soup. The day had been hard on him, and the coming week would be more so, a constant reminder of the ugly job he had been forced to do.

She would not have blamed him if he had left the bodies there. Yet, something inside him had driven him to show them the respect of a burial, despite the cost to himself.

He was learning the lesson the war had tried to teach, that no part of the Law could be ignored at will.

For her part, she was now seeing the man he should have been, and might yet become. And respecting him. Perhaps even liking him.

What was she going to do now?

CHAPTER 13

"And should their fathers or their brothers come to make a complaint against us, we will then tell them, 'Show us favor for their sakes."
Judges 21:22

Men crested the small hill just to the north of their house. Eliab kept an eye on them where he stood by the sheepfold, shearing yet another sheep. He and Aksah had gone out several times over the past weeks, rounding up more flocks that wandered free. Cows and goats had been drawn to their well, and had come through the gate. More work, more fences to build, sheds to expand.

The bulls still roamed the land. He hoped someday they would find their way to his cows. Every day that went by increased the chance they might become more wild and less amenable to being caught, but food and shelter—and females—was a powerful lure. He had particular hopes for one strong animal that had come all the way to the fence, only to back away when Eliab turned toward him.

Ah well. For now he would be content with the herd he had.

Like the flock, plenty large enough to leave any man wealthy. The work it entailed kept him busy from the sunrise until long after sunset. Not just him, but his wife as well. He wished he had more time to watch her, just to see her push her curly hair behind her ears as she moved about the house. Aksah hummed sometimes as she worked, and he would stand out of sight and listen, but those times were rare and to be cherished.

It worried him that she was getting thin. He had become lean from all the work he did, and that alone, but he was a man. He could afford to become just muscle and bone, but he did not want the same for her. "Eat," he said often, just as she had done that awful day when he found his neighbors. "You cook well, your food is delicious. You need to enjoy it."

She would oblige him and take another mouthful, but her thoughts seemed to drift away. He, one of Benjamin's mighty warriors, who had faced swords and arrows and the screams of war, was afraid to ask what thoughts plagued her.

They had a few days left of the twenty-five, and fear clawed at him. He would be shaving a sheep, and panic would strike, driving him to set the animal aside and walk to the house door to look inside, just to make certain Aksah was still there. Those moments came more and more often.

Did she still want to leave?

She had proved herself adept at the household chores. She could cook and spin and weave and sew. In his more hopeful moments, Eliab imagined watching her make clothes for the children to come.

Sons would help with all the work a farm needed, daughters would help her around the house. Those children were only in his mind as yet. Aksah kept faithful count of the days. Ten more to go before the month she had requested was up.

He lifted the razor from the sheep and watched the shapes come closer. Across the span separating them, he saw the grey of a beard on one of the two. Father and son? The grey-bearded man was not tall. The one with him shared his size.

No one had passed their farm since they arrived, but Aksah had assured him her father would come. He had told her he believed it. The decision by the older men of Israel had assumed, even expected, the fathers would come after their captured daughters.

Shading his eyes with the hand that held the razor, Eliab's suspicion grew with every step the men took.

Their arrival could not have come at a worse time. He and Aksah had begun to develop a tentative friendship. Once in a while, when she did not think he was watching, she would peek at him with a puzzling, almost guilty expression. He did not understand what that look meant, but there had been no attempts to run. A good sign, he told himself.

And now, men were coming. From this distance he could not see them clearly, but he was quite certain he knew who they were—and why they were here.

The sheep wriggled in his one hand, and a hoof came free, lashing out with the hard sharp edges. He snagged it and concentrated on getting the last wool off. Nothing could be done until the men arrived and made their plea.

Between swipes, he looked up. They would be here about the time he finished the sheep. He kept the razor going, slicing away clump after clump.

She was loved, his wife, for a father to isolate the man who had captured her, and then to travel all this way. Even the brother had made the journey.

Unless he was not a brother? What if there was a young man who had spoken for her? Aksah had said there was none, but perhaps she had not been informed yet.

It mattered not, he thought as he took another swipe at the wool. Benjaminites had all been warned that the families would want the daughters back. They had all been told, by no less than God himself, what to say. He had it ready, had practiced the right, most respectful way to speak to her family if they did come. The answer would be the same regardless of their pleas, but it was foolish to alienate them.

Especially when his wife early on had every intention of leaving. Whether that was still her intent, he did not know. He only hoped her mind had changed. That goal had been no secret, not from the beginning. He needed the father on his side to ensure she stay.

A tall order, considering the man's bereavement at Benjamin's hand.

The last slide of the razor against the skin, the last clump of wool. He was done, at least with this one. The sheep struggled free. Eliab shoved it through the gate and pulled it shut.

The men walked down the side of the house. Hoary curls peeked from under the older man's turban, dark strands still lingering amid the white.

The other man was younger, as Eliab had thought from his initial sighting, and his rich brown hair matched Aksah's in color, if not in curl. If he had to guess the age, he would put the youth at eight and ten at most.

Two pairs of eyes met his, angry and wary.

They weighed each other as the men came the last few steps. Features became familiar, Aksah's changeable eyes belonged to the father, and her wild hair. The boy had her fine features, cast in a masculine mold and partially hidden by a budding beard.

Both men wore a layer of dust on their undyed robes, the fabric's original milky color showing through here and there. The same evidence of their walk had settled in the creases on their faces, around their eyes, and caked on their lips. A limp waterskin could be seen peeking behind the younger man's arm. It must be empty, or the grit on their mouths would have been washed away by their last drinks. Beneath the fringe of the robes, grime blended in with the hairs there. Eliab remembered the feel of sand and pebbles scraping against the soles of his feet, and knew they endured the same.

The older one's hand holding the staff showed white knuckles. Unless that was just more dust. He suspected it was not the latter. The man had the bulk of one used to hard work. No doubt he could do damage with that staff if he chose.

Someone had to speak first, and Eliab decided it should be himself. "You are Aksah's father and brother. I am Eliab." He caught himself before adding the words *Aksah's husband*. "I bid you welcome. Please, come inside," he waved his left arm toward the house, "and be refreshed. You will want to see Aksah. She is inside."

Her father propped his hands on his hips, and stood, legs braced. "Yes, you are right, I do wish to see my daughter, and make certain she is well."

"Of course." Eliab started toward the door, and looked back, then stopped in place.

Neither of the other two men moved. "I think not, not yet." Aksah's father spoke in a mild voice, but there was iron beneath it. "We have something to settle between us first. You did not think I would be happy to meet you, did you? I wanted Aksah married to a man chosen by her mother and I, one who we knew would value her. You cannot deny the history of your tribe recently has been despicable. I value my daughter, I love her. Only the best man would have been good enough, but because you were there, you took that from her."

Eliab resisted the urge to fold his arms, instead keeping them loose at his side. What else had he expected? The men of Benjamin would be a long time living down their reputation. "Of course we were there. We needed women to rebuild our tribe. If you had not dared challenge the risk, you would have remained safely at home."

The younger man took a sharp breath, and put a hand on the older man's shoulder.

Aksah's father's brows came down in anger and disgust. "What a thing to say! Miss this one chance in a year to gather at Shiloh? No! No! We were there and that cannot be changed. I would not change that part of it even if I could. But this—this I would change! Aksah is a woman of intelligence and—"

Eliab interrupted, "Yes, I have indeed seen her intelligence. She is far too intelligent for her own good some times."

The father's mouth quirked. But he firmed it. "And spirit."

Eliab dared his own smile. "Yes, spirit as well. I think I see from where she gets it. That is what I want in my own daughters and sons. They will need it, and I do know the task I have set for her—and for them. I am also well aware of the rules for the taking of these new brides. I knew you would come. It was expected, even prophesied."

He gestured toward the house. "I know you did not come just to question me, challenge me. I know you desire to see your daughter, and ensure that she has not been mistreated. You wanted her to marry the best man you could find for her. I cannot claim to be the best, that is not my declaration to make, but I assure you," his voice got thick, and Eliab had to clear it. "I value your daughter. Very much."

Now that he could speak again, he went on in a mild voice, "If you are not ready yet to enter my house, I will go get your daughter, so you can see she is well." He moved toward the door, relieved to get away from Aksah's father and his measuring eyes, but was stopped by the man's hand.

"No, call for her. Let her come on her own, and let me see her face."

Muscles tightened on his shoulders, but Eliab appreciated their reasoning. "Aksah!" He shouted but he did not take his gaze from her father, whose name he still did not know. He doubted he would get it before the man was assured Aksah was well. "Will you come? I need you out here." He saw the look on her father's face and added, "If you please."

"One moment! I am coming." Her voice had a touch of impatience in it. He must have interrupted her in the middle of something. Eliab could almost trace her movements with every word.

Her father smiled. "I see she has not lost her spirit."

His wife came around the corner of the house. "The meal will be done—" She broke off and a strange sound, a guttural cry, came from the bottom of her being. "Father!" Her arms opened like sails, as she raced across the space between them.

Her father opened his arms equally wide, in time to catch her with a muffled 'oof.'

"You look well," Aksah's father said.

Her face was wet with tears. She extended one arm to the young man at the father's side. "Gershom, I am so very, very glad to see you."

The boy began weeping, and crowded to her other side. "We worried. We were so afraid. We have been looking for you *everywhere*!" He stepped back after a moment and wiped his nose on his shoulder.

Aksah stood within her father's embrace and burrowed her face in his chest. It was so good to see him, to see Gershom, again. Only now did she realize the size of the hole in her heart, the ache that had remained within. She thought she had known the depth of her sadness, but she must have shut down her emotions in order to make it through.

Now she did not know how she felt. Of course she wanted to see the family again, of course she wanted to go back, but she had found a surprising kind of . . . *respect*, might be the word . . . toward Eliab.

The work had been hard, but newly woven pillow coverings sat around the main room, some filled with fresh grasses and wool, some coverings still empty, waiting for the next batch of filling. They had clothes as well now, new robes for each of them, and new blankets for the nights so the cool air no longer bit. The cupboards were filled with the pots they had found, all cleaned and ready for use, as well as the plates and bowls and cups from both Eliab's family and the house of his neighbors.

She had lain awake night after night, staring into the dark and fighting with herself. Go back, make that treacherous journey alone, risk death every day? If she made it she would remain part of her beloved tribe of Judah, would still keep the possibility, at the very least, of being in the line of the promised Shiloh. Or should she stay here in Benjamin's land and see what developed between herself and this unusual man who could make her laugh and feel protected, could work alongside her like equals?

If she stayed, she gave up her lifetime's dream. She could not guess what that would do to her.

The wild lettuce still grew in the field. Never once had she gone back for it.

It was very confusing. Now, with her father here to take her home, she felt an odd shaking start inside. Delight at going back? Or dread at leaving now, when things were beginning to grow between the two of them?

What did it mean that she had filled pillows instead of a mattress, woven clothes and cushions instead of a mattress? She had promised herself she would not leave before he had a bed to sleep on. Somehow that bed had come to symbolize the end of her time here, a permission to escape and go back to Judah.

And she could not bring herself to finish it. God had sent her father and her brother, she had a way to get back to her family home. Eliab's bed was not done. If she left she would break one vow, if she stayed she would break faith with herself.

And God?

Which was the real truth? Had God given her to Eliab by virtue of his catching her even when she was being alert and watchful? Or had God sent her the way home, the way to remain in the line of Jacob's prophesy?

Even more, would God have allowed her to be captured in the first place if she was the chosen one?

Could she be faithful without the drive of the promise to Judah? She wanted to believe her faith was sincere, bone deep, a part of her heart, but until Eliab she had never been faced with losing what drove her. These last days she had been living in a state of indecision, making a home she was not certain she would live in. Giving Eliab a half-life, a half-home.

Strange flutterings beat about in her chest as she leaned against her father's strength. In a moment Eliab would invite her father and brother in to the house, and she would have to feed them. Right at this moment, Aksah was afraid to pick up so much as a ladle of water for fear her shaking hands would drop it.

The time for decision had arrived, and she could not choose.

Eliab watched warily as, keeping Aksah tucked close, sheltered by his work-hardened arm, Aksah's father turned to him. His face was stern. "No one of Israel was to *give* a daughter to anyone of Benjamin. You made yourselves pariahs to the nation. It will take much effort on the part of all of you to recover any reputation." His eyes narrowed. "You know, of course, the rest of why I am here."

"I am aware of the request you will make." Eliab narrowed his own eyes in return. "You also must know the response I must give."

"What is this?" Aksah looked from her father's face to Eliab and back. "You are here to take me home. I claimed the month for captured brides, Father, and so I am still pure."

He kissed her on the forehead with poignant pride. "I expected nothing less from you." His eyes went moist, and red started to rim them. "There were things we had to keep from you, daughter." Turning his attention back to Eliab, the man said, "I do expect your response, but I will ask regardless."

Eliab watched his wife be shifted away from her father. Hanging on to his robe with a seemingly desperate grip, Aksah moved only far enough to remain sheltered by her brother.

Even though her father had to look up to meet his gaze, Eliab admired the man who had lost none of his dignity.

"I am Saul, Aksah's father, and I ask for my daughter to be returned to me. Her mother grieves for her, her younger sisters are overwhelmed with guilt, and the youngest girl has not stopped crying since the day she was stolen away."

Eliab looked at the little family. Once his was like this, warm and loving. They were all gone, and Aksah's family, or at least her father, knew that much. He respected them for their courage in coming all this way, but the answer did not, could not change.

He took a breath, and kept his voice respectful. "I greet you, Saul of Judah. Show me favor for the sake of the other tribes, because of the provision to keep my tribe alive, the decision of our whole nation. There should be an inheritance for Benjamin, so the tribe may not be wiped out of Israel, and all twelve sons of Jacob may continue. Leave your daughter with me as a gift."

Eliab's words did not make sense right away. Aksah stared at him, surprised by his mild voice, the humility with which he spoke. He towered over her father in height, yet his words were like a request.

What had he said? *Leave your daughter?* Aksah snapped her head over to watch her father, the pride with which he held his head, and then her gaze went back to Eliab. How could her father nod?

"You asked well," Saul said. "I want my daughter back, you know that, but I also knew it was a doomed request. I knew I could not return with her, but this trip will show that she is valued and loved by her family. You have a treasure, young man, and I hope you appreciate her."

A doomed request? Had Eliab been telling the truth all along? She could not be given back? "Father!" Aksah gasped, fighting against the constriction of her lungs to get air. He did not look at her, but still stared at Eliab as if searching for something. "Father?" Her voice cracked at the end. She let go of Gershom. Her fingers clenched tighter on her father's robe.

"I have seen what she can do." Eliab stood, legs apart, standing like the soldier he once was. "She has been well-trained. She is very capable."

Saul's eyebrows came down. "I am not talking about her abilities, broad though they are. She is a woman of deep faith, and you need that here in your tribe. It will take women like her to regain any standing with the rest of the nation. Aksah loves with all her heart. I do not know how long it will take for you to win that, but love is a treasure beyond any gold. I want you to learn that. You men of Benjamin are anxious to get the tribe started again, but do not make the same mistake that caused this war. Do not think of your women as nothing more than a cook and a womb. I will not permit my daughter to be ill-used." His voice dropped. "I will come against you myself to bring vengeance for my daughter."

Aksah looked at Eliab. Her ears were ringing so loudly she feared she would not hear him reply.

"I will not harm her in any way. You have my word. I know who I have, and I know I am the most fortunate of men." He sounded sincere. No, he *was* sincere, she believed that. *The most fortunate of men.* But was she the most fortunate of women?

"Come into my house." Eliab waved toward the front of the house, and Saul bowed his head.

"I thank you. I would like time with my daughter, if you are willing to let me and my son stay for a meal."

"I would be honored." Eliab led the way, and Aksah followed the group toward the door. He stepped aside and let their guests enter. She brought up the rear, trying to remember how she had left their house.

Eliab pulled down a bowl and one of her small woven cloths and invited their guests to sit. Aksah expected the traditional job of washing the feet to fall to her, but Eliab settled himself on the floor and pulled off her father's sandals. They had not been visited yet, and these were their very first visitors in this land that was so barren. She did not expect this assignment to always fall to Eliab, but she understood why he took the task. Leaning against the wall where the food was prepared, she watched the expressions on their faces. Eliab so hopeful of making a good impression, Saul still measuring this new member of their family. Gershom just looked tired, and a bit bored, typical now that he was assured she was well.

"Your feet must be gritty. Please, rest and relax. You must be thirsty. I noticed your waterskins looked empty. We have water, and even wine, if you wish." Eliab continued with his washing.

The food she had been preparing still sat about on the cabinet top, including the meat from the sheep butchered just this morning, one leg ready to be hung over the fire. Dough sat in a bowl, puffier than when she left, and beginning to send a yeasty fragrance into the room. It would be ready to bake soon. She had one fresh round loaf already baked today. What a good thing that she had planned an extra baking.

With two more men to feed and the typical feast for guests to share, the bread might be gone.

Dear God, she prayed, *I have stayed here so long already. Please let me have my own tribe back.* But the prayer, said so often and by habit, brought with it the ugly tang of guilt. And regret.

Aksah forced herself to take a breath, even though it burned in her chest. She had to think and began pulling off the bits of twig from the figs, something to keep her busy while her mind whirled.

Her heart hurt, and she found her hand pressing against that pain before she realized it. Aksah forced her hand back down to her side and glanced around at the men, but no one seemed to have noticed her little movements. They were too busy becoming acquainted.

The promise to Jacob was of God. It had guided her throughout her life, short though that was. And here, just days before the month was over and the decision would be taken from her, came her father and the way home.

In her whole life, God had always outranked the thoughts and plans of man.

What would her father say if he knew of her idea to escape and follow them on the journey? Would he rejoice when he saw her? Or would he send her back to Eliab?

I knew it was a doomed request. I knew I could not return with her. And Eliab's reply: *you have given your response already. The bargain is struck.*

She had never known her father to break his word.

What had they been saying, while her mind was whirling? Aksah looked between the two men, sitting on the benches, leaning against the cushions she had made.

She picked up the leg of lamb and slipped out the door, heading toward the fire that burned night and day. A metal frame sat over it, with the spit that would hold the meat suspended across. Aksah worked the spike through the meat, and braced it across the frame. It would take some time to cook, and give her an excuse to slip away and pray unnoticed.

"Aksah." A deep voice came from behind. Whirling around, she looked up at Eliab. His forehead was wrinkled, his brows drawn together. He ran a hand over his curly hair, then looked at that hand as if he did not know what it was. When he met her gaze, the skin around his eyes seemed tight. "My apologies, I did not mean to frighten you. I see you have the meat ready to cook. I thought to offer help."

She stepped back, then wished she had not when his shoulders slumped. "I thought it best that I get the food cooking as soon as possible."

A faint smile curled his lips. What a pity that his beard hid so much of his mouth. Eliab held out his hand. "Shall we go and make your father and brother feel welcome?"

Aksah took his hand, and held tight. Would this be the last time? How she wished for an obvious answer!

"Your capture has been good for Dinah," Saul said around a fig. He swallowed, smiled at Aksah, and went on, "I nearly despaired of ever teaching her to think, to slow down. All my efforts prior to this had been to no avail. Now, however, she has become much more of a helper to her mother, and I know that is for the good."

Aksah remembered sitting with her mother that last day together, talking about the girls. She also remembered her mother saying, "You always were my most sensible child."

Did Ba'ara still think the same? If only Aksah could look forward and see her mother's face when she came back! More of Ba'ara's words came. *If these last two hundred are to save the tribe, we must allow them to take who they can.*

We must allow.

No.

If only she knew what God—

A burst of laughter interrupted her thoughts. "And then she let the goat's kids into the house!" Her father took a breath, and whooped out, "She said they needed to keep warm! But it was too late by the time I got in, and the three kids were already eating the pillows on the bench!"

All three men laughed heartily. Eliab raised his hand while he fought for composure, reserving the next story for himself.

They would not miss her. "Father, Eliab, I need to get some greens for the meal. I have heard most of these stories, I need not stay and hear them again." She picked up the basket, and slipped out the door.

Eliab was a warrior, alert to every movement even though they slept with a distance between them. Whatever time she tried to slip out, he would hear her.

Unless she could make him sleep deep and long.

The wheat crop had been harvested since the day she first found the clump of wild lettuce. The grain stalks were down to stubble now, and landmarks seemed different without the waving wheat. She kept her eyes lowered, for she had to come back with more than the lettuce. The basket had better be brimming with greens.

If only she had not begun to like him!

Ah. There they were. A few of the green plants had been smashed and ruined, but the rest were still there. She knelt down and looked at them. How much did she need? She did not want to hurt him, to give him too much, just enough to let him sleep while she slipped away.

When the basket was full of greens, purslane and dock and sorrel, with a little wild lettuce on the bottom and her heart tight with guilt, Aksah headed back for the house.

CHAPTER 14

*"These words that I am commanding you today must be on your heart.
Tie them as a reminder on your hand, and they must be like a headband
on your forehead."*
Deuteronomy 6:6,8

Eliab pushed the plate away and leaned back against the chair. The sun was halfway down to the horizon from midday, but there were still several hours of light left. "Will you stay another night?"

Saul shook his head. "I wish I dared, but I have been away from my wife and daughters for several weeks now in my search. It is past time that I made my way home. I can see that Aksah is safe and well, and I am satisfied." He dipped his head toward Eliab. "When this war began, I did not expect to find a man of Benjamin I could respect. I have now. I am pleased to have you in my family."

The two men rose, and as if one, embraced the other. Gershom watched them but his attention seemed to be more on the remnant of that leg of lamb. He caught her eye, and she nodded. That was all it took for him to pick up the bone and begin gnawing.

"Might I have a moment with Aksah?" Her father's voice was respectful and his manner mild. A generous victor? Or humble loser? "Daughter?" Saul held out his hand just as he had done when she was little and he would walk her down the path along their farm. "We have much to say before I leave."

She would not tell him of her plans to follow him, to go back to the shelter of Judah. No, best to catch up with him when they were too far away to return her.

Do not think about those moments of laughter, do not think about working with Eliab to fix the house, do not think about how alone he would be.

They walked out the door and into the warm air. Saul tucked her hand into his elbow. "Out of all of us, you are having the hardest time. You are far from us, and I have seen, perhaps even more than you, just how empty Benjamin's territory is. It will be this way for years and years to come. Your sisters are suffering. Can you not find some way to ease their consciences? Assure them all is well and you are happy?"

Was she happy? Challenged, yes. Frustrated, yes. Maybe even intrigued, fascinated, engrossed. Doing the *right* thing was most important, bigger and greater than doing the *happy* thing, she had to remember that. "I do not blame them. Tell them that. I would have run out to spare any of the other women." That might possibly be true. Could she have seen another girl being chased and done nothing? Her throat was getting tighter and tighter, and her heart began to beat fast. She had to tell him, she had to open her soul, share her dream and the awful confusion of late with her father.

"Yes, that sounds like my daughter." His eyes warmed.

The words would not stay in, but she could not look at him when she started on their walk up the hill in front of their house. Toward home? But what was home now? "Father, if you refuse to take me with you, I will lose my deepest dream. You will rip that away from me." She never thought to tell him, or anyone, but if she was supposed to go back, if that was God's will for her, she had to explain, had to make him see. "I have never told you—"

Her father did not let her finish, but interrupted her. "I can guess, I believe. I understand you better than you think." He looked down and she looked up. The distance between their eyes was much less than it had been when she was a child making a walk like this. "I saw your eyes brighten with covetousness when I read of Judah's blessing. You want the claim on Shiloh, the commander's staff that comes through our tribe."

Aksah felt the air leave her lungs, and she gasped. "Covetousness? But that is a sin! Something that every woman in Judah should long for cannot be a sin!"

"Perhaps I used the wrong word." He still walked, their legs working harder as the land sloped upward. "Perhaps pride is the better word."

"No. That cannot be. I will *not* believe it." She had found a strength inside her in these last few weeks of captivity and struggle, a strength that let her stand up even to this man she had loved her whole life. "It was faith. *My* faith, Father. That is what kept me obedient. Something that powerful cannot be covetousness, nor pride." She wanted him—no, *needed* him, to agree.

He stopped near the top of the hill and turned her to face him. Aksah looked up, afraid to see condemnation in his eyes. She saw, not the condemnation she dreaded, thank goodness, but something firm and resolute. "There are two dreams before you now. The small possibility of being the mother of the promised Shiloh, the Messiah, or the certainty of rescuing the tribe of Benjamin. I am sorry that the first one is now out of reach. You cannot be in the line of the promise now. Let that dream go. You have a *reachable* dream here, that of being the foundation of a new, better, disciplined Benjamin."

His hands were strong on her shoulders as he leaned forward, holding her gaze with his will. "It is every girl's wish to be selected for marriage, to have the man come to her father, to give his credentials, and ask for her. To feel chosen for *herself*, by a man who has watched her or by a matchmaker who knows her worth, not because she was trying to protect others. I, too, wanted to join the procession to your new home with the rest of the village. I wanted the privilege of sitting with your mother and discussing the merits of the men who asked for you. You are my oldest daughter, I wanted to experience the first letting-go with you. Both of us lost dreams."

He pulled her close and held her, rocking from side to side as he had done with all the children when they were little and needed comfort. "I did not get to choose him either, but I do believe he has the makings of a good man. He is hurting right now, even as you are. Do not push him away. Let him heal and grow. It was a hard lesson for his tribe, one he will never recover from in his lifetime. It will take Benjamin's tribe many generations to get back their numbers. This is not our last time. We will see each other at the festival next year, and you can see your mother and sisters then, as well."

He let her go and Gershom was there, waiting his turn for goodbye. She hugged him tight.

Leave? Or stay? Judah? Or Benjamin?

She had to force herself to step back, only to find Eliab at her side. Her skin prickled at his nearness. She was not ready for him to be that close, not yet. Her father's words returned, echoing within. *He is hurting right now, even as you are.* That thought had touched her often, watching him in the house that had once held his family. The first few days of her captivity she could have—and had—lashed out at Eliab without concern, but now?

He had laughed with her, had harvested with her, had sheared the sheep alone for her spinning and weaving. He had been patient with her as she tried to make his house into a home.

He never once tried to violate the month available for captive brides to remain untouched that she had demanded.

Eliab insisted Saul and Gershom fill their skins before the long walk began. Aksah held them open as he poured in the fresh water from the well. Her hands shook too much to wrap the leather tie that kept it closed, and Eliab had to do it for her. His hands were quick and sure, the neck sealed off in but a moment.

Her father and brother slung their skins over their shoulders. There was just the last loaf to send with them, leaving nothing for Eliab later, but he dug into the crock of fresh fig cakes to give them more food for the journey. She scooped out some barley for chewing, as well as dried fruits for their travel pouches. How all the food made it into the sacks she did not know, because she still shook and trembled inside.

Her father and brother were leaving without her.

Those words from her father hurt. *Covetousness. You cannot be in the line. Let that dream go.*

The pain in her heart was getting worse, and it pounded against her lungs as if to smother her. Had her father been sent as a sign to bring her back to Judah? Was she meant to follow him back? Or was she seeing what she wanted to and was he not a sign at all?

The other question, the one that made her heart hurt, was Eliab. She already thought how lonely he would be. She did not want to cause anyone pain, not pain like *this*.

God, tell me what I am to do!

Aksah waved until they were only specks on a distant knoll, as they took the western route direct to Judah and avoided Michmash altogether. Her throat was sore, as if she was fighting sobs. Unless the confusion that roiled inside could do the same thing, make her feel like screaming and weeping when no sound emerged?

"Come inside. Let us get back to work. I think we both need the distraction." Eliab turned her around toward the house. "I enjoyed meeting your father and brother. I feel they are now my father and brother as well. I look forward to seeing them again next year at the festival, and getting to know your mother and sisters."

She hurried inside. He was right, the meal was not done, and she had to get more bread made. Vegetables still sat on the table where she had left them. Aksah picked up the knife but it shook in her hands and she had to set it back down.

Covetousness. The word was sharper to her spirit than the knife that cut her food. Covetousness was a sin, one of the Ten Commandments. But she did not covet something that belonged to someone else. She only wanted a blessing for herself. How could wanting favor from her God be a sin?

And one that she had to give up altogether? She was so confused!

Aksah's gaze was as scattered as her hands were shaky. She needed to move, to get out of this house that suddenly closed around her.

The basket of yesterday's remnants of greens still sat on the preparation table, withered now and spoiled. She knew the wild lettuce at the bottom—unused yesterday because her father and brother had chosen to stay another day and she could hardly make all of them sleep—would no longer be good either.

The answer, at least to her immediate urgency, a way to get out of these four walls before she smothered.

She grabbed the basket and hurried for the door. She would dump out the spoiled food where no one would notice it, and hope the new batch of wild lettuce she was about to pick would still be potent for the evening meal. Eliab would never notice it in his stew.

When she returned to the house, however, she discovered that the relief of being outside was short-lived. Her mind fell back into the hurt left by her father's words.

Was not the promised Shiloh the blessing that all women of Judah were to work for? It had guided her life until now, how hard she listened at the festival, how she tried to remember what she learned. How she tried to answer all the questions her father had asked to see how well they absorbed the priests' instruction.

She remembered the conversation with Dinah and Deborah, safe with the family, their own dreams intact. *What if one of them got to be the mother of the Shiloh, and she did not because she was captured by Benjamin?* Would that be the worst kind of coveting, to be jealous of her own sister?

At last the tears started building, and she began to shudder under her attempt to hold them in. When Eliab's hands came down on her shoulders, Aksah's control snapped. In a harsh, keening cry, the floodgates of tears burst open. Her legs gave out, and she fell to the floor.

Eliab crouched next to her. He did not touch her now, this weeping had been a long time coming and would not stop.

"I did not capture you to hurt you," he said, and his voice sounded as gruff as hers. "You still have a family to see at the annual festival."

. . .

Eliab's arms ached from the control he exerted not to pull her into them. This was far beyond being taken from her family. "Aksah? I promise I will be a good husband. Please tell me what is wrong. If it is within my power, I will fix it for you. You will see your family again. You heard me promise your father that I would take you every year to Shiloh. They will be there, you will have the entire festival period to visit, and show them our children."

Her wailing only increased. What had he said wrong? With a sick feeling in his heart, he asked, "Did you not want children?" The answer came, ugly and unwelcome. "Or is it just children of Benjamin you did not want?"

He found himself on his feet.

"You have taken my dream," she wept, "and my family was supposed to return it to me. I thought they would, I have prayed that they would come and bring me home."

"What is this dream? Tell me, so I can help you." He sat down next to her, but she slid away. "Tell me, and I will do my best to give you a new dream, one you will love as much."

"You cannot!" Her sobs grew deeper.

Perhaps this, more than anything, made him realize what the war had cost her. His need, his tribe's need, had deprived her of something so dear that she wept as if it would never stop. "How do you know that I cannot fix this? Tell me."

"I wanted to be the mother of the Shiloh!" The words struck out like daggers. "It was all I dreamed of since I learned that he would come from my tribe. That I would be so faithful that I could be chosen." She dashed a hand over her cheek.

Eliab sat back, and stared at her. Mother of Shiloh. How did he possibly compete with that? "But we do not even know when he is coming, or even what he will do."

She whirled on him. "That is not the point! The point is that I would be faithful, and I would know that I had done nothing that would make God reject me! That is what I wanted, more than anything. To know that my faith had been sufficient. I did not know that I *would* be chosen, only that I *could have* been."

He stood up and walked around the room, trying to come up with the right way to say what needed to be said. His path circled to her again. Eliab stood close and stretched his hand out for her, but pulled it away. She did not want sympathy, she wanted her dream. He knelt back down, knowing he put himself within reach of a swing, should she want to. Perhaps he even deserved it. "The chance for any woman of Judah of being the mother of Shiloh is small."

That brought her around to him, her poor face blotched with weeping. Aksah opened her mouth, ready to throw words at him, but he took yet another chance and covered it with his hand. "Listen to me. I cannot say that you would have had that privilege, but since our nation does not even know when that one is coming, *neither can you*. There is a prize you *can* have, a sure thing instead of a dream. You *can* be one of the foundations of a new Benjamin. This is a sure promise, a purpose that will help the entire tribe, no, the entire nation. Perhaps this is the dream you were to have instead."

"But that is not the dream I wanted!" Her swollen, wet eyes were empty. "That takes no faith."

"Does it not? There are only six hundred men. With the women added to the count, our whole tribe is down to one thousand two hundred. Before the war our army alone was twenty-six thousand men. Just think what it will take to rebuild the tribe."

"It will take many children," she said, her voice flat. "Women have children all the time. That requires no special effort."

Perhaps, Eliab thought, if he were a better man he would be sad that she was the bride he captured. Instead, he was fiercely glad that of all the women at Shiloh that day, he had caught her. Benjamin had a long way to go, he realized that, to regain any kind of respect in the nation. It would take women like her to keep the men from making a mistake such as the one that had cost them nearly everything.

She would be that kind of woman. She had the principles that would keep him on track. He had the practicality and strength that would prevent her from losing her new goal in life.

Both of them were hurting. Dead family against an unlikely dream? Dreams were for children, not for grown adults who had to live with life as it was.

His dream was practical, children to help build his tribe. He could see why she desired her own dream instead. It was a way to become respected, praised. She might think she only wanted it for the glory of God, only to prove her faith, but no one wanted it just for that! No, she was probably unaware herself of less satisfying, less noble, reasons.

It certainly explained how hard she fought to hold back their marriage. There would be little fame in being the mother of a child of Benjamin.

That stung.

He would have to watch her closely. She was not ready to give up. Re-establish the tribe of Benjamin? How could that compete with the dream of all Judah?

Sitting on the floor, her shoulders slumped, Aksah's anguish had turned her face to grey. They were within days of when he would be released from his promise not to make her his wife in truth.

His touch at this moment might break her spirit. Soon he would begin again getting her used being touched, caressed, but not now. She did not want anything from him that might remind her that she had lost her chance for freedom.

She had clung to her father so tightly before he left! Eliab did not know how long it would be before she saw them again. The yearly celebration at Shiloh, symbol of all she had wanted and lost, would be most likely her next opportunity. Unless she was pregnant at festival time, in which case he would have to make certain she was kept safe. No travels for her then.

If he could get close enough to give her a child! Something to provide her life the purpose she felt it lacked.

CHAPTER 15

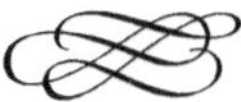

To this [Rebekah's] brother and her mother said: "Let the young woman
stay with us at least ten days. Then she can go."
Genesis 24:55

The animals were quiet as the sun began to lower and Aksah finished the evening meal. The big spoon went around and around as she stirred the soup over the fire, but she did not see it. The spoon banged against the side of the pot, and she pulled herself back. The scent of baking bread drifted by, unleavened as there had been no time for another batch to rise. She stared down at the pot as another series of bubbles broke the surface.

For the sake of the deepest need inside her, the need no one else could feel, she had to try to get home. No one understood that it was not the guarantee to her, but the struggle. Not the prize—so much—but the purpose.

The spoon went around again, bringing up bits of meat and leeks, and the barley that thickened it. Aksah looked down at the slow bubbles in the boiling stew.

There was still time to change her mind. She did not *have* to go through with her plan. She could stay and finish their mattress, become a true wife for Eliab and begin their life.

She brushed at the wetness on her face. Tears kept leaking out. Eliab had seen what she could do. Cook, clean, weave, sew, feed animals, she had even offered to help him shear sheep. The work had been good for her over these past many days, keeping her mind busy. She was not meant for laziness.

The soup was ready, the meat fall-apart tender, the barley thick and full. With the heavy cloth, Aksah took the pot from the small cooking fire stand, carried it into the house, and placed it on the table. The wild lettuce sat in Eliab's bowl, drying as it lingered.

If she poured the soup over those bits, and sprinkled some across the top as a garnish, there would be no turning back. Something made her reach out to snatch the lettuce from his bowl.

"Your bread is burning, I think." Eliab called from outside, his voice rumbling through the windows, and she whirled before her hand closed on the greens.

Her bread! While her thoughts had been traveling through the past and into the future, her bread had continued to cook. Aksah grabbed a cloth to wrap the bread in and protect her hands, then dashed out the door. She was very good at this, she thought as she pried the heavy domed clay oven off. The loaves of flat bread on the hot stone inside were dark golden and crusty, but not as burned as the smell made them seem. It would be easy to wrap one in a cloth and tuck in her sack.

Her father and brother were good walkers. They might have gone quite far already.

She carried the stacked hot bread inside, and stopped, to stare in dismay at Eliab as he poured the soup over his bowl. Aksah glanced over at the cabinet shelf, but no green plants sat there. The lettuce was at the bottom of his bowl.

It was too late now to change things.

Despite her best efforts, she must have given something away because Eliab kept looking up at her, his gaze sharp. She had to pretend to eat as she watched him swallow the pieces of lettuce in his stew, while all she thought every time she looked at him across the table was, *go to bed. Go to sleep.* And of course, *will it work?*

Underlying those emotions, her heart pounded *I am sorry, I am so sorry. Please forgive me.*

Eliab made no attempts to hurry. He had sheep to settle for the night, the coals that heated the bread oven had to be banked to keep any lingering sparks from igniting. Water was carried in for washing the dishes, her chore that she had to do with proper unconcern. All that water carted in, none of which she dared use yet to fill the skin she would take. She scrubbed everything, including the table. She could not leave him with a dirty table. And then there were the two bowls to dry, their two cups to put away.

Two of everything.

Why was she leaving? Her lifelong dream suddenly seemed distant and vague. Was she just afraid of a new life?

CHAPTER 16

When I established my limit for it
And put its bars and doors in place,
Job 38:10

Soft snores came from the other side of the room. Tonight that distance gave her one advantage, and one terrible complication. She had to run, quiet and fast. Thank goodness there were two men to follow. Two would leave tracks where one walker's footprints alone might be missed.

The cooking fire's coals still smoldered outside, she smelled the smoke as it drifted through the lattices, but Eliab made certain it was carefully banked.

How were the other women managing? Were they happy with their Benjaminite husbands? Or were some running, even as she would soon be?

She could not think of that, Aksah thought as she eased herself onto her feet. The blanket had to come with, she had nothing else to keep her warm. As she rolled it into a bundle, she kept watching Eliab, but his breathing never changed.

One step, another, each foot placed with the greatest care and precision. With equal stealth, Aksah unhooked the smaller waterskin from its pegs. A pang of guilt lanced through her, but she shoved it aside. Bread, a few chunks of dried meat, and a handful of early figs went into one of the sacks they had used to carry the fruit harvest. The blanket formed a wall of protection around the edge to keep the flat loaves as intact as possible. She had no desire to pick crumbs out of the sack's bottom.

The food sack went over one shoulder, the waterskin tie's loop over the other. Her sandals were just inside the door. She picked them up, shoving back the waterskin that had slid off her shoulder and down her arm.

Who knew what noise might seep through Eliab's drugged sleep?

One door to slip past. She took extra care lifting the lever that held it shut. That wooden bar had to be lowered back into place from the outside so the door was secure after she left. How would she feel if news came that some hunter among the animals, a lion or a bear, had nudged it open and attacked Eliab when he was too groggy to defend himself?

The door eased open, and Aksah poked the strap that raised and lowered the bar to the outside through the small hole. When she pulled the door back into place, she had to ease that bar into the bracket that kept the door shut, and the leather cord would give her that control.

As long as the bar did not fall into its braces with a *thump.*

Setting her parcels onto the ground, Aksah pulled the wooden handle of the door slowly. The bar whispered against its braces. Aksah pulled the strap and felt the bar raising bit by bit inside. As it cleared those supports the door shifted. One hand on the leather, one on the handle, she eased the door on its pivots until it sighed into place, then let the strap slip through her fingers as the weight of that wooden bar took it down.

The remaining leather strap dangled from her fingers. She could pull it again and raise the bar back up out of the lock, could still push the door back open. She did not have to go, could still stay. It was not too late.

Heaviness weighted her heart, a load that threatened to drop her to the ground.

Forward? Or back?

Breathing around that weight, Aksah pushed the cord until it disappeared inside, slow careful pokes that shoved it into the house where it belonged. Where Eliab would be safe. No one, nothing would get in.

And she had locked herself out. No turning back now.

She slipped her sandals on and eased across the open yard with as much care as she had taken to slip out of the house. This was the first time she had ever done such a thing, and she did not know how effective the lettuce would be. Normally, Eliab's ears were sharp.

No shouts came from inside the house. Now she needed to fill the skin, and worked the leather ties free. Next to let down the bucket, draw it up full and submerge the waterskin into the water, over and over, until most of the air was out and the bucket was nearly empty. Then she sealed the skin back up. One task done.

Her last task was making a torch to see and for protection. All of the torches she was familiar with had the oil-soaked burn source, wool or cloth, even tightly woven straw, slipped into a notch in a pole and wrapped tightly to keep the source firm and slow the burning. Bundles of sheep's wool rich with their oil sat in the shed by the pen. Making a split pole was impossible with the noise of an axe on wood, but there was rope and wool, and sticks aplenty. Aksah dug through the wool, trying to find the biggest clumps heavy with wool fat.

Eliab had been drying leather straps for making a belt. Leather would work well to tie her torch pieces together. Her hands were soft and slippery with the grease when she had enough wrapped tightly against the pole. Hopefully, between the oily wool and the tight bundle she had packed together, the torch would burn for a while. Aksah packed as much more wool into the sack as she could manage.

The cooking fire's coals were dimmer than she expected. It took more time than she had to spare before the glowing coals finally got the wool burning.

Leaning against the side of the shed, a long shepherd's staff seemed to stand at attention, fairly begging her to take it. Aksah remembered practicing with a staff while Eliab slept on the way here. She also remembered him waking and laughing at her efforts.

Those few nights on the trail were all the practice she had managed. She dashed over and grabbed it. The waterskin went over one shoulder, the sack with the wool, bread and the blanket over the other. Now for the torch and pole. A few last adjustments, then with one last glance toward the house, Aksah started running in the direction her father and Gershom had gone.

Wind whistled through her hair, and the torch guttered. Aksah slowed instantly. It would do her no good if the fire blew out, and she was nearing the end of where she had seen the two disappear over the last hill. From here on in, she would need their trail in the dirt. The night was quiet and the moon bright. She prayed it would stay that way.

In the torch's pale light, the tracks showed as murky shadows where the dry top layer of soil had been kicked aside, leaving the more moist dirt showing as a blackish scar in the ground. Without the flickering light to add to the moon's glow, she never would have been able to see even that much. She hated that her torch might burn out during the darkest hours, but what else could she do? Perhaps she would find her father before then.

But she did not think so. Too many hours had passed. Aksah shivered as she slid down the first slope, the dew making her footing unsteady. She had to stop and readjust the waterskin and the other sack after they threatened to throw her more off balance.

The tracks faded into the gully's darkness, and she had to hold the torch close to the scuffed and marked ground to see if they were still there. Ah, yes. Walking bent low, she held the two sacks in place with one hand as she clutched the torch with the other, and followed the scuffed soil back up toward the next hilltop and back into the moonlight.

Faint on the breeze, a lion called and Aksah stopped in place. The lion's call came again, only it sounded closer now. Still far, but the beast was on the prowl. Aksah picked up her pace. Somewhere along here there must be hulks of burned houses. There had to be! They would give shelter if she needed it. The scent of smoke, or man, might yet be enough to keep it away.

The dirt stuck to the moisture and collected between her soles and the sandals, rubbing her feet like a rough cloth.

Aksah started up that small incline and hoped that this time when she reached the top she would see a campfire's glow in the distance. It was a fool's hope, but it made the climb easier, the weight of the sacks lighter for those few hard steps.

CHAPTER 17

Will a lion roar in the forest when it has no prey? Will a young lion growl
from its lair when it has caught nothing?
Amos 3:4

Eliab woke with a strange, pounding headache. He made himself ignore it and opened his eyes. The room was blurry, and light sparked around the edges of his vision. The headache came back, and he closed his eyes again, hoping the odd colors would have faded when he tried again.

He took a deep breath, the sound too loud in his ears, and opened them again. The room was still dark, but daylight could not be far away. As he did every morning, he turned to see his wife.

Her pallet was empty. A chill ran over him, and the hair stood up on his arms. She had never been up this early.

Things had not been normal between them after her family left. His hands clenched on the blanket. Sitting up, he sniffed the air, seeking the scent of cooking and fire. Eliab heard only silence, and smelled nothing but faint traces of last night's baking.

No, something *did* tease him, some whisper of a new scent he could not place. It smelled a bit like scorched fabric.

Or burning wool! That was it, a smell he should never have forgotten after the fires of the war, the torched cities, burned houses, and all who lived in them. He should have, *would have*, recognized it at once, but for the nuisance of the pain in his head. Had his wife burned herself while stoking the fire?

He rolled to his feet, his body moving slower than his thoughts, and almost went down on one knee. Catching himself on the table, Eliab struggled to find his balance and staggered for the door, flipped the bar and jerked it open. The cool air slapped at him, clearing away some of the odd sensations that hounded him. Eliab braced himself against the door's frame and scrubbed at his face.

What was wrong with him? Was he becoming ill? He stumbled toward the well, and plunged his hands into the near-empty bucket, then splashed the water on his face. Between the cold air and the colder water, he felt the world begin to right itself. There was still no sight or sound of his wife. He looked around the area.

Aksah was nowhere to be seen, but the traces of burning wool on the air were stronger here. He looked toward the pen, but the sheep showed no signs of distress, or even concern.

His staff was missing from the side of the shed.

Suspicion prodded him. What a fool he was not to have prepared for this! His sleeping so soundly, the headache—his scheming wife had drugged him!

How far ahead was she?

He needed to think. How long had he been asleep? The last he remembered, it had been heading toward dark. Now it would soon be morning. Foolish woman! Did she still not know the dangers of the night?

Eliab ran back to the house and began preparations. Sandals, robe, cloak, his large waterskin. His weapons belt. The small skin was missing, so at least she had water. The smell of burning wool made sense now. A torch.

Despite his annoyance, he felt a prickle of pride at her. She had planned for only the things she was able to carry. That still left her unarmed. Just the staff, in her hands more of a detriment than an advantage. A staff against the creatures of the night.

Eliab strapped on his belt, and straightened his sword. Each loop still full except for the axe. The axe was outside by the sheepfold. He rolled the cloak into a tight bundle and tied it around his waist. His bow went over one shoulder, and the quiver over the other, ready to grab an arrow. He had almost reached the door when he remembered the waterskin, and hurried back for it.

Eliab ran out to the shed by the sheepfold and grabbed his axe from the wooden stump where he kept it, pulling it free in one movement, and slid it into its loop on his belt with a skill that came back easily.

Fretting at the time it took, he poured water down the narrow neck of the skin, and tied it off. He would need a torch, at least for the first part of the run before the sun took over, and that took more time.

His hands kept wanting to shake.

He looked down at the dirt before he realized that she would follow her father's route. That would save him some time. Clutching the torch, Eliab started down the trail, certain he was on the right path from the roughed dirt at his feet.

Grateful for the moon's light to speed his way, he picked up his pace. No torch bobbed up ahead. Clouds moved in, faint tracings of grey across the blackness overhead. They would bring no rain, but they hid the moon from time to time and forced him to slow. He dared not lose the trail, and was grateful for the marks three pairs of feet left on the dusty ground.

Eliab did not let himself think how much time had passed. The moon, when it shone bright, combined with the light of his torch and still showed the footprints that led him.

The sky began to brighten, the first signs of sunrise. It would help, he would be able to run along the marks, but how far ahead was his wife? The same light that sped his way would do the same for her.

A roar rumbled through the ground. In these hills where the sound could bounce and hide, it was impossible to tell how far away an animal was. Four legs moved much faster than his two, and those animals had the advantage of smell.

He picked up his speed, skimming the ground for the faint marks, the darkness in the lighter soil.

The sun topped the horizon, and color seeped into the landscape, painting the trees with greens, and turning the pale soil into a light brown. Eliab stopped and bent to get a better look at the tracks. Three people? Or two? Had she gone off the trail, was she following something else now?

No. Three pairs of feet still marked the path, but it was impossible to tell how much time separated them.

He took one step to every two of hers. He should have found her already. She must have slipped out shortly after he went to sleep! His jaw clenched.

Growling rumbled along the ground again, raising the hairs on his arms. *Aksah, where are you?*

With his hard-learned warrior's stride he loped along in the rising sun, never losing sight of the scuffs on the ground, praying as he ran that some of those prints were hers.

Eliab skidded to a halt, and stared down at the dirt. The three sets of tracks were now two, and both much too large for his wife. He had lost her trail! How long had he been running the wrong direction?

Eyes fixed on the marks, Eliab began walking back the way he came, following his own steps in the dust and scraped pebbles. Later in the summer, the ground might have been too hard to show the marks, but now the footsteps were clear.

Marking time with the rising of the sun, Eliab walked back along the tracks that had led him this far. His heart screamed to move fast, to run, but he knew he dared not. Small drying plants woke as the day dawned, and leaves lifted. A clump of green to the side caught his eye. Broken leaves and smashed blossoms went off to the right. He had not even noticed them on the initial run, his gaze so fixed on the soil ahead, but now he realized they blocked the trail. Enough so someone inexperienced might lose the path?

Scuff marks led away, scrapings on the ground made by some hooved animal. One of the bulls he had been trying to catch, no doubt.

A bull gone wild could kill as easily as the lion whose roars had frozen his heart.

Bull tracks were one thing, a marker of movement, but he would not leave the main path until he was certain Aksah's prints were here as well. Staying low and keeping the original trail in sight, Eliab followed the broken leaves and scrapes on the ground until a print showed. Small, just her size. Then a second and a third, and he began to pick up his speed.

Another growl rolled through the air, and he wished he dared run, race to find her, but he had lost her marks once, he would not do it again.

Her prints kept going. It took all his training to keep walking. Faint whiffs of smoke teased his nose. Her torch? Would she know the fire would hold animals away?

A memory, tantalizing amid all the emptiness of his land, whispered in the back of his mind. A town had been nearby, where a carpenter and a baker had lived, along with a weaver of large textiles, and a blacksmith. He had seldom needed to visit, his family's farm had provided for most of their needs, so the road there was not well-known and the months of abandonment had erased most of the markings.

Hope lifted his heart a little, just enough for a pain-free breath. Eliab did not know how hard breathing had been until then. In a town, however destroyed, there would be places to hide, and some shelter.

Her prints were deeper now, the stride further apart, like a woman running, and Eliab released the chain on his restraint and picked up his own speed.

Aksah crouched low, her back to the bits of standing stones, and shivered behind the wall that remained. She was so grateful for even this much cover. What a fool she had been! No weapons, the torch long burned out and useless by her side.

Her thoughts went back to Eliab. Was he awake? Did he know she had fled? Did he care? Would he even want to find her now? Or had her stubborn insistence—and resistance—driven him away for good? Dinah, for all her young silliness, would have had the sense to stay with a husband. Would have done a much better job of accepting her new life course.

Would probably never have even considered herself worthy of being the mother of the Shiloh.

As Aksah had walked along, trying to keep her eyes on the trail her father and brother left, there had been too much time to think. No distractions of cooking and cleaning to keep her busy. Alone in the dark, it was just herself and her thoughts.

And they had not been comfortable ones.

She had been so determined to remain in Judah that she had not seen the many ways her God had been telling her 'No.' All she could see then was the distant chance, her overwhelming hope, her prideful desire.

Her father had told her that it was pride, but had even his words stopped her? No. Not only had she fled, she had poisoned Eliab to ensure she could get away clean.

God was not so easy to manipulate. She knew that, had known that all along. Yet that was what her actions said, that she could bend God to her will instead of bowing to his.

She had come to that conclusion just before the first growl echoed along the hills.

And now here she was, hiding in a burned out shell of a house with nothing usable to defend herself, hoping the lion would not smell her scent over the remnant of smoke that clung to the town and find her.

Eliab, I am so sorry. Eliab, please forgive me and find me. And an even greater prayer though not as likely to be answered because of her stubbornness, *God, forgive me and rescue me.*

Her father would be so disappointed in her. He had been right, that God had given her a new chance, a real and reachable goal. Eliab had said the same thing and he, too, had been right. Her blindness and the damage she had done to her marriage, to Eliab, slashed at her. This hurt might last a while, she thought, and shoved a hand against her mouth to hold in the sob.

Would she ever live long enough to become the wife he had wanted, needed? To be the mother to his children, the foundation of a new Benjamin?

What a fool she was!

Aksah turned her head just enough to peek through a gap in the charred wood around her. The lion had lingered at the village edge, but his roars announced how determined he was to cross the barrier of smoke and come into man's realm. At first she did not see the tawny shape, but no—there he was. Only instead of standing, mane puffed to intimidate the victim and ready to release another howl, he was low and still, his eyes fixed on something, his tail twitching at the end.

A movement at the edge of her vision, along the direct line of the lion's sight, drew her gaze as it had drawn his. She shifted just a little, just enough—and clenched her jaw tight to catch her scream.

In the golden light of earning morning, Eliab knelt behind a broken wall, his gaze as fixed on the lion as its was on him, and fitted an arrow into the bow. No wasted movement, but no unnecessary haste. The bow came up and the string stretched—and Aksah could not breathe. Her throat was so tight air was pinned inside. Her hand groped for the spent torch, found it, clenched.

The bowstring released with a twang, but before she turned her gaze back to the target, Aksah knew her husband had been one second too late. The lion sprang nearly straight up, and the arrow zipped right beneath it, missing it by the width of a mane's hair. It stuck in the brittle wood beneath and behind the lion's leap and shivered there.

She could not watch, she did not want to see Eliab suffer for her stupidity. Before she knew what she was doing, Aksah leapt to her own feet, waving her arms, anything to distract the animal. The tightness in her throat gave way to the sound that burst out of her mouth. *"Yaagh!"*

"Aksah, no!" Eliab's own shout drowned out hers. He swung an axe she had not even seen as the lion came over the top, but low, tight to the barrier, and Aksah saw red open on Eliab's right shoulder. Time seemed to slow. Eliab gripped the axe harder and still crouching, swiveled on his feet to face the animal as it slid to a stop, apparently surprised to find empty air. It turned, ominous, growling, fangs showing on a wide open mouth as a snarl tore through the air.

Eliab motioned with his hand, *down, hide,* but said nothing. She thought she saw red run down Eliab's right arm as he faced the beast. Her head turned without any will on her part toward that snarling mouth.

The lion's mane was marred with red, too. Eliab's blood? Or his own? Had Eliab's swing managed to connect?

Words ran through her head, whether a prayer or not she could not say, *please make it go, make it go, make it go.* What was wrong with her? She was still standing, her arms spread wide!

From the dirt on the opposite side of the broken wall, a curl of smoke rose. She did not know what it was from, had not seen a fire, but another puff swirled over the top of the wall, curling up from somewhere near Eliab. The beast yelped, and backed away, releasing another roar that made Aksah's ears ring, but instead of charging, it turned and ran through the blackened and broken town before disappearing into the trees that dotted the tawny hills.

She hurried on shaking legs around the chunks of wall to Eliab, dropping to her knees in the dirt at his side. "You are hurt! How badly? Let me see." Her hands shook as she peeled his robe, soggy with blood, away from the wound.

The skin was split clear across from his neck to the top part of his right arm. Aksah gritted her teeth against the gasp that fought to burst loose. "Where is the village well? Do you know this town? Where would it be?"

He tried to rise, and she pushed his chest, a firm hold. *"Stay here."* To her relief, he leaned back against the rock. His other hand came up and fingered the gash with a hesitant touch, then he held blood-stained fingers in front of his face and stared.

That left hand was more solid than hers had been. Did he not feel the pain?

"How bad is it?" Her very question, only from his mouth this time. He looked up at her, his eyes still clear, but she knew that would not last.

"Bad enough." He moved as if to touch that mutilated skin again. Aksah caught his hand, and dabbed the blood off his fingers and palm with her robe. "Eliab." He was stubborn, though, and turned his head away, trying to see what the lion had done with his own eyes. Aksah needed his knowledge, she had to get his attention off the wound. *"Eliab!* Where is the village well?"

"You are not going to wander about to find it, do you hear me?" For an injured man, his voice was strong enough to make his point. "Aksah? Did you hear me? No wandering about." He took a breath, and she thought she heard it shake as he let it out before speaking again. "That lion could well be waiting for a new opportunity. Check about the nearby houses." Another shivering breath. "Rain might have filled what containers remain intact, if there are any left. Stay close enough that I can see you."

She had heard tales of the cleverness of lions, but Eliab's reminder sent an unwanted shiver over her despite the day's warmth. "I will."

"Give me my bow, and the arrows. And take the staff. It is still burning, and will give some protection." He pointed, and this time his hand shook. Not much, but Aksah had him fixed firmly in her gaze. The pain had begun, she knew, reaching past the first moments of protective shock, the startled wondering, *did this happen to me?*

He wanted the weapons. Whether he could use them or not. She picked them up from where they had been knocked away by the attack and set them close.

Pointing down what was left of the street, half-houses, scorched bricks fallen outside the broken walls, upper stories missing, and the wooden roofs nowhere to be seen, she leaned down to make certain he heard her through the pain. "I will start on this side. Call if you see anything." Then she went for the staff smoldering in the dirt.

Her shaking fingers could hardly close on the pole. At last she managed to grip it. Her own body was reacting now, just like Eliab's.

If the lion came back, would her husband be able to fight it off a second time? Aksah turned and ran across the space to the first house, the staff trailing smoke behind her.

At the doorway she paused for a brief moment, afraid of the noxious smell of death that had clung to their neighbor's house and the bodies Eliab had buried. But all that remained was the ash coating the opening, the wooden door shattered and black. With cautious steps, Aksah walked over it to get inside. Charred wood cracked beneath her feet, and snapped, throwing her off balance. Flinging out an arm, she caught herself against a broken wall, and more grey dust puffed out, landing on her hand, her stained robe, her legs.

Food crocks lay on the floor, smashed, whatever food they had once held now charred clumps. Large jars, the kind for water, were broken and only more black powder remained. He was correct, rain had found its way through the opening where the roof had once been. Any water—or wine—must have burned away with the first flames. What once had been a family's home was completely destroyed. She glanced over the house's fragmented wall. Eliab still leaned against the stone barrier that had saved his life. Somehow he had gotten himself into a half crouch, his eyes moving left to right as if he would be able to spring up if danger appeared.

She hurried out of the first house with less care than she had entered, ignoring the scrapes of cracked wood against her ankles, and moved to the next. It was much the same, as was the house beyond that. She still saw Eliab over the remnants of the walls, the bricks that had tumbled outward.

This house was in better shape than the previous three. Apparently the fire had run out of energy before it got here. The walls were higher, blocking her view of him. Although she had promised to stay within sight, this might be their best chance for water, perhaps even oil to bind his wounds. Aksah fought down the urgency that pounded at her, snapping at her to *hurry, hurry, hurry.* She could not afford to miss anything.

While the walls were intact, the fire and the soldiers had left their mark. Grey covered everything. The shelves in the eating room, much like her own house, were still intact, and some dishes on the bottom of the pile remained in one piece, although those on the top had shattered. Dampness lingered in the broken bowls, just a slickness on the fingers, but not water. Handles had broken off the mugs, but a pitcher, although on its side on the floor beneath the shelf, seemed to be intact.

She picked it up with care, in case this handle dropped off as well, relieved to notice that both handle and pitcher felt solid, and a small bit of water sloshed in the bottom. Taking a better look at the shelves, Aksah found a few unbroken mugs. Handle-less though they were, they still held remnants of the rain that had poured through the gaping roof.

It was enough, poured together, to rinse the pitcher.

As she lifted her head from watching the water splatter its last onto the floor, a small corked jar in the corner of the wall caught her eye. It looked intact, and although singed, the cork was still in good condition. She set the pitcher on the shelf and walked over to that jar. The lid stuck, but as she worked it loose, the sweet scent of honey drifted out.

Honey! The perfect healer. If she could just find more water, with it, some rags and honey, she could wash and bind Eliab's wounds, and perhaps prevent infection.

This house might even have cloth for rags. Setting the honey pot down as carefully as she had the pitcher, Aksah braced herself and walked deeper inside. The back of the building was surprisingly intact. She should move Eliab someplace more protected, so he could become better healed before they went back home.

And she would go back with him. She was a Benjaminite, no longer of Judah. Eliab had faced her father and brother with courtesy and humility. Had fed her, had come after her, had faced a lion for her, had taken its claws for her.

And now suffered for her.

Remember Eliab, his wound, his pain, and the lion that might still be nearby. He needs you, needs your knowledge, your hands, your head.

Think, she told herself.

A blanket lay on the bed, streaked with ash. They would need that, and she would have to wash it. Robes hung on pegs on the wall, and she grabbed those as well. They would work as covering for the night and bandages, maybe even fresh clothes for both of them.

She had everything now but water.

No matter the danger, she had to find the well.

A rumble shivered across her skin. The lion was coming back. Grabbing the treasures, Aksah hurried back to the main room and shoved the pitcher and the honey inside.

She could not carry the staff at the same time. With a lingering glance, Aksah marked where it stood, still smoking, and slipped out the door, then ran down the street.

Eliab was on his feet. His wounded right arm hung at his side, and she saw it rise, saw the exposed muscles flex as he worked it, preparing it for attack. How could he move it with those awful gashes?

Her foot hit something and she stumbled, glancing down by reflex. A small metal case bounced a few bounces, then stopped in a puff of grey powder from the fire-blackened ground. Her mind recognized it and she bent to grab it up before running again.

The roar was closer.

Eliab's left hand clenched on the axe, his wounded right closed on the short dagger in his weapons belt and slid it free. The lion would have to be so close, so terribly close, to use either. Unless he thought he could catch it in mid-air with a mighty throw, but Aksah did not believe he was capable of a throw that violent, not with the awful pain that must be wracking him.

The sword still dangled from his belt. The bow leaned against the stone wall at his back, the arrows hung in their quiver over his shoulder. He would never leave that weapon unused unless he knew he could not pull the string, never leave the sword unless he knew he could not swing it.

She knew how to shoot an arrow, but had never handled a bow the size of his. Eliab stood light on his feet, ready, while blood dripped from his shoulder.

Time was running out. Please let everything she needed be in that box! If she had been thinking, she would have looked for that while in the house, surely they had one there, but her God must be on her side, to have had a soldier drop just what she needed, and have her trip over it. Sliding to a stop, keeping her hand clenched on that precious box, Aksah dropped to her knees, and shoved the blanket and all its treasures behind her husband. Then she opened the lid. Yes! Flint and oily wool, what they needed for a fire. Plucking the honey and pitcher out of the blanket, she set the wool tinder on top of the ash-covered cloth and began chipping away with the small stones, hoping for a flicker. *Please, please, please, light,* she thought as she worked.

She had to slow down. Mistakes in haste would not help them.

"What have you done with the staff?" Eliab spoke over his shoulder as he remained in place, waiting with soldier's patience.

"I know where it is. There is no time right now." Her hands kept going, *snap, snap, snap,* bits of flint popping off as she fought to make a spark.

"I need the distance the staff will give me." Tension poured off him, through his voice, though she heard no movement, not even the shuffle of a foot. Despite his pain, he stood like a warrior.

Yes! Smoke curled from the tinder. Aksah leaned over and blew carefully, fighting the tightness of her lungs, locked from the urgency inside. The smoke sputtered, then lifted, as she blew again. And then yellow, deep inside the oily clump.

That would have to do. She looked up at Eliab's back. "Should I go get it? I know exactly where it is."

A roar came again, and Eliab shifted, cocked his head, following the sound. The howl came from a new direction, away from her path to the house. Aksah leapt to her feet and ran as if the beast was at her heels, skidding through the doorway of that house so fast she knocked the pole from its support. It slipped out of her fingers on the first grab, but the second time she caught it and ignored the ash that ground into her nails as she snagged it from the floor.

Then back out, running, holding the staff at her side. The far end dragged the ground every other step, but she did not let that slow her. The roar came again, too close, and she ran harder. Eliab suddenly swung to the side, looking toward the next street.

"Eliab!" She screamed and braced herself, letting the staff fly even though it headed straight for his wounded right arm. He saw her intent and shoved the dagger back into its loop. The heavy spike flew through the air, but her throw was not enough, the rod began to dip, the momentum slowing, as it neared him. He jumped a step, caught it and straightened, but she was close enough to see him wince. "The fire!" she yelled as she drew near, and pointed. The flames out of the oil source had reached the blanket and would begin to burn that away. Eliab glanced behind, flipped the pole over and held it near the dancing yellow.

Aksah slid to a stop and picked up the bow. "An arrow," she gasped, and he leaned just far enough for her to snatch one out.

A wide, shaggy head popped around the far corner of the house across the street from where she had been. Four houses. That was all the distance he had to come. She nocked the arrow.

"You take this." Eliab handed her the burning pole, and pulled the loaded bow from her hand.

Aksah heard him hiss as he pulled the bowstring back, back, back. She took her place at his side, and held the torch out, saw the yellow flare behind them. The blanket had caught. Flames were fluttering higher, stabbing into the air. With the staff in one hand, she backed and crouched, catching the untouched fabric. Pulling it through the dirt, she crossed in front of her husband, the blanket burning behind her, until the fire's flame and the remaining fuel of fabric ringed them.

Eliab gave her a smile. "Good."

She took her place again, and waved the stake back and forth, back and forth, using both hands to hold it slow and steady.

The lion came out from behind the broken house, the head followed by the body, then the tail. It never took its attention from them, slowly stalking down one house, two, as the fire moved with the same slowness along the blanket that surrounded them. Eliab was behind the flames now, and she had the pole. The staff's heavy wood could not burn fast, it would hold out a good time.

Where was her dead torch? There was not much left of the lashed wool, but two burning stakes would help. It had to be in her first hiding place, the broken house in which she hid when she first sighted Eliab.

Their lives depended on how long that blanket held out. And on Eliab's strength and skill.

The lion stopped with two houses to go before the open area in front of them. Aksah stopped breathing. Would it charge? *Dear God*, was all her mind said, and she only hoped it was enough for Him to understand her.

The beast let out a roar. Aksah's ears rang, she could not even hear the thunder of her heart.

And then the animal lifted its head, no doubt smelling the smoke, turned and disappeared between the two shattered homes. The air went quiet, but over the fire a hint of the lion's scent lingered, musky and angry, its frustration remaining behind in warning.

Eliab lowered the bow, and slid to the ground as if all his strength had seeped into the dirt, landing on the quiver. Aksah laid the staff onto the blanket, letting it burn, and turned, then dropped beside him. "Eliab?" she sobbed. "Eliab? Wake up, please! Say something! Talk to me!" She touched his cheek, his neck, his chest, gasping with relief when a thump patted against her palm.

He did not respond, but his chest lifted and fell, lifted and fell. A frown formed between his eyes, so he still felt the pain even though not awake.

Blood pooled off his wound and dripped into the soil. She pulled herself together. He needed the bleeding stopped before they could make the journey back home. That meager fire of wool and robes would have to do its job protecting him because she needed water, and more cloth for bandages, and another blanket for warmth.

She would have to hope the lion was gone, and work fast. She needed to carry a weapon now, his life depended on her remaining alive. The sword did not leave its scabbard easily, so she let it be and raced back to that broken wall where she had hidden with her blanket, the empty waterskin, the bits of bread. And the torch.

Fire. Her only weapon, but it had worked before.

The wood beneath the wool padding was blackened, none of her wool itself remained, she saw as she dashed back to Eliab, but there was plenty of the stick yet to burn and she intended to lay the stick on the fire.

When all the preparations she could think of were made, Aksah touched Eliab's chest, and let her palm linger there in hopes he would feel it. Picking up the burning torch in one hand, the pitcher in the other, she jumped over the flames, and ran back down the street.

CHAPTER 18

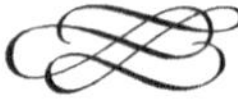

*O God, you are aware of my foolishness, and my guilt is not hidden
from you*
Psalms 69:5

Not much was left once a city had been burned and looted, Aksah learned as she searched again. This was the last house on the street. Every sound made her jump and grab up the sputtering torch, but the sounds were soft and small, mice and rats, maybe a badger or an owl flying through the open rafters.

She had done three trips, moving fast each time, and still no well. No water left in any of the large jars, those that had not shattered from the fire. Perhaps she was going too fast, she might be overlooking something, but she feared Eliab waking and injuring himself more.

His breathing sounded normal. She had bound the gaping wound as best she could with some of the cloth she had found, tying it tight, but it continued to show red, so the bleeding had not stopped.

There must be a well somewhere. Who ever heard of a city without a well? True, she had stayed on this same street, within sight of Eliab, which rather limited the possibilities of finding one.

It was time to venture farther, move out of sight of him.

She took a deep breath, and looked down the street, where he lay behind the dancing flames. She had brought some broken chair legs on one of the trips. Wood should hold the fire a while. Even if the lion came back, he would hesitate to go near.

A staff with its glowing tip against a lion. Eliab needed her help, and she would give it. Aksah stopped at the corner of that last house, and peeked around the edge. More broken, blackened houses, shattered pots, the detritus of war. She walked along the side walls until the next street, and looked down it.

At last. There, at the far end, was a waist-high ring of stones. It had to be a well, or at the very least, the opening to a cistern. No brace remained over it for the bucket and rope, but the possibility that the wooden pieces might have fallen away from her vision in the city's destruction moved her forward. The urge to toss aside caution and run for that stone circle pushed at her. Only knowing Eliab's life depended on her held her back. As she passed the gap between houses, Aksah paused for a look, watching for any tawny shadow, any movement, the glint of an eye before scurrying to the protection of the wall.

So far she was safe. House by house, she moved forward until she reached the span between the last one in the row and the well. She smelled the water from where she stood, a hint of fresh moistness. Two wagons could pass between the houses here, the ones she had crept down and those opposite. Plenty of room for wagons to pull up with their large jars waiting to be filled.

Unfortunately for her, once she reached the well, on both her left and right was a straight run, perfect for the lion to build up speed. No ready shelter, no walls to hide behind without racing back across that gap.

A deep breath for courage, and Aksah stepped out into the open, crossing toward the well with deliberate steps, steady movement, one foot after the other.

She was there. The brace had been indeed been shattered, she saw the wide logs laying in the dirt, but the bucket seemed intact, and best of all, the rope, although singed, had not burned through.

Now she could move fast. Pick up the bucket and the rope, check the knot that kept them linked, and drop over the stone edge. A splash, the water so close, the sound clear, then she let the pail sink. Up, into her pitcher wedged against the well, and down again. All the while, Aksah kept her gaze moving, listening for sounds that should not be there. The torch glowed, but no flames remained. Hopefully, if she needed to wave it, the embers would wake.

The bucket was full, she pulled it up and worked the wet knot loose. Two containers, brimming with water. Aksah propped her hands on her hips and looked down at her treasures. How to carry both vessels and the torch?

She turned back to the brace where it lay on the ground, and studied the cracks in the wood and the position of the crosspiece where the bucket had been tied. If she stood on one side support and used her back to push up the opposite piece, she might be able to break that middle section loose. The crosspiece then would fit over her shoulders like a yoke, and she could hang the pitcher and bucket on either end. She would have to keep it on a single shoulder, the two containers hanging front and behind. With one hand holding the yoke in place, the other hand would be free to grip the smoldering torch.

The singed wood came apart easily, and in a matter of moments, it was done. The bar balanced over one shoulder. She decided to keep the pail and the pitcher close to her body, front and behind, just to limit the chances of either sliding off.

Somehow despite the added weight, the return trip felt shorter, even though she took the same care crossing every open space. Perhaps because she now knew the path.

Eliab was awake, but barely. He only blinked when the two vessels landed at his side. When she worked the torch end into the dirt and crouched beside him, however, his eyes popped wide. He looked at her. "Where have you been? I thought I told you to stay here."

"I never heard those words." She held back her smile as she looked up at him while starting her first step, tearing one of the recovered robes into strips. "Perhaps you only thought them, because you never said them."

"Would you have obeyed if I had?" His voice was rough from pain, his face so pale it worried her. Sweat stained his robe. The scent of blood was now heavy and thick.

"Probably not." Aksah made herself breathe through her mouth to avoid the smell. The strips of robe were set aside, and she went to work at the knots on his bindings. The fabric was thick with blood, heavy and wet. When she peeled it off, it was impossible to tell if the bleeding had even begun to slow, because more blood rushed out. *You must not die,* she thought, but did not say the words aloud.

She could not think about that, could not take the time to worry other than the constant refrain in her head. *You must not die, you must not die.* Aksah started washing the long gash, one piece of cloth after another dipped into the water, trying to get out the bits of dirt and grasses the lion's paw had left behind.

More than that, though, she wanted the streaks of blood gone, wanted the wound to stop looking like it took up his entire shoulder and arm. Perhaps if it appeared smaller, her fear would subside.

People died from animal wounds. She would not let that happen to Eliab.

"The painful part is over now," she said. At the words, Aksah saw Eliab's body relax, the muscles release from their tight knots. Time for the honey. "This will help you heal. My mother always used it on my father and brothers, even Dinah, Deborah and myself when we got cut." She poured it, a thin golden line, all along the raw red gash. More clean strips from the robe with the least soot, tied together to make a bandage that could go around and around, cover everything and let it heal.

He caught her hand with his uninjured one. "Now I *do* tell you, stay here. Do not wander off again." He winced at even that movement, and released her. "I need to know you are safe."

"One of us *must* get water. We *do* have to drink, after all." Aksah patted his hand like a mother would a child.

"I will go with you. We cannot wander about without being armed." He sank back against the short stone wall, meager protection, as they both had learned. "I need to sleep, just for a short while. Keep my sword nearby and build up the fire."

Aksah nodded, but the wood she had brought earlier would not last much longer. They needed food as well, if there was any to be found in the wasted village. "You should lay down on the ground. I have enough robes to cover you while you sleep."

He looked at the fabric she held out, and frowned. "Since I do not recognize those, I assume they are more of your scavenging? I find I cannot complain about the results, just your foolishness." Eliab closed his eyes. "Wake me if the lion comes back."

"Yes, certainly. Eliab? There are some crumbs of unleavened bread in the blanket, the one not burning."

He grunted, but did not open his eyes. She did not know if he had even heard her. His breathing was too light, she knew he would hear if she started walking. Instead, she began sorting what she had gathered so far, hoping the sound of her movements would help him relax.

Aksah looked down at the small piles she had made, pieces of wood for the fire, three more robes, the pot of honey, sorely depleted now, and the two vessels for water. These sparse supplies were not much. They might be here several days, until he was strong enough to take on the long walk back.

And for that, she *did* feel guilt. Had she listened to her God's reply at the beginning, to the resignation of her fellow captives who accepted their new future with at least a semblance of grace, Eliab would be well now. He would not have a scar to bear for the rest of his life.

She would remember how he fought for her the rest of her own life as well. Their children would want to know. Somehow the two of them needed to decide how much to say when those questions came. His chest rose and fell in catches filled with pain.

If only she could ease him! Aksah set her hand in the lightest of touches on his chest. The skin beneath her palm shivered, as if it too suffered even while he slept. Somehow, though, she could not make herself lift that hand, but let it stay.

His breathing finally smoothed out. It was safe to venture out again.

· · ·

Eliab opened his eyes a slit, and let his gaze wander until he found his wife. Aksah put a piece of wood on the fire, and turned toward him. How many times had she checked in the hours past? She had been up the whole night on her ill-fated flight, he would insist on taking the nighttime watch. No doubt she would try to take his place. And after being awake all day? It would be folly. No matter how hard she tried, his wife would not be able to avoid sleep.

One of them must be alert during darkness, when the wild animals came out to feed. After its second stalking, the lion had apparently given up during the day. The attack had happened just after daybreak, but he feared it would try again during the normal hunting time. In spite of the pain in his shoulder and neck, he felt surprisingly well. No fever. He knew what that felt like. He had fought off fever before.

Whatever other skills his wife had, she made an excellent healer. Now that he saw the reason for her risks, he understood why she had disobeyed, even though her wandering about without his protection still irritated him.

If he was truly honest with himself, he had to admit that he slept as well as he had because he knew she was standing watch.

He said nothing, just watched her putter about with some piles around the fire. Piles much larger than what he remembered from before. She had disobeyed him. *Do not wander off again,* seemed like clear instruction to him. Of course she had disobeyed him. But she was resourceful, and he had no doubt he would find himself grateful for her scavenging.

Eliab waited until she turned to check on him.

Her eyes were large with what looked like relief. "Yes, I feel much better," he said in answer to the question in her raised eyebrows and ignoring the pain that still throbbed down his arm. "What do I see?" He waved his left hand toward the pile of treasures she had found, then wondered if she had ever noticed he could use his left hand as easily as his right.

Having both hands strong, agile, and healthy would be better, but they would just have to rely on what they had. His skill and her determination.

"Yes, I did go and find us more supplies." She poked at something, set down a spoon—a spoon!—and came over to kneel at his side. His wife had certainly been busy searching the town.

Begrudgingly, he had to admit that without her willfulness, he would be in much worse shape.

Aksah touched his forehead, his cheek, feeling for fever. The month he had granted her was nearly over. His injury would help him pass the last few days, as he did not want to have anything interfere or distract either of them when this marriage was finally sealed. He wanted her absorbed in his attentions, not checking to ensure the wound did not reopen.

After one more check, Aksah said, "You do not have a fever."

"Thanks to your good care." He caught her hand and brought it to his lips. "I might well have one now, or worse. I might be dead, if not for your quick work."

Guilt washed over her face, and she turned her head away as she rose. Her tumbled, dark hair with its messy curls hid her expression but even so, Eliab could see she did not look straight ahead. Her shoulders, even her spine, sagged under her blood-spotted, ash-streaked gown of plain linen. He doubted it would ever come clean now. In a muffled voice, she said, "You would never have been injured if not for me. Your wound is all my fault."

Something was different. The Aksah of the captivity would speak her mind and lash back rather than turn away and accept guilt for something hardly her responsibility.

Unless—what was she trying to say?

The remembrance of this morning's headache nagged at him, his slowness in waking, the sluggishness of his reaction to the lion. He looked at her averted face. "If you had not run away, yes, things would be different." He had to speak with care. A wrong word would lock her in guilt, and seal her mouth, fearful of his retribution. "Lions frequently stalk wherever there is prey. We should return home as soon as possible, as we know now that our flock is in danger."

Then he rubbed the back of his neck. "Had I felt more—myself, I would have been able to better acquit myself against the beast." Her head remained turned away. Eliab caught her hand, trying not to jar the injury that lashed his shoulder with pain and rose to his feet to join her, ignoring the dizziness that followed him. "Listen to me, Aksah. I am glad it was I who got hurt, and not you."

Aksah's hand tightened on his. "I drugged your food." Her head came up, he saw the courage it took her to meet his eyes. "I put wild lettuce in your bowl of stew. I wanted you to sleep so I could catch up with my father and brother." A tear trickled down her cheek, leaving one clear trail in the dust that covered her face. "I did not know you would be hurt. It was only to ensure you slept."

Ah. Things began to make sense. Wild lettuce. He knew very little about it, just that his mother had warned him never to touch it. "Were you that eager to leave me? Have I been so cruel to you?"

She shook her head. "It was not you. It was *me*. I did not want to be of Benjamin. I wanted the life I would have had, and I wanted to be part of the prophecy. There was no man waiting for me in Judah, but I knew there could be. I kept telling myself I would never let myself be part of the tribe that did such cruel things. Not even in my mind could I accept such a fate."

That again. Eliab bit back the growl that threatened in his throat. "I have put the war behind me. The rest of the nation put the war behind them. Are you going to hold—"

She interrupted him, putting a hand over his mouth. Eliab complied, closing his lips. "I did something to you I would not have done if my mind had not been so fixed on my own dreams. I was not ready to give them up. Because I let them grow and fester, I caused you to be hurt. If I had not fed you the wild lettuce, you would not have slept through my leaving. Or you would have been closer behind me. I would never have made it this far, I would never have gotten lost."

Her hand slid away, and clenched on her stained gown, crumpling the fabric as she twisted her fingers into the wrinkles. Her head dropped down again. "It is all my fault. I do not know how I can possibly atone for what I have done to you. Can you ever forgive me?" A silver drop fell through the space between her drooping head and the ground below.

In an attempt to lighten her heart, he said, "Remind me never to make you angry." Then he sobered. "You are forgiven, Aksah, my beautiful wife."

She did not smile at his loving words. Instead, in a voice so soft and sad he could barely hear it, she said again, "It *is* all my fault, every bit. My mother had tried to tell me first, even before my father tried, but I did not want to listen."

Now, *this* piqued his interest. He lifted Aksah's chin with a finger. Speaking as quietly as she so as not to shut down her thoughts, he asked, "What did your mother tell you?"

Her lashes glistened with unshed tears, and a soft color washed up her cheeks. "She said Benjamin was still our brother, that it was wrong to want you to be gone. And that if the last survivors were to save the tribe, we must allow them to take what and who they can." One of those hanging tears broke loose, to match the other of a moment ago, and slid down her face, and she brushed at it with a fierce stroke. "I was not to be one of those women. I was determined not to be caught. And because I could not accept what had happened, I nearly had your blood on my conscience."

Something caught her attention, her eyes shifted a little and her hand came up. He felt it touch his wound through her layers of bandages. "I *do* have your blood on my conscience. See?" Her gaze went to his, and she lifted her hand. Her fingers were tinged with pink. "You are bleeding again."

He looked down at the faint color that stained her hand. "I have bled worse practicing with my sword. You need not worry."

"We are running low on honey. If you are to heal, I must find more." Red rushed up her cheeks. "I shudder to even mention it, the name now makes my heart hurt, but wild lettuce wrapped on the wound helps heal."

He wiped off the tears that lingered with a careful, lingering touch. "The honey seems to be doing well enough. Better we be inside a wall if we are going to stay another night. We are too open here. The houses are the only place to look for more honey. No hives are anywhere near here, especially after the fire." He smiled at another thought. "I would rather not add bee stings to the list of wounds you need to treat."

"I found a fire holder," Aksah said, looking toward her pile. "We will not need to start another, we can carry the fire to a safer place."

"Good. Scoop up as many of the coals as you can. I will roll the supplies in a blanket. If you can carry the flint box and the fire holder, I will carry the rest."

"Be careful with the honey pot." She smiled. He had to stop and stare at that smile, so open, so without reserve, lighting up her face despite the dust and blood. "That is nearly the most important thing right now."

They had been through much this day, they had a night and maybe another day yet to struggle through before Eliab was ready for the long trip home.

Their only roof was the collapsed plaster-and-stone wall of a nearby building that had landed in just the right place, but the walls of this house were still adequate. The homeowner had not used wood except for the roof, so despite being cracked and blackened from fire, they still stood. The furniture had shattered and burned when the roof collapsed, but there was still enough to make a fire.

Best of all, the crocks of food had been well sealed. Nuts and dried figs and grains not yet turned into flour.

Eliab kept his right side away from her as he pulled a burned wooden plank that might have been part of the roof over an opening too wide and jagged to be a door. He pushed the plank's bottom against the wall, and winced as he straightened.

He was bleeding again. Aksah watched his eyes, waiting for the glittering brightness that announced fever. So far it had not happened. He knelt on one knee on the stone floor and set out the fireholder. She shifted behind him, trying to get a better look at the bandages, but he seemed to know what she was doing, and managed to be always one move ahead of her. If it had not been so serious, it would have been funny, watching Eliab constantly twisting and turning to keep his wound hidden as he looked for wood chips and windblown grasses to feed the coals. The fire caught, small yellow flames casting light and throwing shadows aside.

She would get a good view eventually if she was patient. He turned and the fire's growing brightness caught the spreading red along his arm, the glistening wetness of fresh blood along his neck.

As he broke off another piece of something wooden to add to the small fire, a drip of blood fell into the flames with a sizzle. She could take it no longer. "Eliab. Let me see your arm."

"No. It is well enough."

"Eliab. Let me see it." She strode over, crossing the small room that was their shelter, and put her hand on his arm just below the wrapping. His skin was slightly warm, but she did not know if that was from starting the fire, or the beginnings of a fever. "You are in pain. Your wound has likely ripped back open, if it ever closed."

He jerked away. "Aksah. Leave be."

She cradled his arm from underneath with more force. "I will not. You know as well as I the scent of blood will draw that lion back, so the sooner this wound is sealed, the better for both of us. I know what I am doing, Eliab." It was only a little lie. She had seen it done. Once. Surely that had to count as some knowledge.

His hand clenched, she felt the muscles tighten. Wetness brushed against her palm, and determination turned into alarm.

Holding her hand up in front of his face, even though he turned his head away, she raised her voice. "You are bleeding badly! Eliab, we have to burn the wound. Now!" With a determination that surprised even herself, she grabbed his arm and pushed him toward some rubble by one of the walls, rubble that seemed solid enough to hold him.

He sat down. Of course, having her hand on the wound, or at least the bandage over the wound, might have caused enough pain to induce him to obey.

It was tempting to smile. For the first time, she actually had him in her power.

"Your dagger, please." She held out her hand.

He leaned to the left and pulled the dagger from its loop on his right hip. The meaning of the movement struck her. The dagger was for close work, and held in the strongest hand. "You are left-handed." Why had she not noticed before?

"Many in Benjamin are. Did no one tell you?" The words scraped out as he thrust the dagger, hilt first, toward her. His voice was rough with pain.

She looked down at the knife she held, as if it was a poisonous snake. Long, narrow blade, thick handle with finger grips carved into the wood, and a round guard to keep the hand from slipping onto the sharp edge.

Smoke drifted past her face. Giving Eliab one more stern look, Aksah went over and knelt by the fire. Sealing a wound with hot metal! She was going to have to do it herself, alone, with no one to ask for advice, she would have to touch his open wound with a knife so hot it would burn the flesh! Her stomach twisted, but she did not dare put her hand on it for fear he would see and guess her nerves.

He did not know that, though. Being a warrior, Eliab no doubt had the skill to sear that wound, but she was as certain as she could be that fever had begun. Was someone already suffering fever steady enough to do what needed to be done?

In her mind, the answer was, *No*. Whether she could do it herself, she did not know, but he could not keep bleeding like this.

With a deep breath for courage, Aksah shoved the blade into the coals. Now to unwrap his arm. She knew about the dangers of red streaks that radiated out from the wound, and to watch for a foul smell. Saying a quick prayer as she went over to Eliab's side, she braced herself for whatever lay beneath the bloody cloths.

Bleeding had an advantage, she discovered as she peeled away the bandaging. As wet as they were, soaked with blood and honey, the strips did not stick. At least in opening the coverings, she would not do any more damage than was already done. The flesh beneath still appeared healthy, if a broad and bleeding gash could be called healthy.

And she had to press that hot knife against his skin. For the first time, Aksah looked, really *looked*, at Eliab's skin, the golden color, the soft hairs that covered his arms, the ridges of muscles that moved and shifted, and the scars, long healed, from earlier injuries.

A sob tore out of her, just one, but more were building behind it. She fought them back, desperate to be brave, to be strong. To save him.

Eliab turned to her with one quick movement. Aksah looked up, surprised at the suddenness of his reaction. His arm came around her, his wounded arm, the one she now had to burn. It dripped blood down her, she felt the warmth trickling along her skin.

Aksah wished she could burrow against him, make what she had to do go away. Instead, with that arm holding her, and the pain he must feel from that bit of movement, she wept.

A few moments later, washed clean inside, Aksah eased away from Eliab. She made herself meet his eyes. "Thank you."

"The first time I had to put a hot blade to a man's flesh, I lost all the food in my stomach." His dark eyes twinkled, even though she saw the pain underneath. A muscle tightened on his jaw, and Aksah wondered if it was for the pain he already endured, or if a man as big as he even dreaded what she had to do, or if it was just one more wound. His uninjured left hand came up and cupped her face. He went on, "You do not have to do this. I can do it myself, at least some of it."

Eliab lifted his shoulder, and she looked at the gash that marred it. He could see what ran down farther along his arm, but getting the knife in the right spot on that shoulder—no, someone who could see everything and see well, had to do it.

The fire spat out a spark. Aksah pull herself out of his arms. It was hard to do. They were warm and strong and gentle, and some of his strength must have seeped from them into her.

"I can do it." As she rose to her feet, she added fiercely, "I *will* do it."

The knife blade glowed a pale red-orange. She had delayed long enough, washing the wound, checking the knife, and washing the wound again. Now, with no more excuses, she picked up the wooden handle with the skirt of her robe, it was too hot to touch, and carried it over to her husband.

He caught her skirt with his good hand and gave a tug. "Listen to my instructions. Once you touch that to me, I probably will not be able to talk for a while, not making sense at any rate."

Tightness clenched at her heart, but she nodded, and tried to pay attention. It was different, she realized, watching it done at a distance when one need not absorb every movement, or count every touch of the knife. She wished for someone to guide her. She just never expected the help and counsel to come from him.

"Short touches," Eliab said, holding her gaze with urgency, as if to ignore the glowing blade she held above his arm. On the edge of her vision, she saw a short stick, one of the few unburned bits they had, sitting in his lap. She thought she saw the marks of his teeth already there, but that could not be. "Make sure it is no longer bleeding before you go to the next bit. But do not hold it too long."

Did a 'please' hide beneath his words? *Do not hold it too long, please?*

"If it starts to cool, heat it back up." The stick went between his teeth, and she flinched. He reached for a broken bit of wall to his right, clenching his hand on it as tightly as his teeth held the wood. Aksah watched his knuckles go white with the force of his grip. Then he closed his eyes, and took a breath. The order came out, muffled but unmistakable. "Now."

Now. Aksah took her own breath. "I need to see," she said, part truth and part the frantic need for one last delay. She pressed Eliab's head out of the way, exposing that awful wound, and watched her hand and that glowing blade come down on his shoulder. A horrible sound came from his throat, his body stiffened, his head pressed so hard against the burned wall Aksah feared it would shatter, but he never opened his mouth. Just that taut body and rigid jaw and that awful sound in his throat.

One knife-size section, another, another, counting each time the blade touched his arm. The smell made her want to retch, but she forced herself to continue. She stopped twice to heat the blade back up, and the two of them took advantage of the rest to get their shaking under control.

She would not let herself stop now until the burns were completely covered. Aksah took the honey, grateful she had found more in her searching, and dribbled it just as she had done before, then wrapped down his arm with a cloth she had scrubbed clean. Around and around, she followed that awful scar.

At last, she was done. Over the buzzing in her ears, she remembered to turn and check on Eliab. His face was the color of the ash that dusted the floor. Even his lips were grey. His jaw remained clenched and he took several deep breaths that shivered as they came back out. He slumped against the wall behind him, shaking hard enough to rattle the pile of detritus on which he sat.

That alarmed her. Crawling, pulling her robe out from under her knees to cross that last cubit, Aksah reached his side. "Eliab?"

His left hand, the one without the scar, twitched, then came up and pulled his right arm up against himself. He spat out the wood and she heard his teeth chatter.

"Eliab?"

He took a deep, shuddering breath. "I forgot how much that hurts." His beard twitched on one side. Was he smiling?

Aksah pulled away to get a better look. Yes, that was a smile. Rather thin and strained, his lips still pale, but . . . "What did you just say?" *He forgot how much—?* "This was done to you before? I thought you said you had done it to someone else!"

A great gust of air hissed in his throat. Aksah waited, knowing he was fighting the pain she had inflicted. After a smaller, more normal breath, he said, "Both have happened. One can hardly be a soldier without wounds." The smile, more of a grimace but he was trying, crept back. "When we finally become one flesh, you will see my other scar. I had a hard time sitting for a while."

Heat rushed up her cheeks. "It is on your—" She could not bring herself to say the word.

"Yes. I was cut on my hip with a sword, and it was sealed with the knife."

"Your hip! You!" She raised her hand to give him a playful shove, remembered that was his bad side and stopped in time. "You know what I was thinking!"

"Of course!" A strained laugh bubbled out of his mouth, followed by a groan. "I should not be laughing yet."

"I thought it was on your—where you sit down." She began to laugh as well, sheer relief that the horrible task was over giving it more humor than she expected.

He gave one more wan laugh, then groaned and held his arm tighter against his flat belly. "I assure you, it hurts just as much wherever the wound." His lips were white with pain.

They both looked at each other and smiled. The smiles faded. Aksah stared into his dark eyes and then away, down at her hands that were clenched together. The knuckles were white. When had she done that?

It was time to speak while he sat there, wounded, burned, and quiet. He had a right to hear the words from her, and perhaps this was what God wanted. If she said it out loud, maybe it would make everything more complete. Settled. Absolute. "I have come to a decision."

Eliab looked down at the top of his wife's head. A pain formed in his stomach, nearly worse than the one in his arm. She could not go back her family. Despite hearing it from her father's own mouth, look what she had still done. What if she still wanted to return to Judah? When he said *No* this time—well, he did not want to have to do that.

After what they had been through on this day—had this all happened before the sun could even set? It seemed more time must have passed—surely they had bonded. His arm gave a sharp twinge. "Aksah, do not be afraid to look at me."

Her head came up, but slowly. Then those eyes met his, green this time, not dark, and the courage there made his heart swell with pride. In a voice he could feel her fight not to let tremble, she said, "I will not run away again. I have decided. Or perhaps more, I have accepted. True, this was not the way I would have picked to find a husband—"

She said it! She said the word he had longed to hear from her. *Husband.* He knew it was impossible at the moment but how he wished to jump up and grab her, swing her wide, laugh until his laughter rang off the skies . . .

But Aksah was still speaking. "—but you are the one God has chosen for me. I told you of my dreams of being the mother of the Shiloh. You and my father both said I was given a different dream, but it has taken me all this time to accept it."

Then her mouth turned up again. A little smile, but a smile nonetheless. "My father said he had wanted to have a man come and ask for me, prove himself for me. That perhaps I wanted the same." She looked away, then back, a shy peek under her lashes. "I do not know how much more clearly any man could have proven himself to me than what you did today."

His chest was tight, but from deep inside not from the muscles he had worked today, emotion building. This was happiness, he thought. He had not really been happy since his family was destroyed. Not even the moments he and Aksah had laughed together, worked together, were truly happy.

This, *this* was what he had been waiting for. And now that she had said what he needed to hear, she was sitting on his wounded right side, where he could not touch her. "Can you come over to my other side?"

The smile still tilted her mouth. Aksah rose and stepped over his feet, to sit down. His hand fit easily in the space she left between their bodies. Before the old doubts could slip back in and taint the moment, he slid his left arm around her and, with one pull, tugged her close.

"Oh!" Surprise replaced the teasing look. Her eyes were big, her skin still glowed with the last traces of her sweat. Moving his right arm with the greatest care, refusing to let himself think of the pain, Eliab caught her chin. Maybe tomorrow the seared arm would have enough strength to lift her face to his, but now he had to hope she would follow his lead.

She did. Their lips met for the first time. Her mouth was so soft, He wanted to crush her to him, wrap her in his arms, and do nothing but kiss until he memorized every breath, every sigh.

Pain flashed down his stretched neck and across his shoulder and he jerked away from her, shuddering. His head banged against the wall, and he held it there until the torment eased and he could breathe again.

"I am so sorry! What did I do?"

When he could open his eyes, he saw Aksah on her knees beside him. Her hand hung in the air just above his chest as if afraid any touch would cause more agony.

Thank goodness for one able arm! He caught her hand and held it, clung to it, while he found his voice. "Nothing. You did nothing. I was too enthusiastic, and moved when I should have remained still."

She did not smile with her mouth, but her eyes lost some of the worry.

The night birds chirped and whistled their chorus, even though the sun had not gone down yet. He did not know when they had started. The shadows in this small room gave no hint of the time, with the fire still holding them at bay.

"We are not going home tomorrow, are we?" Her eyes had darkened.

It seemed they both could not remove the lion from their thoughts. "No.

Not if I am to be of any use to you at all." He looked at the fire. "That has to be built up. We need it to keep the beasts away all night—and not just the lion."

Trying not to turn his head and repeat the pain that had interrupted their long-awaited kiss, Eliab looked around the room. There was enough for one night's fire. Tomorrow's cares would have to wait.

The sun finally rose enough to eat the last of the shadows and make the fire's light unnecessary. Aksah yawned, stretched, and when that did not release the strain in her muscles, dug her knuckles into the small of her back and arched into the pressure. Her eyes felt gritty from staring into the darkness during her turn at watch.

Whether it was the size of the fire they built or if the way they fought back had sent him off for easier prey, even the possibility of it being wounded, they could not guess, but the lion had not returned.

It was time. They were going home. Yesterday Eliab had slept most of the sunlight hours, except for when she had to get more water and scrounge for more food. He walked with her, carrying the bow at his side, the arrows in their quiver hanging from his left shoulder.

He had begun moving his arm, with only the greatest care, but as he told her time and again yesterday when she fretted, "I cannot risk it healing locked in position, and this is all I know to keep it moving."

Her improvised water yoke had more than proved its worth. Water for drinking, water for washing, water for boiling the rags used on the healing wound. If there were any honey pots or oil jars left in this part of the city, they could not find them.

But the oil and the honey they did find, and the warm water with which she washed the ash away, had done their job. Eliab's wound remained clean. So today they would make the journey back.

"I hope the flock is not going thirsty." His voice came from behind her, but she did not jump. She knew he was awake, had sensed it in his breathing, in the faint shifting of his body on the floor.

How had this happened, that in the span of but a single day they had gone from awkward acquaintances in an unsettled arrangement to husband and wife?

He pushed himself to his feet, gave a sideways stretch, and walked over to her, leaning down to press a kiss to her hair. "Good morning, wife. I trust the night's watch was uneventful?"

"Only the small creatures were out," she answered, and leaned back, knowing he would be there to support her.

His left arm came across her front, and he pulled her against his uninjured side. His chin settled on her head, and another yawn rumbled along her scalp. As he chuckled, new shivers ran through her from back to front. "You must sleep a little before we leave. I will not risk you falling because of exhaustion." Withdrawing his arm, Eliab turned her toward the bed of smoky rags. "Rest."

Aksah smiled at him, and settled onto the floor. Her eyes, gritty though they were, did not want to close yet. She watched her husband from this odd vantage point. He looked taller than ever, towering over the fire as he laid on more bits of wood. His movements were smooth, almost flowing despite the red gash that marked his arm and should have impeded his actions.

This marriage had started with bloodshed, yet blood seemed to be what drew them together. It was remotely possible that out of all the men in Benjamin, he might have killed her brother. On the other hand, her brother might as easily have been the one to kill any of Eliab's family. He had suffered far more losses than she.

The woman at the core of everything, that poor dead concubine, seemed distant now. Aksah knew she would never be able to wipe the city of Gibeah from her memory, would never excuse their actions, and would never deny the righteousness of Israel's response.

But in Benjamin, if there was only one such man as Eliab, the tribe had been worth saving.

As if he heard her thoughts, her husband turned and smiled down at her. "Go to sleep," he said with mock displeasure. "I promise I can handle the guard."

She smiled, and closed her eyes.

CHAPTER 19

For he has clothed me with the garments of salvation; He has wrapped me with the robe of righteousness, just like a bridegroom who wears a turban like that of a priest, and like a bride who adorns herself with her ornaments.
Isaiah 61:10

"You are not going to the celebration this year." Eliab propped his hands on his hips and drew himself to his full height. Aksah had her back to him as she put another robe into the carrying sack, so his intimidating stance was wasted.

But then, she never did seem impressed with his size, except when it served her purposes.

"Of course I am going." She reached for the next robe. "Have you wrapped the loaves in oiled cloth yet? Are the waterskins filled?"

"Aksah, I will not risk your health, nor that of our child." If it was only one inside her. As he had watched her grow ever larger, his worries had grown at the same rate.

That brought her around to face him. How she managed to stand upright and not topple over onto her nose he did not know. Although her nose would never be able to reach the floor with that belly in the way.

"You would leave me alone, here in this vast empty space? Who would I call on for help? We have no servants to send for aid, and no neighbors to send them to." With ponderous steps so unlike her former light gait, she thumped over to him. "Eliab, we both know there is a safe path there, we know the best midwives in Israel will be there, and we also know I am not ready to give birth. I have two months to go. So of course I will go with you."

Giving his chest a pat, Aksah turned and made to waddle back to the bed where her packing remained. Eliab caught her arm, and drew her close, her back to his front, fitting his arms between her swollen breasts and belly. It was the only way they managed to stand close now.

He could hardly wait for the child to be born, so he could pull her close and feel her arms go around him again, instead of having to settle with half an embrace. Two months, if their count was right.

Of course he would not leave her here while he went off for the joyful annual celebration. It was the first time since that horrible crime that Benjamin would be welcomed as a full part of Israel.

Plus, her family would want to see her, to see she was well and happy.

"Are you happy, Aksah?" The need to hear her answer pushed the words out.

Her head settled against his chest. Eliab thought he could feel her smile flow through her body, a softening of her joints and muscles as if to be absorbed into him. "I am. Very."

"I wish we had met differently. I wish our starting had been with joy, that we could tell this child and the others to come how we smiled across the marketplace the first time our eyes met, or spoke to each other while at a gathering." His chin came down on her head. A memory came back, standing in a smoky, broken room with a collapsed wall for a roof and holding her like this.

Aksah's chest rose and fell against his arms as she took a deep breath. She insisted she could not get enough air lately, although it was not possible to tell if that was so. There was so much extra at her front.

"Instead we will tell them about how you rescued me from a lion, and how you were hurt in the attempt. And we will tell them, daughters and sons alike, that any man or woman you would not be willing to give your life for is not worth the having." She stroked the scar that ran down his right arm. "I wish I had not been forced to mar your body like this, but every time I look at it I remember the risks you took to find me, and the courage you showed in protecting me."

One final pat, not a caress but an emphasis, and she stepped forward. He let her go, and gave up the battle of wills. "Very well. Pack what you will need. Just remember, if this child is born in Shiloh at the celebration and not here at home in our bed where he was conceived, I did warn you."

"Two months yet." She smiled over her shoulder and went back to her robes and carrying sacks.

The dancers made moving flowers of color on the tiered hillside, swaying between the layers of vines. Aksah sat on the bench outside her father's tent, enjoying the sunshine with her mother.

"How much has changed in one year's time!" She looked up at the dancers and remembered as if from a distance last year, the fear and grief that dogged her as she circled with the other women.

Chileab's widow had a new husband now, and hopes of another child, though none was on the way yet. Aksah had seen her sister-in-law give envious looks as she stole glances at the bulge that got in the way of every embrace.

"It was a hard time." Ba'ara sighed. "Even one year is not enough for a mother to stop grieving." She reached over and patted Aksah's womb. "How wonderful that another is coming. Birth goes a long way to ease a mother's grief."

The baby kicked hard against its grandmother's hand, and Ba'ara grew thoughtful. "I know you must be thinking the same thing, so I will say it aloud.

There are two babies in there. You remind me of myself with the girls." Leaving her hand in place, she looked at Aksah with a firm gaze. "When your time is closer, you must make Eliab send for me. If I do not hear from him, I will come on my own. I had several children already when the twins were born, but this is your first time. You need an experienced woman at your side."

Then Ba'ara smiled. "Twins or not, I intend be there and see your husband as you labor. Men are so funny, and he is such a large one. I admit the unworthy thought of needing to watch him suffer."

"Oh, Mother!" Despite the insult to Eliab, Aksah had to laugh. "I truly am happy with him." She sobered. "It was not easy, we had many an argument, but he worked hard to prove himself."

Ba'ara gave her thighs a slap and rose to her feet. "I have to get the meal ready for your father and sisters. Stay here if you wish, watch the dancers." Her eyes twinkled. "I know it seems far away, but one day you will have your slender body back and be able to move freely again. I cannot wait to see you busy running after babies." She laughed and opened the tent door to disappear inside.

Aksah observed the dancers for a few moments, but the sound of her mother's bustling reminded her of her own food and her own husband. Without the tent cord and a healthy pull, she doubted she would have been able to rise to her feet. "I will come back later," she called through the curtain's gap, and started down the row of cloth shelters toward their own.

Music drifted over the camp like the smoke from the sacrifices at the Sanctuary's altar as she wandered through the brightly colored temporary city. Fabric walls in colors of yellows and reds, blacks and blues mirrored the robes of circles of women on the inclines, and the last of the glowing flowers that carpeted the valley floor and crept up the vineyard tiers.

She remembered the flowers that passed beneath her feet as Eliab dragged her away, remembered the drying edges and the thorns he had managed to sidestep. A name caught her attention, and she stopped to listen.

A young woman's voice, piercing and cold. "The Benjaminites are here. Can you believe it?"

Trembling crept up Aksah's legs, and down her arms as the months slipped away. One year ago that might have been her own voice, her own inflection. Her own attitude.

Anger and regret pushed away the weakness. She followed the voice and the words as they went on. "As if they expect us to forget the past year!"

Around the corner of a faded blue tent, a group of four women stood gossiping in the same spiteful tones. They were not as young as Aksah had assumed them to be. One even had a sleeping baby over her shoulder, and was swaying back and forth to keep the child from waking. Light hair and dark hair, tall and short, two of their bodies had the ripeness of motherhood, two were as lithe as maidens.

For a moment, Aksah just stood there and listened, hearing her own words coming back at her, her thoughts and words of those early days. The crime that caused her own fury and this lingering schism in the nation could not be wiped out. Down until the end of the nation's memory, if that day ever came, that crime would remain.

But she could stand up for Eliab as a man. "Hello."

The women turned and noticed her for the first time. "Hello." Their faces were warm and welcoming.

"I heard your words. They were not meant for me, but I was walking past."

Four faces lit up at the prospect of another sympathetic listener. "Certainly. Our conversation was not private. Everyone here is thinking the same thing. Those six hundred men walk about in the camp as if all is forgiven. Perhaps the men find it easy to forget, but we women will never excuse them."

"You are talking of Gibeah?"

"Gibeah, yes, but the monsters compounded it by stealing our friends and sisters."

"Nothing can erase the crime, I agree. But those six hundred are still part of Israel. My mother said that to me a year ago though the war was barely over." Aksah had to take a quick breath, fighting down old memories, new loyalties. "The arrangement was approved by God, no matter how hard the decision was to accept."

Memories battered her, those first days when she fought so relentlessly.

The ropes and the rebellion, the cutting words and the cruel walk. And ah, the hardest thing, the loss of her dream.

How had she put them all behind her? How had Eliab put those awful first days, those cruel words and her heartfelt tears, behind *him*?

The four were snapping like geese. "Are you saying it was a good thing?" "You cannot defend Gibeah!" "That is easy for you, you did not lose a friend to the monsters!"

That was the second time someone had used that awful word. Aksah would not let it go. "The *monsters* are dead! The city was burned. All Israel suffered. I lost a brother in the war, who was both husband and father. But you cannot condemn all of Benjamin. It is not fair!"

The other woman stared at her, past her, as if she had said the most vile of blasphemies.

"I am a captured wife of Benjamin. I made my husband pay, I assure you, but he fought a lion for me and will bear the scar for the rest of his life. That is not the action of a monster. He has earned his place back in Israel."

Familiar hands came down on Aksah's shoulders. "My dear, you have defended me well. I think we should leave them to their own conversation." Eliab turned her around, never lifting his hands from her shoulders, as if one would steer a handled cart.

Aksah turned and smiled at the women behind them. She did not even care if it looked smug.

As soon as they were out of sight of the women, Eliab stopped Aksah, and turned her back to face him. There was so much to say, he did not know where to start. She stood in front of him, her belly protruding so far it stretched the fabric of her robe. She looked as dangerous as a mouse, yet her eyes sparkled with life despite the dark circles beneath them.

"You defended me." The words were weak for all that was in his heart. Was her memory filled with the frightening, awful first days, as his was? This place reminded him of where his life had been twelve months ago. Empty, grieving, and angry.

She had run into that barrenness, bringing zeal and honor and truth, and since then nothing had been the same. She had tried to start a revolt to keep her principles, had called every man in their group to account by her vehement stand. She had helped him put his broken home together, and in the process helped put his broken soul together.

She cocked her head to the side, and smiled at him. "Yes, I did."

"Why?" Somehow the answer seemed very important. Months had gone by when it was just the two of them. Now, among the rest of the nation, he had been afraid of what she would say, what she would do. "They might be of Judah, you do realize that?"

Aksah's eyes flickered, as if the thought was new to her. "I suppose that is true, they might have been."

He could not let it go. "So why did you defend Benjamin?"

A smile turned up her mouth. "Ah, but I did not defend *Benjamin*, I defended *you*. I still am hurt by Gibeah, and the woman's fate. That will be with me always."

Her hand came up to his chest, a gesture she did often. "And before you ask again, I defended you because of who you are." Lines etched her mouth, creased between her eyes. Determination crept into her voice. "Had you been unworthy, I would have found a way to leave. No one would have made me return." She rose on her toes and, resting her hands on his strong chest, stole a kiss. "But you are worthy, so very worthy, and I am blessed."

Eliab simply had to smile. "Now this is the Aksah I know. I was just thinking it is your very principles and your zeal for truth that I prize."

Her entire body softened at his words. "Say that again. Please."

He leaned forward and pressed his lips to her forehead. "I prize you. I love you. I will never get tired of saying that. Out of all the ugliness and grief, I got you."

Aksah smiled. "And I got you, my love." She had said it before, but never felt like she said it enough. She framed his face with her hands and looked deep into his eyes. "I wish I could go back and do it better, be more kind to you. Every time I think about what you had to endure because I was so stubborn, I weep. God gave me a man of gold, a prize, and I am so grateful he made me stay until I saw what a treasure I had. How amazing it is, that it worked."

Sobering, Eliab said, "It did not work by itself. We made it work."

Tilting her head to the side again, Aksah draped one arm, and then the other, over his shoulders, and leaned forward as far as her belly would let her. "It might have been work in the beginning, but it became much more fun later on." She linked her fingertips behind his head, all that could connect with the distance between his height and her protruding womb. "Eliab?"

"Yes, Aksah?"

"Stop talking and kiss me."

So he did.

CHAPTER 20

Your father and your mother will rejoice,
And she who gave birth to you will be joyful.
Proverbs 23:25

The last of the day's light had almost faded when Eliab heard the clump of a donkey's hooves outside. His heart leaped. It had to be. It simply had to be. "Aksah? I will be right back."

One hand flopped as she seemed to acknowledge his words.

He ran to the door, and pulled it open, then sagged against the wall in relief. "Ba'ara! I am so grateful you could come! I did not know you would get my message in time." Eliab had to force himself not to grab Aksah's mother and drag her into the house.

"After your letter? How much did you pay the runner to reach me? I assumed things had gone very wrong." Ba'ara shrugged off her wrap and caught it on a peg. "My daughter, Eliab. Where is Aksah? Is she well?"

A moan snapped his attention to the room behind the open door.

"Come!" He ran toward the doorway, not even waiting to see if she was following.

They bumped together beside the bed, and Eliab found himself grabbing Ba'ara's hand. "Every day for the past several weeks she awakened with pains." His words came faster. "So I sent for you and I feared you would be too late and then she began laboring this morning but today the pains did not stop so I have been watching the hills around the house praying to see you." He gasped for air. Did that make sense? "You came. You must take care of her. I cannot live without her."

Ba'ara shook a finger at him and scowled. "Nonsense! There is no need for talk like that. I have birthed six children, each of them safely. All will be well."

He could not remember even now what he said. Aksah moaned again, and then her eyes popped open. "Mother? Mother, I have to get up, I think I have to push now."

Eliab gestured behind him, never moving his gaze from his wife. "I made a birthing stool." It sat in the corner of the room. He had expected to need to use it before today, but he had feared he would be using it alone. Well, alone except for Aksah, but she would be very busy with the birth, and would depend on him to do the rest.

Ba'ara patted him on the back, as one would a child. At the moment, he felt almost as weak. "She will be very thirsty when she is done, so do you have water from the well?"

"Aksah always keeps water in the house." He did not look toward the sleeping room door, either. He was not leaving his wife now, so if Ba'ara wanted water, she would have to go get it herself. And if she was trying to get him out of the room, well, that plot would not work.

"Get me up!" Aksah screamed at the both of them, and pushed with one arm, managing to get her shoulder off the mattress.

He leaned down and caught both Aksah's hands. After months of practicing, they had learned together how best to get her out of bed. It took very little time now to realize their method ran into difficulties when the woman was deep in labor. Finally, Eliab leaned down and caught her under her armpits, then straightened, easing her up bit by bit until she was on her feet.

Her knees promptly buckled. "The chair," Eliab gasped out as he tried to hold Aksah's limp body. The birthing chair appeared almost immediately though with considerable scraping and screeching across the floor, Ba'ara pulling it with quick steps into place.

He backed Aksah to its edge. "Can you sit if I let go?" The seat was wide across the sides, but shallow, the chair back sloped away to allow her to lean if she weakened, and there were handholds both in that seat and on the arms for her to grab. Aksah immediately pressed herself against that sloping back, grabbed the arms, braced her feet, gave a deep groan, and began to strain.

Time ceased to have meaning. The night stretched long, room was dark except for some oil lamps Ba'ara insisted be placed on the floor. She had set out tools, a knife, some string, and small blankets she had made herself.

Eliab's world narrowed to his wife, pressed tight against the chair's back, her hands clenched on the armholds, the knuckles white with effort, and Ba'ara, kneeling on the floor watching with interest. Aksah strained so hard he feared the chair would either fall over backward or break in two.

He stood behind that chair, pretending to hold it in place, and stroked his wife's hair, rubbed her shoulders and arms, anything to give her ease. "I love you," he whispered into her ear, hoping it would help, but other than grabbing his hand once, she seemed locked in her body.

He stayed where he was as the night moved on and watched his mother-in-law, hoping for reassurance. From time to time, she would feel Aksah's tight belly and nod.

He asked Ba'ara about that nod once, but she merely shrugged. "We will see what we see," was all she said.

All of a sudden, something was different. Aksah's groans reached a crescendo of frightening noise, like a long drawn-out scream, and a small head popped into Eliab's view. After that things went fast, and it seemed Ba'ara was scarcely able to catch the child as the rest of it came slithering out. Waving legs and arms and gurgling, and at last a high-pitched cry.

"A son!" Ba'ara laughed as she held the babe in her lap with casual experience, grabbed string and the knife and tied and cut. "Take your boy, Eliab, because we are not done."

A son! He and Aksah had made a baby! There was another being in the world who needed him, but his legs did not remember how to move and he could only stare at it.

"Eliab!" Ba'ara snapped his name, and he managed to force himself away from the chair and over to the wiggling infant in his mother-in-law's arms.

As he took the baby, he suddenly realized Aksah was indeed straining again. He sat down on the bed with a plop, his tiny son still safe in his arms, and watched his wife go through the groaning and pushing and clutching again.

It was one thing to watch his wife's body swell beyond all expectation and have the thought of twins drift through his mind, to be promptly banished. It was quite another to wait and watch the second child slide into the world and realize in one night his family had gone from two to four.

Aksah rolled her head against his well-built birthing chair and smiled at him. Her face was mottled, blotched with red and spots of white, shiny with sweat, her lips trembled with exhaustion, but the smile was strong and filled with joy. "Eliab, we have sons! Two!"

He looked from the tiny red faced baby in his arms crying to make himself known to the world, to the second matching child with matching cries in its grandmother's arms. "Aksah . . ." he had to take a trembling breath before he could speak more, "you have given me a family again."

And then Eliab wept.

The account of the rape and death of the concubine in Judges 19-21 is one of the most graphic—and hated—accounts in the Bible. Many view it as a sign that Biblically, women were lesser beings.

I disagree. While the account is indeed heartbreaking, I find the fact that the entire nation of Israel was sent to avenge the death of a single woman to be instead proof that women were *valued*. The account also makes a point—twice—that there was no king, once connecting it with the idea that a king might have kept the people obedient. (Judges 19:1; 21:25) The final verse of Judges makes the statement, "What was right in his eyes was what each one was accustomed to do," clearing God of any complicity in those events.

Something very interesting is that the account is out of sequence in Judges, which to me implies that the compilers of the book nearly did not put it in, and then decided at the end to include it. We know this because Judges 20:28 lists the high priest during this event as Phineas, son of Eleazar, and grandson of Aaron. That puts its place at the very beginning of Judges, as Phineas would have become the anointed high priest in the last verse of the previous book of Joshua.

So why put it in at all? The city of Gibeah is referred to twice in the book of Hosea (Hosea 9:9; 10:9), and connected with a great sin that put the nation in line for judgment. Since no other crime is mentioned in this city, it appears to refer to this account.

One other reason to add the account is one could hardly claim to have written the history of a nation and forget to include a civil war that divided the country, and resulted in the near extermination of a portion of the population.

As far as Benjamin's fate, the tribe that had been nearly wiped out for *disobedience* later became known for its *obedience*. When the nation split into two, only Benjamin joined David's tribe of Judah, and remained part of that two-tribe kingdom until their captivity in Babylon. (1 Kings 12:21) The very first king, Saul, came from Benjamin, as did Mordecai and Esther, who set examples of faithfulness during the captivity. (Esther 2:5-7)

I preferred to focus on the last chapter of Judges, the solution, rather than on the crime. How would a chastised tribe treat the women they were granted by the nation? I could only assume they would have treated them as women are, as good gifts from God.

ALSO BY MARY ELLEN BOYD

Temper the Wind

His Brother's Wife

Days of the Judges box set

Regency Romance - available on Amazon Kindle

Fortune's Flower

The Thief's Daughter

ABOUT THE AUTHOR

Mary Ellen Boyd is a romance author whose passions are in Regency and most important to herself, Biblical fiction, although if the muse strikes, she will happily branch into other genres. Her special passion is building a fictional story around a factual account. She is always on the lookout for another tidbit that begs to become a novel.

She lives in the beautiful state of Minnesota (and yes, it does get hot there in the summer). She and her husband have been happily married since 1982, in May, the prettiest month of the year. They have one son, who is now married himself to his high school sweetheart.

To follow her and receive news of any upcoming releases, you can follow her here:

http://www.maryellenboyd.com/newsletter/

She can also be found on Facebook, Goodreads, BookBub, Twitter, Pinterest, & Instagram.

www.ingramcontent.com/pod-product-compliance
Lightning Source LLC
Chambersburg PA
CBHW071509110726
47908CB00003B/783